Susan Leigh Stevens

BLACK EYE, BLUE SKY

A NOVEL

ALLISON LEIGH STEVENS

© 2020 Allison Leigh Stevens
Black Eye, Blue Sky
First edition, Month 2020

JustOneYou Books
Grand Rapids, MI
allisonleighstevens.com

Editing: Shayla Raquel, shaylaraquel.com
Cover Design & Interior Formatting: Melinda Martin, melin-damartin.me

This is a work of fiction. Names, characters, businesses, places, events, locales, and incidents are either the products of the author's imagination or used in a fictitious manner. Any resemblance to actual persons, living or dead, or actual events is purely coincidental.

ISBN: 978-1-7351958-0-3 paperback, 978-1-7351958-1-0 epub

To my loving husband,
who believed in me long before I knew I could.

1

In the Beginning

My husband Bryce persisted with his plans for us to go camping in West Virginia on our honeymoon, even though he knew I was more than apprehensive about sleeping in a tent. He also hated the word *honeymoon*, so he called it a *vacation*. It stung a little every time I heard him say it, but I went along with everything because I told myself these were silly things to get upset about and that to sacrifice for others, especially your spouse, was the truest expression of love.

We drove south in my black Jeep, and my mind drifted back to the only other camping experience I had. I was about eight years old. It stormed that night as if the gods were in an all-out war against each other, ear-shattering thunder and lightning every few seconds. The tent my parents and sisters and I shared leaked and finally collapsed under the heavy rains, sending us clamoring in different directions in the dark to find safety in my aunt and uncle's small camper. I haven't been camping since.

Bryce and I had close to an eight-hour drive from

Indiana. Hundreds of cars and trucks pulling boats and campers followed too closely behind each other. Even the guy with the "Sorry for driving so close in front of you" bumper sticker was tailgaiting the person in front of him. When one driver stepped on their brakes, we all did, and even I pressed down hard on the passenger-side floor, also offering assistance. I glanced over at Bryce a few times to make sure his eyes were on the road, which they were, and then dreaming about our first night together, I reached over and ran my fingers through his soft, wavy brown hair. I let my hand travel down his strong arm and rested it on his thigh. His hands were firmly set on the steering wheel as we switched lanes. He looked over at me with his sapphire eyes and said, "Don't distract me *too* much." When we finally escaped the flow of other drivers and cut into the heart of West Virginia, I let out a long sigh of relief.

It wasn't long before we were engulfed in a world of green. I rested my head on the window as the sun burst through the leafy ceiling of a thousand different hues: jade evergreens, lime hickories, and emerald maples. The sun hit my wedding ring, and I held it up to catch more of the sun's rays. I grinned at Bryce and said, "I can't believe we're married!"

"Do you like your ring?" he asked.

"Of course I love it! Look how it shines. I feel like a queen."

"*My* queen. Don't forget that." He grinned tightly, and I felt a twinge of unease.

The huge ravines at the bottom of the dark, twisty

roads made my stomach do flips. I imagined our Jeep careening down into the bottom where no one would find our upside-down broken bodies for months, if ever, because Bryce didn't want me to tell my family where we were going on our vacation. He insisted they were being too intrusive.

"Your parents are too controlling. Can't you see that, Savannah?" he'd said a week before our wedding. His eyebrows furrowed when he added, "They need to let you be an adult for once. I'm not going to continue having this conversation with you." He softened his tone, walked over close to me, and cupped both of his hands around my face. He looked down at me with those eyes of his and kissed me. He said, "We need to start our lives together, as husband and wife, don't you agree?" *Mrs. Bryce Clark. Not quite two years ago, I was Mrs. Raymond Pearson; and before that, I was Savannah Young. Do I even know who I am, apart from being a man's wife?*

I nodded, and he walked back to the table where he was looking at camping brochures. Opening up a trifold pamphlet, he said, "But I'm very concerned that your mother is going to get in between us, and all I want is for us to be a unified front. You understand that, right?"

It's true that my parents could be intrusive, especially my mother. She dialed my phone several times a day, and if I didn't call back right away, her voice was cold and distant. She got me a job at the law office she managed, for which I was grateful. And she continued to beg us to attend her and Dad's church even though I kept telling her no. Bryce adamantly refused to go.

3

As I looked down the ravine, my stomach dove forward. *At least Chelsea will have an idea of where to look for our bodies if we fall down this mountain.* I wasn't sure exactly where Bryce was taking me, but I knew the general area, so I told Chelsea, my younger sister, we were staying somewhere near Summersville because I wanted her to know where I was. The more I thought about it, the more it bothered me that I couldn't give my family a specific location—so much so, that my heart started racing and I fidgeted in my seat.

The terrain leveled off, and I distracted myself looking at the run-down houses that peppered the landscape. Each home's front porch propped an old, faded couch or an unusable oven. Rusty vans and other appliances were strewn about in the tiny yards. I imagined that if we needed assistance, if our car broke down or something, someone in long underwear would rush out with a shotgun, yelling, "Get the hell off my property!" Bryce and I lived in Indiana, but I grew up in the South, and both of my parents were born and raised in Georgia. I understood southern folks. No matter what walk of life, there was a beam of light coming through southern people as if they'd won the lottery by being born in the South; that pride mixed with a distrust of northerners made up the heart of many southern men and women.

"Ya ever wonder about the people who live in those houses?" I wondered out loud.

"Not really. They're just people like you and me, Savannah." He rubbed his head and gritted his teeth. "Aren't much different than us."

"Aren't they, though? I mean, what's with the appliances outside? Personally, I like cooking in a kitchen." I looked at him, smiling, inviting him into my jesting with the expectation of getting him to laugh.

"Well, I guess everyone isn't as privileged as you, now are they?" He put both hands back squarely on the steering wheel and squeezed.

"What do you mean by that?" I said with a defensive tone.

"They don't have a daddy who pays for their college education, buys them a car, basically pays for everything." He glanced my way, then back at the road. "It must be nice to be you."

I studied him, thinking at first that he was teasing me, and I waited for him to start laughing. But one look at his face, and I knew he wasn't joking. He was grinding his jaw, and his eyes were cold, unblinking.

"I-I didn't mean it that way," I stuttered. "I just think about these things—how different people are." I sank lower in my seat and glanced out the window, fighting back tears. I didn't want him to see me cry, not on our honeymoon-vacation. I put my window down for a moment to feel the breeze, but instantly the coolness in the car was replaced with thick, outside clammy air.

"Put your window up!" Bryce spat. I rolled up my window without a word, and the sides of my head pulsated with every rotation of the handle.

I couldn't understand what was wrong. Bryce had grown moody since we left Indiana. Did I say something back then that upset him? I thought about our conversations during the trip and came up with little that would have angered him so much as to warrant him snapping at me like he did. Several minutes passed, and he reached over and took my hand. He said, "I'm sorry. I'm just stressed out about finding this campsite and getting set up before dark."

My dad used to yell at us kids and my mom a lot on vacation; my mother would always explain that Dad snapped at us because he was responsible for getting us where we were going safely. *Maybe that's what Bryce is experiencing—a lot of pressure.* Even so, I accepted his apology, but his response seemed more than just being stressed. I slunk down in my seat and closed my eyes.

I remembered Bryce was reluctant to have me meet his parents the first time. He kept saying, "I wasn't raised like you." To which I replied, "That doesn't matter to me." After a few months of my asking to meet his family, he arranged the visit with his parents and me and we made the three-and-a-half-hour drive to his childhood home in Bloomington, Indiana. He was quiet as we pulled into the short dirt drive up to the house. It was a tiny, white, low-roofed bungalow, where his mother and stepfather raised him and his brothers. One brother was in jail for drug possession and the other had moved out to Washington years ago, but Bryce never had any contact with either of them.

The yard was tidy and mowed, a huge oak tree flanked the half-acre front lawn, and there were a few wildflowers growing and clematis climbing a wood trellis on the south side of the house. We walked up to the front, and the screened door squeaked and wobbled as Bryce pulled it open. There was no foyer; we walked right into the small living room. When my eyes finally adjusted to being inside, I figured out why it was so dark: the few windows this bungalow had were blocked by old boxes. The dusty shelves were filled to the ceiling with books, old magazines, jars full of marbles, and broken toys, while a handgun sat on an end table. My mouth dropped, and his stepfather noticed me staring at it. He got up from his recliner, grabbed the gun, and said, "Not used to guns, are ya." It was a statement rather than a question, and in his tattered sweatpants and T-shirt, he mumbled something about putting it in the safe. I watched him enter a back bedroom, and he didn't come out for about fifteen minutes.

Cobwebs and dust clung to the curtains in the kitchen, and dirty dishes and pots were piled high like a cityscape behind his mother sitting at the kitchen table, heaped with papers and stained coffee cups and an ashtray with a smoldering cigarette. She didn't stand to say hello, but I walked over anyway to shake her hand. She only took the ends of my fingers as if I had a communicable disease and released them quickly to grab her cigarette out of the ashtray, and looked back to her magazine. This memory made me wonder if this was also part of the reason for Bryce's strong reaction. Did Bryce think my comments were a judgment against his family?

I continued to feel hurt by what Bryce said to me as we pulled into Gauley River National Forest. A wash of relief poured over me when I saw other people camping as well because I didn't want to be camping alone with Bryce. He said he was sorry, but the burning sensation in my chest hadn't let up. Sure, I could understand where his response came from, given his family history, but his words cut me deeply. I had no idea how to bridge the gap between us, and he was making little effort. Still, we unpacked the car and put up the tent together, without much conversation and, surprisingly, without too much difficulty. He started a campfire while I pulled out hot dogs and opened a can of beans, and that was our first dinner together as husband and wife.

Darkness covered the woods, making the moon and the fire the only sources of natural light. We sprayed ourselves with Deet, I wrapped a light blanket around my shoulders, and we sat in camp chairs around the crackling fire, our faces glowing from the light.

"What are your dreams, Savannah?" Bryce asked. His eyes were tender for the first time in hours.

I was taken aback by his penetrating question. He hadn't spoken much since he apologized, but at this moment, he seemed to be reaching out to me for closeness.

I shifted in my chair and cleared my throat, as this particular question made me a little uncomfortable. A cloud of confusion hovered over me and settled on my brain whenever I was asked about my hopes, my dreams, my goals in life. So much had happened, so many dreams crushed; I didn't know if I had any big dreams anymore. One wish I still hung on to, though, was that I wanted children.

"You know one of my biggest dreams is to have children someday," I said, mesmerized by the fire.

"And you know that's one of mine too," he responded, chuckling. "I've always wanted a family, especially a son." The fire popped, and he leaned away. "What are some other dreams you have?"

I twirled my hair with my fingers. "Hm, well, I'd like a nice house someday."

"A nice house. Huh. Okay. Is that all?" He fussed with the collar of his shirt and grinned and squinted at me as if there were a better answer.

"I'd like a nicer car too. My Jeep is okay, but we could use another car, a little nicer. Yours is on its last leg."

Bryce turned back to watch the fire. His hard smile faded away, and he rubbed his eyes as the smoke blew in his direction.

I toyed with my wedding ring as the firelight reflected on the gold and princess cut diamond. *Bryce seems disappointed in my answers.*

Several seconds went by, and I tried again. "Well, I don't know, I guess I hope we have good jobs."

Bryce had picked up a long stick and was moving logs around in the fire. He shook his head and said, "I want our lives to be about helping others, not about living in a big house in the suburbs and driving expensive cars, like your parents. That's why I choose to work part time so my remaining time can be used to build my ministry to help underprivileged kids. That's why we rented the apartment near the city." His eyes rested on me, and he waited for me to say something.

I moved my shoulders up and down but stopped short of a full-on shrug. "I want to help people too. I just think we could help people in a nice house in the suburbs just as easily as an apartment." I smiled, hoping to quell the tension building between us. I'd learned years ago that smiling and laughing, even when you're not feeling happy, can ease the tension in high-conflict situations.

"You care too much about material things. I can't blame you completely, though; it's how you were raised. I guess we'll just have to work on that together, huh?" Bryce winked at me.

He stood up and grabbed the bucket sitting near him and poured the small amount of water on the fire. I was about to protest that I wasn't ready to leave the warmth of the fire, that I wanted to continue our conversation, but instead I grabbed my flashlight and followed Bryce into the tent.

Bryce purchased an air mattress for the trip, which helped with comfort from the rocky ground, but it did little to help with balance or firm footing. This wasn't how I imagined the first night of my honeymoon, but I didn't say anything because I didn't want to hurt Bryce's feelings. The upside, if there was one, was that it developed a slow leak, so by the end of our five-day getaway, it was easier to deflate.

We lay down on the mattress, and Bryce immediately rolled over with his back toward me. We had never been intimate before marriage, believing we were following Christian ethics, but now, here, when we were *supposed* to be intimate, he didn't show the slightest interest. I put my hand on his back and said, "Bryce? Don't you want to, you know, kiss me?"

"Not tonight. I'm exhausted."

I took my hand back and stared up at the tent ceiling. I clutched my blanket for warmth rather than the bare chest of my husband, longing for him to wrap his strong arms around me.

I thought Bryce was my last chance at having a family, and I'd given up on ever finding true love again. The unexpected failure of my first marriage the previous year sent me reeling, and my heart was still mending when I met and married Bryce. It was a daily fear of mine to end up alone and childless; I was twenty-seven years old, after all.

I was at his apartment the first night we kissed. As I was leaving, we stood on his porch, our eyes locked, and he leaned in and kissed me. We pulled away from the kiss, laughed awkwardly, and I said, "Well, I'd better be going." I turned away, confused that there was no chemistry in the kiss. I walked down the few brick steps to the sidewalk to my car thinking, *Sparks should be flying! Something is off. But what? I think he likes me, so what is wrong with me? I don't feel anything.*

Oh, here I go overthinking again. I just need to let this go and see how things play out. I want to find love, I want to start a family, and Bryce seems like he might be the man I've been looking for.

Not being intimate on our honeymoon ripped me in two. It was a hard shock to ignore. Three days into our honeymoon, still no sex. I held my hand over my mouth to hide my crying from Bryce as he breathed heavily beside me. The next morning, I looked at myself in the mirror, and my skin was pale and my eyes were puffy. I didn't know how to talk about it with my husband, so for the rest of the week, I did what I had done since I was a little girl: I put a smile on my face and pretended everything was okay.

Every morning of our vacation, he chose our activities for the day, which mostly consisted of hiking. The first night, my muscles ached from our hike up and down mountainous trails. He also insisted on driving everywhere we went and got angry when I asked to drive one day.

"Hey, where are the keys? I'd like to drive to the little general store in town."

"What? No, I'll drive."

"Bryce, I just want to drive to the store. It's just a short trip." We needed eggs and bread for breakfast the following morning.

"Don't you think you're being a little childish for wanting to drive?" he chided. "I'm your husband. I should be the one driving. It's weird that you want to drive suddenly."

What? He'd never expressed these kinds of archaic patriarchal views before the wedding. Not only was I with a man who didn't want me in a way a husband should want to be with his wife, but now it seemed he was suggesting that I need his "permission" to drive my own car. I had no control over what was happening. He was in charge of it all, and I had no say. A sense of powerlessness was creeping up on me, and its weight on my chest constricted my breathing.

Walking through the trails that morning gave me a respite from the ugly truth that my honeymoon was nothing like I'd expected it to be, and that I didn't understand my husband. I had a small camera with me, and I took photo after photo, getting as close as I could to capture the essence of one leaf's splendor; then, a mountain so glorious that I couldn't take it all in. Several times I had to stop walking simply to try to grasp the beauty that my heart and mind were trying to perceive.

Still, in the midst of such beauty, something felt off with my second marriage. I was getting lost in this relationship. It was happening quickly, and I needed to do something to change it. One morning, I was straightening up the tent while Bryce was in the shower, and I spotted my car keys sitting on the floor of the tent near his backpack. I took them and dropped them in my jacket pocket.

He had planned a canoe trip for later that day, and we had to drive a short distance to the rental place. When it came time to leave, he was searching for something; he checked his pants pockets from the night before, his rain jacket, and his backpack. He even lifted up the air mattress to check underneath. I said, "If you're looking for these, I have them." I held the keys in front of me.

The keys in my hand caused his eyes to change from

his usual light blue to dark, almost black. I'd never seen that before, but it sent chills up my spine. I swallowed, and before I could react, he let go of the mattress and ran up to me. "Give me the keys!" Spit flew from his mouth as he barked his demand loud enough for the family two sites down to hear. He grabbed my hand, squeezed, and ripped the keys from me.

"God, Bryce! That hurt!" I pulled my hand away. "The keys were on the ground when I was straightening up this morning, and I thought I would like to drive to the rental place." I said this as an intense whisper and held my burning hand, fighting back tears, as I didn't want anyone to hear us arguing. I was embarrassed that my new husband was yelling at me. I wanted to drive, yes, but it really wasn't about the driving anymore; it was about wondering if he loved or respected me.

Bryce ignored me and marched toward the parking lot. My fingers were red and the skin had ripped and was bleeding a little. Tears started pooling in my eyes and my ears grew hot. I wanted to go home. I wondered if I should go canoeing with him or not. I stood there for a few seconds with my hands shaking and my stomach burning with anxiety.

While I was somewhat like my father, the former marine who fought like a bulldog, I was also like my mother, who clammed up when she got her feelings hurt. I couldn't speak up for myself when it mattered most.

I decided I'd better follow Bryce. I walked quickly to try to catch up; I wondered if he'd drive off without me, and then what would I do? I'd be left alone in a tent all afternoon. But he didn't; he waited the thirty seconds it took me to get to the Jeep, and then he drove out of the parking lot too fast.

My hands were shaking; I was shaking all over. I couldn't get my body to calm down. I wanted to jump out of the Jeep. Why had I gotten in this vehicle with him? What am I going to do? *I want to go home.* I at least wanted to call my parents, or Chelsea, but I couldn't.

Instead of waking up each morning, excited to spend the day with the love of my life, I woke up every morning of our honeymoon with a feeling of alarm. *What have I gotten myself into? Is this my future with him?*

Sadness creeped inside me like kudzu vines, wrapping itself around any joy I had left.

2

The First Bruise

I started to breathe easier upon seeing the WELCOME TO INDIANA sign. Bryce tried to joke around a little on the long trip back home, and he held my hand for a while, but I had been on edge and anxious ever since the first night of our "vacation." Getting closer to Chelsea and the familiar surroundings of home were the only things putting my mind more at ease.

It was a cloudy, warm day when we pulled into the parking lot of our new apartment. I walked up the stairs, dragging my duffle bag, into our matchbox-size apartment, and sighed at the beige carpet, walls, counters, and cabinets. I took a deep breath in and wondered, *Is this what my life has come to?*

We had opened many of our wedding gifts at the small reception after the ceremony, so I needed to put them away. I decided to fill the kitchen cabinets with our new white dishes and the new toaster, coffee maker, blender, and pots and pans. I enjoyed organizing my kitchen, and it distract-ed me from my racing negative thoughts.

I reached into one of the boxes and pulled out the cast iron skillet my mother gave me upon my first marriage. It was a hand-me-down from my grandmother, whom I loved. I'd snap beans from her garden, roll pin curls in her hair on Saturday night, and go to church with her on Sundays. She taught me how to make corn bread in her cast iron skillet and chocolate chip cookies and, best of all, she never yelled at me. At bedtime, I'd hold her hand as she told me stories about when she was a child, and we'd wait for the train to blow its whistle as it rumbled by her house.

I wrapped my hand around the cool iron handle, and my grandmother's love came through like an electric current, bringing light into my gloomy heart as I remembered her standing in front of the stove in her housecoat making delicious dishes for our family. She used the skillet every day, sometimes three or four times depending on what she was preparing. Using it in my kitchen united me to my past, to people I loved, and to parts of me I thought I'd lost. It was a rite of passage, an honor that signified I was ready to provide for my family, food made with love from the heart of a southern cook. I wanted to leave it sitting out on my stove, just like it sat out on my grandmother's and mother's stoves, so I placed it on a back burner, just as I had with my first husband, with no problems.

Bryce walked over and said, "You're not going to leave that out, are you? A pan sitting out all the time makes the kitchen look trashed. We need to put this thing away."

That first visit to his parents' home popped into my mind: Dishes, pots, and pans were everywhere, clean and dirty, with not one inch of counter space available for a cutting board to chop vegetables or even to open a can of soup. I could understand his need to have things neat and tidy, to put appliances away, I truly did, but he was insisting on his way for everything. He wasn't discussing anything with me.

I grew cold inside as I reluctantly put the skillet in the drawer of the stove, just to placate him. Every time he spoke, I stiffened and started to get a tension headache. I wanted to scream, but I was afraid to speak up. All week, I had mostly shut down my feelings, thoughts, and desires, but I was beginning to bubble over with putrid sensations in my gut. I'd become so irritated with him that I decided to speak up the next time he made some ridiculous request I disagreed with. It didn't take long before the opportunity came along.

"I have to return some things to the store and then stop at Todd's house. I need you to sweep out the tent for me so I can return it to the rental place in the morning," he said while holding *my keys*. His car was a rusty heap of crap that might break down any second, so naturally, he preferred my car.

"Now?" I asked. "I'm busy with the kitchen stuff. Can't I do that in the morning?"

"I need it done before the sun sets, so no, it needs to be done soon, in the next hour or so."

"I'm so tired, Bryce. I really don't want to do it now. I was hoping to go to bed early tonight. I'd rather get up early tomorrow and do it. Or can you do it before you go to Todd's?" I rubbed my eyes and fought back a full yawn.

Bryce took a step closer to me, so close that he could touch me, and his eyes grew dark, implying that I had no right whatsoever to suggest he do the chore. "No, I can't do it," he spat. "I have so many other things I need to do. Do I have to do everything?"

Like what? Stop at your best friend's house and play video games? I thought, but I didn't dare say it. I couldn't believe he was acting this way. I clearly couldn't do anything right in his eyes.

I can't take this! my mind shouted. The anger and resentment rose up in me and, a little louder than I'd intended, I said, "I'll do it tomorrow! Right now, I don't give a damn about that tent!"

I didn't see it coming. The back of Bryce's left hand slammed against my mouth, his wedding band cracking against my teeth. My head jolted, and I fell backward into the cabinets.

Did he just hit me? I was dazed, and time slowed down to a crawl. My face pounded as the blood rushed toward the injury, and I slid down to the floor, crying out at the taste of blood. My tongue wrapped itself around my front teeth as if to keep them in their place. None of them were chipped or broken, thank God. But I held my face together with my hands, afraid that if I let go, at least one of my teeth would fall out.

"Don't you ever swear at me like that again!" he said, spit flying out of his tight-lipped mouth. His eyes were wide with anger, his face was red, and a vein on the side of his neck pulsed.

The second he backhanded me, my life turned ugly and gruesome, like something out of a horror movie. Darkness enveloped me, yet there was still a part of me that wanted to swing and fight back and hit him with all the strength in my 105-pound body. He was only five-foot-ten and about 165 pounds, but he worked out and was much stronger. I went still. Utterly quiet. I went into a state of paralysis. I didn't run from him. I didn't fight him. I froze. I was certain I'd married the devil.

I could barely make out Bryce's face through the tears in my eyes, pouring over my cheeks as my lip swelled to twice its size.

He was now a shadow over me. "Do you hear me? Do you?"

I wanted to shout, "How dare you! Don't you ever hit me again!" But fear froze me; I nodded, my tongue still wrapped around my teeth. I whimpered, "Mhm."

He backed away from me, my keys jingling in his hand, and then my car rumbled to life and screeched out of the parking lot. Part of me was relieved he was gone; the other part was livid he took my car and thought he could do whatever he wanted. The other part of me retreated so far back into a place, a dark place I never knew existed until that moment—or maybe I did. It was a place where I couldn't be heard or seen. I went into hiding, and the apartment became my prison.

The weight of what just happened made it difficult to move, but I knew I needed ice on my injuries. I was crying and I couldn't stop. I slowly stood up and got a glimpse of myself in the hallway mirror Bryce had hung. My mind couldn't take in my own reflection, the person staring back at me. *This can't be. This can't be me.* My upper lip was cut and was swollen and bruised, so I got ice from the freezer, put it in a plastic grocery bag, and wrapped it in a kitchen towel to put on my lip.

I lay down on our bed, curled my legs up, and buried my head in my pillow on my uninjured side. I finally stopped crying and then got lost in my racing mind. I was shocked at how angry Bryce got, and so fast.

Should I see a doctor?

Do I need stitches?

Should I call the police?

I worried what would happen if I told anyone. *Would he go to jail?* His arm swinging toward my face played over in my mind, and suddenly I noticed that I was digging my fingernails into my skin. I pulled the comforter up near my chin and prayed this would never happen again.

I must have dozed off, but the turning of the key in our front door woke me. Our bedroom door was unusually quiet, but I watched the door handle turning, and then Bryce's face appeared. He smiled at me, I'm sure hoping I'd smile back and that it would expunge his record. He walked in the bedroom and sat on the bed next to me. I moved away a little, too afraid to do what I wanted to do, which was jump off the bed and scream at him to leave. The wrinkle between his eyes was deep. He rubbed my arm and said, "I'm sorry for hitting you. I don't know what got into me. It will never happen again, I swear. I just hate it when someone swears at me, especially my wife."

Calling me "his wife" made me think maybe he did love me, that he didn't regret marrying me like my first husband did. Maybe he's just a regular guy who got too angry. I remember my dad used to get angry too. He hit us with his leather belt and hit my mother a few times. He'd get an inch from her face and yell at her, and she'd run off crying, Dad in hot pursuit. But then later, out of the same mouth, he'd say sweet things to her and to us kids about her, as if his words erased the spine-chilling way he had behaved earlier. And Mother seemed happy again, so I grew up thinking it was normal to be married to a Tasmanian devil–type guy who apologized and moved on, as if this is how life was going to go, this insane and terrifying roller-coaster ride—and we'd better just hold on and accept it.

Bryce's eyes and voice were soft when he apologized, and that gave me some assurance that he was sincere. I hoped he was, I needed him to be. I needed him to love me; I was starved for it. *Oh, God, please, please let him love me. Let this marriage be a good one. I need someone to love me.*

He went on, "My mom and stepdad argued all the time, and he'd yell and swear at her, and then he'd do the same to me. He didn't like me because I wasn't outdoorsy enough for him. He loved hunting and fishing, but I didn't. I was really close to my mom—still am—and I think that made him jealous. So, he would swear and call me names all the time." He wiped his eyes at tears that I didn't see. *Is he really crying?* "Swearing is, I don't know, like a trigger for my anger. Probably a good idea if you don't use curse words around me, ya know?"

He moved closer to me on the bed, but I stared at him, as if he were speaking a language I didn't understand. I didn't know how to respond. I wanted his apology to be true, and part of me believed him, while a mixture of fear and powerlessness branded me and made me *his*. I was still in shock. Plus, I was holding my teeth in place with my tongue. I held the bag of room-temperature water on my lip as he hugged me. Then he said, "I'll make dinner, and we can watch a movie, okay?" He didn't wait for my response and stood up to go into the kitchen.

Dinner and a movie wasn't as much of a request as it was a command. After someone hits you, you either fight back, run, or freeze like I did, and then you comply; if you don't, there will be more hitting, pushing, humiliation. Using his fist against my face was a crime that was unforgivable in marriage, I knew, but my first marriage failure weighed heavier on me than that of marrying an abusive bully. I didn't want to add yet another nuptial strike-out to my list of mistakes. I knew what my mother thought about people who divorced. I'd heard her judgment and condemnation about people with moral failures.

"Did you hear about your cousin Susan? She's getting another divorce. You know, all the grandchildren on your dad's side of the family have all been divorced at least once." She would remind me of this with a heavy sigh, as if she were the only one left on the planet who could make a

24

long-term commitment.

The weight of shame pushed down on me. *Why can't I find a husband who loves me?* Were my parents right all along, that no one would ever love me as much as they did? I had already married one man my mother didn't like, and his leaving me proved she was right about him, that he never really loved me. Now, I married another man she didn't like, and I started to wonder, *Was she right again?* Or was this just one really bad mistake that Bryce made and won't do again? I didn't want to admit my mother might be right, because then all hope would be lost of ever finding love. I lay back down in the fetal position and waited.

Bryce popped his head into the bedroom as if we were celebrating something and announced with a smile that dinner was ready. He pulled a bouquet of flowers out from behind his back and handed them to me. I tried to smile back, but the soreness shot through the side of my face. Two of my teeth were loose, and the skin on my lip might burst open if I moved it. I got off the bed, took the flowers, and walked into the bathroom. *Oh, God, I don't look like myself.* My eyes were red and puffy, and the bruise had inched its way up my cheek, turning blue, black, and purple. I continued to feel the impact of the back of Bryce's hand slamming into my mouth and his wedding ring tinging my teeth.

I didn't say anything throughout dinner; I stared at my food on the plate, pushed it around some, not eating anything, and sat like a corpse close by him. I didn't want to anger him again, yet I couldn't get my body or spirit to warm up to him. And my head ached.

Bryce cleared our plates, the ones my parents gave us for our wedding, and put them in the dishwasher. He came over to me and took me by the hand. "I gotta pee. When I get back, let's sit on the couch together and watch a movie."

Sitting at the table, I had a premonition that I had some power that night, albeit miniscule, and I needed to use it because tomorrow it would be gone. When the bathroom door closed, I walked over to the stove, opened the drawer, and pulled out my grandmother's skillet. I laid the heavy black skillet down gently on the stove where I wanted it. I had made my move, daring him to put it back in the drawer. That skillet was going to stay out on my stove, and I wanted Bryce to know it. My heart raced as I did it, partly out of fear, but also exhilaration that I had some sort of say-so.

I was afraid to push this moment much further, so I sat back down, and as soon as I did, he came out of the bathroom. As he approached me, his eyes darted past me and caught sight of the skillet. He didn't say a word; he simply took my hand and walked toward our worn leather couch. I waited, but he didn't mention the skillet. *One for me, a million for him.*

He wanted to lie together on the couch, so I tried the best I could without touching my cut lip or sore jaw. My eyes were on the television screen, but I saw nothing as my lip pulsed with its own heartbeat.

I needed more ice, but I couldn't move; fear had me by the throat as it pushed me up against this wall, its cold fingers squeezing, its long arm threatening to crush my chest until all air was gone.

How was I ever going to show my face at work on Monday? The bruise and cut would still be there, and people would notice. I thought about calling in sick, but I'd already missed the previous week and we needed the money. *I'll have to come up with some story to explain my bruises if I can't hide them with makeup; anything but the truth, but something believable.*

I trudged through the weekend, telling Kay, my best friend, I had a bad cold and avoided seeing anyone I knew until the inevitable Monday morning. I knew I had to face my coworkers, the worst one being my mother. I dreaded seeing her most of all. I didn't want her to know what a terrible choice in a husband I'd made *again*. I didn't want her to turn away from me like there was nothing she could do to help me.

Monday morning came, and I woke up with a pit in my stomach. I had tossed and turned all night, thinking of the daunting task before me, the deception I needed to pull off. I reconsidered all the lies I could tell to keep me from having to go to work, but I knew I had to go. I was sure the bruise on my face was going to be there all week like a bad cruise ship comedian.

I pulled my tired, achy body out of bed and dragged my feet to the bathroom to assess my face. The swelling was down, and the split lip had mostly healed, but the bruise, which had crept up to my cheek, was a greenish color. *Oh my God, this is bad. I hope my makeup can cover this.*

I showered, got dressed, and began the layering of cover-up, foundation, and powder until I looked dangerously close to a marionette. The right side of my face still ached, and now I had an unnatural greenish tint on my cheek. *I'll have to keep my face turned away from everyone as much as I can.*

"What happened? It looks like you have a bruise on your cheek," asked Debbie, a paralegal, one of my coworkers. She had her own troubling life, an ex-husband who never paid child support on time and a proclivity toward bar-room drama. Of course, she'd be the first not only to notice the bruise, but to say something loud enough for everyone to hear. If others in the office noticed, they had the social awareness not to ask me in front of God and everybody. But not Debbie. I stumbled a bit in my reply, but because I had rehearsed it over and over, the lie came out easier than I thought.

"Oh, I slipped and fell and hit the railing outside our apartment as I came down. Yes, yes, it hurt, and I put ice on it right away." Then: "Oh, yes, I'll have to be more careful next time." *Oh, God, get me out of this conversation. Just let the earth open up and swallow me whole. God. Please. Just take me now.*

The office was open, with two cubicles, one being my mother's. As the receptionist, I sat up front where everyone could see and hear me. Because of the open floor plan, everyone's conversations carried through the entire office, and I'm sure my mother made out every word.

The morning continued on, clients coming and going, and I was able to make it through without anyone else, so far, saying anything about my face. Then, my mother called my desk. "I need to talk to you about some of these files when you have a break."

Oh, my God, this is it. I didn't want to admit to her that my husband did this to me. She didn't like Bryce anyway, so if she knew he did this to me, I didn't know what would happen. Maybe I'd find a way out, I don't know. My mind was blurry, and I didn't know how I could avoid this conversation.

About fifteen minutes later, I gathered up my courage and fake cheerfulness and walked into my mother's office. She wore black pants, a pink sweater, and her pearls. She was slim, and her hair was perfectly put together. And there I was, an emotional and physical mess. "Is there a problem with some of the files?" I made sure to keep the greenish-blue side of my face away from her.

"Here, sit down. No, there's no problem, but do you see these boxes here? They all need to be taken to the storage facility and kept there." She shuffled papers around on her desk and signed a check. She asked, "Can you do that? Of course, the firm will pay you."

I made a slight turn of my head to count the boxes and, in so doing, exposed my battered mouth and cheek. I quickly realized my mistake and caught her eyes zoomed in on my injury. She met my eyes too, and for a second, we sat there, with nothing to say, as I gazed off in shame.

Maybe she recognized herself in me, or maybe she was silently judging me.

I filled the silence between me and my mother/office manager with, "Oh. Yeah, sure, I'll do that. When do you need it done?"

She played with her necklace as if deep in thought and said, "Anytime by the end of the month is fine." She swallowed and then turned away to resume her accounts payable.

I'm sure she saw it. I pulled my hair forward to hide the bruise and said with as much positivity in my voice as I could collect, "Okay, I can get started tomorrow afternoon." I lingered, but when it was clear that Mother had nothing more to say, I left her office.

I was relieved when the day was over, but on the way home, I wondered how I ended up so unhappy, aching for love without conditions and expectations. The sadness in my heart didn't add up with the way I was raised, because my parents always told me that we had a good family and they loved us. So, why did love seem so impossible for me, the one thing in life I longed for, but could never get?

I walked into our apartment, and Bryce was there with dinner on the table and more fresh flowers for me.

"Hey, honey, I missed you today. How was your day?" He kissed my non-bruised cheek and hugged me. He held me and rubbed my back for several minutes.

"It was okay. To be honest, it was hard hiding this bruise, and it still really hurts."

He pulled me away and his eyes wandered over my face.

"I'm so sorry. You are beautiful to me. Hey, after dinner, I'll clean up, and then you want to go on a walk on that trail you're always talking about?"

All this kindness made me start to warm up to him. I liked this Bryce, the one who paid attention to me and said sweet things. *Maybe he really is sorry. Maybe he just made a mistake and won't let it happen again. Maybe we could have a good marriage after all.* Discounting the bruise peering through my makeup, I replied, "Sure, I'd like that."

3

A Leather Belt

" Mother, where are you going? Can I go too? I don't want to stay here with Daddy." I was days away from turning five years old and I was attached to my mother, wanting to be with her every moment of every day. This afternoon, she was dressed up in her silky gold and green flowery pants outfit, and I thought it was the prettiest thing she'd worn all week. My mother had a laugh and an energy that was infectious. Everyone wanted to be in her presence, including me.

"I'm going to choir practice, honey, you can't go with me. And then after that, I have a Bible study with a few ladies from choir. It's going to be late when I get home, so you'll be in bed already."

My head rested in my hands as I watched her tease her bleached-blond hair and spray it; I had to leave the bathroom, though, so I could breathe. I walked into their closet to play with Daddy's electric shoe shiner. It had a red side and a black side, and I loved the way the fuzzy material tickled my palms when it spun around fast. I took a pair of

Daddy's black wingtip shoes that he wore every day to work and pretended to buff them. "Savannah, get out of our closet!" Mother yelled from the bathroom. "Stop playing with that shoe buffer! I've told you a thousand times that's not a toy."

I went back into the bathroom and watched her apply makeup. My most favorite part was when, with black liquid eyeliner, she added a tiny dot on the left side of her mouth, like Elizabeth Taylor. I wanted her to do that to me, so I asked, "Mother, can I have a dot like you? Is that a mole?"

She pulled her chin in and laughed as if I had caught her in a lie. "It's not a mole! It's a beauty mark."

"A beauty mark?" I asked.

"Yes, a beauty mark. You're almost five years old now, and all women have one, somewhere." She winked at me. I wasn't sure what she meant by that, but I liked how she cupped my face with her right hand and drew a dot above my lip with her left hand. I liked my beauty mole and I tried not to touch it so it would stay on for a long time, but my face itched and I scratched it, which made the mole look like I drew on my face with black marker.

I thought my mother was the prettiest of all my friends' mothers. I loved her clothes, her makeup, the sparkly necklace she wore, and the matching earrings, tiny chandeliers hanging down from her ears, catching the light and shimmering. She touched people on the arm and leaned into them when she laughed, and hugged people, leaving her Norell perfume to linger long after she was gone. She had a lot of friends and I wanted to be just like her.

"Savannah! Your beauty mark's already messed up!" She threw her eyeliner on the counter and made a sound like she was exasperated. I followed her as she walked through the house talking. "Daddy's going to babysit you, Michelle, and Chelsea, okay? I expect you to be good for Daddy." Michelle was my older sister. She was nine, and Chelsea was only two. Mother kissed Daddy goodbye, walked out the door, and drove off to church, where she spent the better part of Sundays and Wednesday nights. My mother loved church and Jesus. And just maybe she enjoyed the break from my dad and us kids.

I didn't want Daddy to babysit. He never let me do anything. He wanted me to stay inside and play quietly, but I loved being outside, getting dirt under my fingernails. Andy, my best friend across the street, and I wanted to go next door because there was a big pile of red clay that we couldn't wait to run up and down. We lived in Alabama, where within the soil, oxygen, iron, and water combine to create bright-red clay. If there was one thing Andy and I had in common, it was clay-dirt; we both loved getting our hands in it.

I asked Daddy if I could play with Andy, and he said, "After dinner, but don't go next door and play in the dirt, do you hear me?"

The dirt pile was the whole point of going outside to play, and I wanted to go over there so badly I could die. "Yes, sir," I mumbled.

I ate dinner with Daddy, Chelsea, and Michelle and then walked over to my friend's house. He came out scratching his head full of red curls and asked, "You wanna go play in the dirt?"

As if I'd never had a conversation with my daddy, I said "Yes!" and off we went to the forbidden dirt pile.

I loved Andy and knew he'd be my best buddy till the end of time. He understood me. He shared my love of dirt and bugs and Indians. He came over almost every day and rang our doorbell and asked if I could play. I missed him the days he didn't come over. It was rare that my mother allowed me to go to his house and ask if he could play. "No daughter of mine will chase boys," she told me.

When we played, we'd run around the yard shooting at imaginary bad guys with our cap guns. I imagined that I was a cowgirl with a hat and a white-and-brown paint horse. He was a cowboy, and we had Indian friends. We'd explore the red canyons and deserts together and fight "the bad guys," dirty, dusty cowboys gone bad. After a long day of riding, when the sun went down, we'd huddle around a pretend campfire that we'd built with sticks and talk about the day and sing songs.

Andy and I skipped over to the mountain of red-orange clay that stained anything that came within an inch of it, but it was the most fun two five-year-olds could have. As we made our way next door, I was giggling and glowing and Daddy didn't enter my mind, not even when I was elbow-deep in the dirt.

I stooped down to play in the cool clay. I liked how it stained my skin, my hands turning reddish. I stuck my little white arms in the pile of dirt and pulled out little pink arms. My heart soared as I ran up the side of the clay mountain; we ran up and down the hill, rolled down it, and ran back up, and now we were covered in dirt. I believed I was strong, capable, and part of the earth. I loved being outdoors—the air, the smell, the trees, dirt, snails, roly-polies, the green grass, and the blue sky. My hands muddy with the terracotta earth, I reached up and rubbed my nose till the itch was gone and then wiped the sweat from my forehead. The wind blew my hair, and I pretended I was a wild horse running free.

Until "Savannah! Savannah!" ripped through the backyards and stopped me in my tracks. My daddy didn't sound very happy. He was a marine, and very tough. I had a bad feeling that I was about to find out just how tough he was. I told Andy I had to go home. He slumped his shoulders and kicked at the gravel driveway as he trudged back to his house.

I ran back to my house but walked backward through the door and closed it as if someone were sleeping. I turned to find Daddy standing right there. My red-stained sneakers, arms, and face betrayed me. His cheeks exploded red, and his eyes twitched. I tried to bolt up the stairs, but he grabbed my pink arm, almost picking me up off the ground, and yelled loud enough for the neighborhood to hear, "Didn't I tell you not to go over there?" He shook me by my arm. "Didn't I? And you went anyway?"

I knew what was coming. He wrangled with his belt, and before I could react, he grabbed the buckle, pulled the belt loose from his pants, and made a loop. Then the madness started. He started swinging like he was cutting weeds, clearing a trail, and with every swipe, the belt stung my tender flesh. I screamed and cried out and jumped with every swing. He yelled, "I'll show you what happens when you disobey me! You'll never do that again, will you?" When I didn't answer fast enough for him, because I was trying to breathe, he yelled, "Huh? Do you hear me? I'm talking to you! You'll never do that again, do you understand me?"

"Y-Y-Yes s-s-sir," I stuttered between sobs. My tiny frame was shaking, and my skin was burning. I couldn't touch the wounds; they would hurt worse. I needed ice, but I didn't dare ask for that.

He said, "Take your shoes off and leave them by the door." I did as he said and stood there crying, and I thought the mayhem was over, but Daddy was volcanic, out of control. He started swinging his belt again.

I tried to run from him, but he was faster and my socks slowed me down and the leather belt caught my flesh with each swipe. My bottom and legs were on fire—they felt singed. He kept hitting me as he chased me up the stairs and into my bedroom.

"Find your pajamas and stop that crying!" he yelled over my wailing. I stood in front of my dresser and I saw my red swollen face in the mirror and thought, *Daddy is going to feel sorry for hurting me.* But instead, he said, "Stop your crying, or I'll give you something to cry about!"

I could feel the welts and heat growing on my legs as my daddy continued barking orders. I opened my dresser drawer and found my pajama shorts. When I slid my legs into the cloth; every movement, every swipe of the material on my skin burned my bottom and legs as if they were on fire.

I lay in my bed, tears streaming down my face, and tried to cover my legs, but even the light top sheet stung. "It hurts, the sheet hurts," I cried.

"Cover your legs! I won't tell you again!" Daddy yelled.

I pulled the sheet over my legs and I held my breath as the sheet floated down over me. I lay as still as a corpse until Daddy turned and left the room, slamming the door behind him. As soon as I thought that he wouldn't come storming back in, I softly lifted the top sheet off my legs.

I longed for my mom to come home or for my sisters to come visit with me, but no one came. *Where are my sisters?* The house was quiet. With every staccato-inhaled breath, I believed my daddy was the meanest man on earth. I thought my mom would come home any minute and tell me that Daddy was wrong for what he did. I pictured Mother comforting me and vindicating me. I waited. I waited even as the light waned and turned to night.

My legs continued to smolder, even without any covering and with them bent. My bottom ached, and I tried to lie on my side, but I couldn't find a painless position. I lay—alone, crying, and in pain—waiting for my mother.

With each beam of headlight that floated across my bedroom walls and ceiling, hope rose that my mom was home to save me, but she never came. I was sure the burning pain and my desire for my mommy to comfort me would keep me awake, but finally sleep overtook me. Before

I fell into that dark nocturnal abyss, I stuck my thumb in my mouth and wondered, *Where is Mother?*

Mother clanging metal spoons in pots and pans woke me the next morning. I lay in my bed staring at my door, wondering if Mother knew what happened last night. I wondered if Daddy was still mad and if he would have his belt ready to start whipping me again.

I lay in bed awhile longer until I heard Michelle's shuffle down the hall. As I crawled out of bed, I winced when the sheets rubbed against the red marks on my legs. My mother's arms around me would wash away the worry I had about Daddy. But when I crept into the kitchen, she squinted at me and her mouth was as straight as a line. I knew not to go to her, so I slowed my pace and sat at the table.

I rubbed my burning eyes as I sat in the chair closest to Chelsea. She was in her high chair giggling and kicking her legs while Michelle fed her eggs. The smell of coffee and warm biscuits in the oven brought Daddy into the kitchen, and I stopped breathing for a second.

He walked right up to Mother and gave her a kiss. She smiled at him and asked if he wanted coffee and scurried around plopping eggs, sausage, and biscuits on his plate. My chest tightened when Daddy sat down next to me with his food and said, "Why aren't you eating? Aren't you hungry?" He dipped his knife in the butter and spread it across the warm biscuit.

Mother said, "I offered her food, but she said no."

I wondered when she offered me food. Did I not hear her? I was hungry, but I looked away from my parents and the empty spot on the table in front of me.

I sat on the far edge of my chair because the back of my legs hurt, and also because I didn't want to sit close to my daddy. My eyes were wide, and I stared at the back of Mother's head, wishing she'd put her spatula down and give me a hug. She didn't, so I put my thumb in my mouth and sucked it like I was nine days old.

When Mother turned back around, she pointed the spatula at me and said in a shrill voice, "And take that thumb out of your mouth this minute!" I took it out but put it right back in as soon as Mother turned back to the stove. I tried so hard to hide it, but I was addicted to my thumb. It comforted me.

"After breakfast, I'm going to put that stuff on your thumb, Savannah!" Mother threatened.

No! Not the *stuff*! It was a clear liquid that, when put on the skin, dried quickly but had a bitter taste. When I'd forget it was on my thumb and stick my thumb in my mouth, the most repulsive taste would be all over my tongue and I couldn't get rid of it. I hated it, and my mother was cruel for putting it on my most precious beloved thumb.

Daddy looked at me, and I pulled my thumb, with a string of spit attached like a thread, out of my mouth. He said, "Are you going to go play next door in the dirt anymore?" His eyes were wild, like they were going to pop out of his head.

"N-No sir," I said, terrified from last night's horror.

"If you're not going to eat, you can go," Daddy said with a mouthful of breakfast. Mother averted her eyes.

I went outside and sat on the front porch where the cold cement soothed my burned thighs from last night's leather lashes. I looked over at Andy's house and wondered if he could play. Just then, he and his mom pulled into their driveway, and one of Michelle's friends, Lisa, walked over to play with her. I ran to the edge of my yard waving my arms to flag Andy down as he got out of the car. I yelled, "Hi, Andy, can you play?" He shuffled his feet and glanced at his mother.

She said, "No, honey, I'm sorry. We have family plans today. Maybe another time."

I dropped my head and meandered back to our front porch, kicking pebbles and pinecones. I crunched through the pine straw near the side of our house to a honeysuckle bush and pulled off a honeysuckle flower to taste its sweet nectar. I plucked another one off to bring to Michelle.

Mother was changing Chelsea's diaper, so I went down the hall to Michelle's room. Her door was closed, and I knocked. There was no answer, and it was oddly quiet. I knocked louder, and she shouted, "Leave me alone! Lisa and I are playing now, and we don't want you to bug us."

I leaned on the wall, popping off the end of the honeysuckle flower and licking it. I slid to the floor, and Mother stepped over me with a laundry basket in her arms walking directly into Michelle's room without knocking. Michelle said, "Hey!" and Mother said, "Don't 'hey' me." I stood up to peek in Michelle's room, and I flinched because the carpet swiped one of my burns.

"Lisa, your mother called and wants you to head

home," Mother said.

Lisa groaned.

"You just got here. I wish you could stay longer!" Michelle whined.

I followed along as Mother and Michelle walked Lisa to the front door. After the girls said goodbye, promising to hang out later that afternoon, my sister, Mom, and I headed into the kitchen. Michelle said, "Mother, I'd like to get a pair of jodhpurs. Lisa's getting some today with her mom."

Mother laughed as she got out bowls and the mixer. "Jodhpurs? Oh, Michelle, you can't wear those. Your legs are too much like your nanna's. They're too short, and jodhpurs would make you look even shorter."

Michelle's shoulders rounded, and she hung her head. "I still want a pair. Lisa says I'll look good in them."

"Friends tell us what they think we want to hear, Michelle. She's not being honest with you like I am. I'm sorry, honey, but it's only because I love you that I'm telling you this." Mother smiled.

Michelle's face reddened.

Mother said, "Now, come on over here and let's bake that cake we talked about."

I perked up. "Can I help too?"

Michelle said matter-of-factly, "No, I'm doing it right now."

Mother pulled out a stool for my sister and said, "Here, you need this. You know, there's nothing wrong with being long-waisted like your dad's side of the family."

Michelle said, "It looks like Chelsea is too."

"Yes, it looks like it," Mother replied sadly. "But what matters is on the inside, not the outside, girls."

Michelle climbed up on the stool, one step at a time, and then Mother explained that she had to sift two cups of flour and pour it in another bowl.

I sat at the kitchen table while Chelsea played in her playpen. I watched my mother prepare the pans for the cake by putting Crisco all over them, and Michelle was at the end of her sifting flour. She stood there with the sifter in her hand and she had those little balls of flour that collect at the bottom. Michelle didn't know what to do with them, so she dumped the tiny balls of flour into the bowl of sifted flour.

Mother saw her do it and said, as if Michelle's hair was on fire, "Michelle! No! Why would you do that? You've ruined the flour now! You have to do it all over again. How stupid!"

Michelle jumped down from the stool and ran up to her room crying, slamming her bedroom door.

I said, "I'll do it, Mother. I know how to sift." I stood up and got up on the stool and took over the sifting job. I wanted to run after Michelle and tell her it was okay, but I wanted Mother to be happy and I knew sifted flour would make her happy. Usually my efforts at comforting Michelle didn't work, but that didn't stop me from trying. I heard a sniffle behind me, and there stood Michelle with puffy eyes and a red nose.

"Michelle, come here, and I'll show you how to sift if you want," I said, trying to remain cheerful.

"Shut up, Savannah. I know how to sift flour, you little twerp."

Mother snapped, "Michelle, don't you speak to your sister that way!"

But Michelle only glared at me, and her dislike for me grew.

About four years into Alabama, my dad got a job promotion and moved us to Atlanta. I was sad to leave Andy, and Michelle had friends she had to leave too, but my parents were excited because it put them close to their families. Mom found a trilevel house for us, and we nestled into a neighborhood with lots of other young families where we made new friends.

Mother immediately found a church for us to attend, twice on Sunday, plus Wednesday night prayer service. She joined the choir and a women's Bible study and served on the board of the Christian Women's Club. All of her friends were Christians, and they called often to ask her to pray for them. My mom was an Eagle Scout Christian.

One afternoon, I relaxed on the couch beside my mother, and as she rubbed my back, our doorbell rang. It was my aunt Louise and uncle Mike and their two children, seven-year-old Mary and six-year-old Bobby. We kids immediately ran upstairs to play, while the adults sat in the living room talking and laughing.

After about an hour or so, I heard Mother yell, "Savannah! Come down here! We want you to do your

Edith Ann impression."

I didn't want to be torn away from my cousins. Mother yelled for me a second time, and I groaned and walked down the stairs to the living room where Aunt Louise and Uncle Mike sat on our blue velvet couch, anticipatory smiles stuck on their faces as they waited for me to do my shtick.

"Come on, come on. You can sit over there," instructed my mother as she pointed to the overly large rocking chair. My dad sat off to the side, drinking his Schlitz malt liquor beer.

"I wanna go back upstairs and play," I told Mother.

"Oh, now, it'll only be a minute. Go on, and do some Edith Ann," Mother urged.

"You're so funny, Savannah." My aunt Louise laughed and slapped her knee. She loved my antics and wanted to see me do my thing. She said to my mother, "Carol, she is very talented. You oughta get that girl into some acting classes."

My cousins and Chelsea ran by the living room, taking snacks back upstairs to the bedroom where we'd created an imaginary world. They were laughing and talking, and I muttered, "I'm coming back—wait for me."

Once, I'd refused to sing a song for one of Mother's friends, and she ignored me for a week, so I knew this was a situation that could easily go sideways for me. But seeing my cousins and sisters have so much fun drove me to say softly, "Mother, can I please go back upstairs?"

Daddy slammed down his can of beer on the table. My heart raced because his face was red, his eyes big and round, and I thought if I didn't comply, he'd take off his belt and spank me.

I hurried over to the rocking chair and scooted all the way back. I choked back the tears, wiped my hair out of my eyes, sniffled, and cleared my throat. "My name is Edith Ann, and I'm five and a half years old," I began, making it sound like I had a cold. A couple of tears escaped my eyes, but I quickly wiped them away and got back into character.

"Oh, this is so cute and funny," Uncle Mike said. He was laughing and drinking his bourbon on the rocks.

I tried to recall the skits I'd seen from the Rowan and Martin's Laugh-In television show, repeating Lily Tomlin's performance and adding my own particular spice to it, reading my audience much like I read my parents' reactions to life. If a chuckle slipped out from my aunt or uncle, I knew I had something, and I reeled that line in, ending my skit with the famous "and that's the truth!" and then sticking my tongue out and blowing.

The roar of adult laughter turned out to be mind-altering for me; I looked around the room and smiled. The tightness in my chest released, and a warm feeling of approval washed over me. Mother said, "Ah, Savannah, you're so funny! That was great! Do you have any more you can do? What about your Red Skelton walk you do? Do that for them. And then play your piano recital pieces you've been working on."

My mother's pride spread like a peacock's feathers. It gave me pleasure to see my mom smile and hear her brag about me to her friends and our extended family. I breathed in the perfume of her approval, and with every inhale,

I became higher on her endorsement of me. I noticed that my sisters had come into the room and that Michelle was giving me a cold stare.

I didn't mean to be an attention hog; it's just that I liked to make Mother and Daddy happy. They were a lot nicer to live with when they were laughing and bragging on their daughter than when they were yelling and blaming us for everything that went wrong and chasing us with belts. It was a good thing to joke around and do impressions in front of them. They enjoyed it, and it kept them in a good mood.

It was bizarre living with these people. One minute everything was okay, the next it was violent chaos, then everything settled back down again to its quiet doldrum. But it wasn't really okay; it's just what Mother and Daddy wanted us and everyone to believe.

4

The Black Sheep

I woke Saturday morning to the usual smell of frying bacon. Mother accepted the job of cooking every meal in our home as part of her God-given responsibility, as if she had read the contract beforehand, weighed the pros and cons, signed the thing, and then proceeded to fulfill her duties, no questions asked.

Even after she started working full time as a secretary, before leaving the house, she remembered to take meat, hard as a rock, out of the freezer for dinner. She then rushed home to fry the thawed meat, peel, cut, and boil potatoes, open a can of green beans, and make corn bread and sweet tea—staples of every dinner. My mother's job of taking care of us girls, making all the meals for the family, and all the housework never changed, even after taking on a forty-hour-per-week job.

I was the oldest of our little neighborhood friend group. I was the six-year-old leader of the pack. Michelle was twelve, and she thought she was too old to play with us. She had her own friends, anyway. Chelsea and I spent our summers racing to the swing set at night, swinging as high as we could before the pole nearly came out of the ground. We'd sing Bobby Vinton's song "Sealed with a Kiss" at the tops of our lungs. And on more nights than I can count, we ran around with our friends catching fireflies.

Still, there were times I wanted to be with Michelle and her friends. This particular Saturday morning, after we ate and Daddy had left for work, Michelle was outside with her friends, Kathy, Tommy, and Luke, and they were planning on walking to the five-and-dime, about ten minutes away from our house. They were all in the seventh grade and old enough to go hang out at the Ben Franklin store.

I ran outside too and called out, "Can I go? I wanna go with y'all."

"No! You can't go with us," Michelle said, annoyance in her voice. "You're too young."

"Please, I won't talk or anything. Please?" I begged her.

"Savannah, I said no! I hate when you're always trying to tag along. I just want to be with my friends."

Mother had walked out and overheard what Michelle said. She yelled, "Michelle, you let Savannah go with you! You need to include her. Don't be so mean."

Michelle rolled her eyes, tilted her head, and groaned. When Mother went back inside, Michelle took the chance to say, "Fine, you little brat, but don't talk. Just walk behind us. Got it?"

I was thrilled that Michelle was letting me join her gang of cool friends. I knew she didn't like me, but I wanted her to, so I vowed quietly to myself to be as cool as they were.

Luke and Tommy rolled their eyes too.

We left for the store, and within five minutes, beads of sweat formed on my forehead. It was only ten in the morning, but the temperature had already climbed to ninety-five degrees. With no reprieve of shade, the late-summer heat beat down on us. The air was thick, and it was hard to breathe as I counted the squares of sidewalk cement. I took as big of steps as my little legs could take to keep up with Michelle and the gang, and yet stay behind them. I was just coming close to regretting the trip when we reached the store and Kathy opened the door. I walked into the air-conditioning, and it was like easing into a cool bath. Every one of us kids said some version of "Ah!" or "Oh, it feels so good in here!"

Unfortunately, we didn't stay in the store that long. I didn't have any money, and whatever Michelle and her friends had come for, they either got, or the store didn't have, I wasn't sure. I held a plastic ballerina necklace between my fingers when Michelle found me and said, "Come on, Savannah, let's go."

Instead of going home the same way we came, Tommy, in his baggy jeans and white T-shirt, said, "Let's go this way." And we all followed him, as if he was our trusted leader.

We rounded the corner of the back of the building, and Tommy and Luke stopped walking, reached into their front pockets, and pulled out cigarettes. Michelle, anticipating this scene to happen, pulled out a lighter, flicked it, and lit a cigarette for Tommy as if she'd been doing it since learning her ABCs. They each lit cigarettes, leaned on the brick wall, and smoked.

Smoking was something Daddy did, but Mother made it absolutely clear that smoking was off-limits to us girls forever. She added it to the list of immoral activities, but I'd sneak a smell of an old cigarette butt in Daddy's ashtray, and I loved the initial odor from the match when he'd first light up. Or when he used a lighter, I'd open up the lid and take a whiff of the fluid inside. But to see my sister participate in this forbidden activity—that was unthinkable. I knew that Michelle was smoking, because Mother and Daddy had screamed at her that she'd better not *ever* smoke in *their* house again, but I'd never witnessed this wonder with my own eyes. She held the cigarette between her fingers like Daddy did, lit it up, took a pull, inhaled, and blew out a smoke ring. I was enthralled with my big sister and captured by the fact that at twelve years old, she was smoking like Rita Hayworth.

"Can I try?" The words came out of my mouth before I realized what I was saying. But I wanted to try it. I wanted to do what she was doing. I wanted to be cool like Michelle.

"No! Mom would kill me," she snapped back.

"Please? I just want to try one! I won't tell. Just let me try one. Please?"

"Come on, Michelle, let her try just one. It'll be fun to watch her!" Tommy said as he puffed his own chimney of smoke.

After I wore her down, or she wanted to make Tommy happy, she said okay. She handed me the white stick, and I held it between my little fingers, almost dropping it. I got the right end in my mouth, and she lit it for me, but I didn't know what to do.

"You have to breathe in. Like this," Michelle explained. And she showed me how abnormally one inhales smoke. I imitated her and almost coughed to death.

I hated it, the bitter burning in my mouth and throat. I all but threw the cigarette at her. I wanted no more of it as I coughed so hard that I thought I broke a rib. The older kids laughed, Michelle included, and she had quite a loud laugh that lingered longer than the others'. But I wanted to impress her and do what she was doing, so after my coughing fit died down, I extended my hand for her to give me another try at it. She handed the cigarette back to me, and I tried it again and again, coughing like an emphysema patient, until I got the hang of breathing in smoke into my virgin lungs. Before long, we lounged by the brick wall, unhurriedly finishing our cigarettes, like old souls who'd seen more of life than the average elementary school-age child.

And then, this urge for *more*. It came up slowly through my lungs and then into my brain. I finished the one cigarette and wanted another. "Can I have another one?" I asked.

"No! One is enough," Michelle chided. Turning to Tommy, she said, "Can you believe her?" They roared with laughter.

"Oh, just one more. I need it!" I begged.

That got them really going. Luke and Tommy were pushing each other and laughing so hard I thought they were going to fall over. Kathy was laughing too, but not nearly as hysterically. She said, "I think we should go back to your house now, Michelle." I started begging Michelle for another, but she wouldn't give it to me. Instead, she laughed at my insistence.

"You're crazy, Savannah. You're my crazy little sister." They thought it was hilarious to watch a six-year-old become an expert smoker right before their eyes. I thought I'd grown six inches taller and gained their respect.

As we walked back to our house, I started to feel a little nauseated. I went to my room and plopped down in my chair and put my head down on my white French provincial desk. When the bile entered my throat, I ran to the bathroom, but I couldn't vomit. I put cold water on my face, then went and lay down on my bed. Mother came in and said, "Did you have fun?"

"Uh-huh," I muffled.

"What's wrong? Are you sick?" She came over and rested her hand on my forehead. "Huh, you feel a little warm, but it could just be the heat. Just stay in here for a while, and you'll feel better."

A fog of guilt overcame me. I knew my parents didn't like smoking, in spite of the fact that my daddy smoked two and a half packs a day. He smoked in the house and in the car with only his window cracked a quarter of an inch, while we kids suffocated in the back. But my mother—she'd be so hurt and angry and disappointed in me. I thought I might go to hell for what I'd done, and I believed the only way to escape that fate was to confess my sin to Mother. A chasm had formed in our family that divided us between the good and the bad. Mother was on the good side, and when I smoked, I was different from her; it put me on the bad side, and I couldn't take it. The separation was similar to when she ignored me. I felt cut off from her, an unbearable pain.

I'd forgotten about my promise to Michelle not to tell our parents, and I didn't consider the ramifications for her if I told. I worried about the punishment I would receive, but I needed relief from the shame and alienation that burned in my chest.

The lawn mower sputtered across the lawn, and I knew Daddy was home. Michelle and Kathy were laughing and talking in Michelle's bedroom.

"Do you want to play a game?" I asked Chelsea, who was drawing pictures on her bed across from me.

"No, I'm drawing. But you can draw with me."

I sat on the bed next to her, and we drew pictures together for about thirty minutes, and then the lawn mower cut off. My stomach churned as I thought about telling my parents what I had done.

Kathy went home, and when she did, I hunted for Mother; she'd be easier to tell than Daddy. I found her in the laundry room, shoving sheets into the washer. She asked, "How are you feeling, honey?"

"Good." I put my foot in an empty clothes basket and moved it around nervously. "I smoked today."

She stopped stuffing and shoving. "What did you do?" Her eyes were wrinkled together.

My hands were clammy, and my throat was dry. I swallowed and said, "I smoked a cigarette."

"You . . . you smoked a cigarette?" Her voice got louder and higher-pitched by the time she got out the word *cigarette*. She closed her eyes, grimaced, and turned away with her hand on her heart. After a few seconds, she turned toward me and asked, "You smoked with Michelle, didn't you?"

"Yes ma'am," my voice quivered. I was breathing heavier and I thought my heart was going to beat out of my chest. She could make a shiver run up my spine, even on a hot Georgia July afternoon.

"I'm gonna kill Michelle!" Mother dropped the shirt she was folding and pushed past me screaming, "Michelle! Michelle!"

By the time Mother was done yelling, Michelle, Daddy, Mother, and I were all in the kitchen having a family meeting.

Daddy said to Michelle, "Why would you give your six-year-old sister a cigarette? What is wrong with you?"

Mother was crying, like she always did, and said, "I never thought you'd stoop this low, Michelle. I knew you didn't like Savannah, but to do *this* to her? I'm just sickened by this. You make me sick!"

Dad turned to his crying wife and said, "Who let Savannah go with Michelle, anyway? Did you give her permission?" His eyes bulged out of their sockets.

"No! I most certainly did not!" Mother lied.

My eyes grew wide, and I tried to steady my breathing. Michelle glanced at me nervously and said, her voice quivering, "Yes, you did, Mother. You told me I had to let her come with me."

Mother's tears magically dried up. She stood up from the kitchen table, lips puckered, and as indignant as a person can be, she shouted, "How dare you! You little liar! I never gave her permission! I would *never* do that. I told you to include her and to stop being mean to her, but I never told you to take her to the store and smoke with her! Never! I swear, as God as my witness, I don't know what I did to deserve this. I don't know what I did to deserve a child like you, Michelle." She walked out of the kitchen, stomped up the stairs, and slammed her door so hard that the kitchen light above the table shook.

Even though Mother was so upset, in a strange way, I was absolved of any wrongdoing, as if I had confessed to the pope. I was a "good girl" again, like I was on the good side of things, connected with Mother.

My daddy said to Michelle, "You're grounded for two weeks. Now go to your room."

"What about her?" Michelle pointed her finger at me, and I froze with fear. She was trying to get him to punish me? I hope he doesn't take off his belt!

"You don't worry about her—you worry about yourself! You've got enough problems of your own, young lady," Daddy yelled.

"I hate it here! Savannah never gets in trouble. I can't wait to move out of here the day I turn eighteen." *Michelle hates it here because of me?*

My dad yelled back at her, "Go ahead and leave, but

leave everything, even the clothes on your back, because I own it all, you ungrateful brat! You think you'd make it a day out there by yourself? Go ahead and try. But don't you ever come crawling back to me or your mother when it all falls apart." He slammed his fists down on the table right in front of Michelle, and it made us both jump.

I was very confused and scared. *Is Michelle leaving? Where would she go? And why is Daddy trying to get her to take off her clothes? Will she be naked on the street? Oh, God, I'm scared, and I don't like this.* I hunkered down in my chair and lowered my head, wondering what my punishment was going to be.

Daddy stood up straight, and when he did, his hand hit a drinking glass that was on the edge of the table and it fell off and shattered.

I thought Daddy was angry before, but he actually growled. "Look what you made me do!" He started wrangling with his belt, and I knew exactly what was coming; both Michelle and I tried to get out of our chairs as fast as we could to run up the stairs, but Daddy was always faster at getting his belt off than we were at running up the stairs. He started swinging and yelling, "If I ever catch you two smoking again, I swear to God, I'm going to spank you till you can't sit down for a week! Do you hear me?"

Michelle and I reached our bedrooms about the same time, and we both slammed our doors shut, hoping that would keep him out. It worked, and I wondered if he needed to go smoke a cigarette to calm down. I'd heard my mother once tell him to go smoke when he was getting angry. With all the excitement, I didn't notice if he'd hit me or not. I examined my legs and only saw two stripes forming on the back of my right calf. *Two's not too bad.*

Chelsea was still drawing, staring down at her paper, as if she hadn't been bothered at all by any of the screaming and fighting and door-slamming.

I used to fantasize that we sisters rallied together, met in our bedrooms underneath the covers with a flashlight, coming up with a plan of collaboration and bravery to stand up to our parents and protect each another and end the abuse. The problem with that fantasy, however, is that we didn't know we were being abused. Our parents told us that everything they did, they did because they loved us and that no one would ever love us as much as they did; thus, our lives seemed normal to us. In addition, part of Mother's strategy was to turn us against each other. She wanted to keep us apart so she could have us to herself when she needed us.

The next morning was Sunday, and we all went to church, even Daddy. Mother was ignoring all of us, but as soon as we got to church, she put on her best smile and started chatting with everyone and made sure she talked with the ladies from her choir and Bible study. We played our part by wearing our best clothes and smiles too so they'd think we were a nice, happy Christian family. From my viewpoint, people seemed to believe us; no one ever suspected that anything was wrong.

At home, the smiles disappeared, and as we sat down for lunch, Mother insisted that we hold hands and say a prayer. "Dear Heavenly Father, thank you for this beautiful day and thank you for this food. I pray for Michelle, that you will help her give her life to you, Lord Jesus. Please help us always glorify and honor you in all we do and say. In your precious Son's name, I pray, Amen."

I peeked at Michelle during the prayer, and her eyes were wide open, staring straight ahead at nothing, really, just staring.

Chelsea said, "I made a bean cross today."

"Oh, how nice. Did you bring it home?" Mother asked.

Chelsea hopped up out of her seat and ran to get it. She brought back a piece of paper with beans glued on it in the shape of a cross, or a plus sign, either way. We all told her how good it was, and then Mother put it on the refrigerator. It was the perfect opportunity for one of Mother's lectures.

"When we do what Jesus wants us to do, then our lives are happier, girls. If we don't, then our lives are full of trouble. You remember my second cousin, Ruth, don't you, the one who's been married twice and has three children from three different men? Well, her daughter got herself pregnant and now she's going to have a child out of wedlock." She shook her head and adjusted her plate, as if the food made her sad.

"What's 'out of wedlock' mean?" I asked.

"It means they're not married, and you shouldn't have children until you're married," Mother answered. "That makes the Lord very angry."

I wondered what the Lord did when he was angry. Did he have a leather belt? Did he slam his fists down on tables?

Did he ignore his children? I really didn't know this God my mother loved so much, but he seemed like he might be a lot like my parents.

Daddy weighed in. "When your mother and I get angry with you kids, it's because we love you. And when we spank you, it's out of love. You won't believe this, but it hurts us much more than it hurts you." They gave each other knowing nods. I wanted to protest, but I was afraid to. Even then, I knew that was rubbish. How could it be possible that having someone three times your size swinging his hand or a belt hitting you be more painful, emotional or otherwise, for the hitter than for the one being hit? That just didn't make sense, but I wasn't about to make my thoughts known to this unpredictable audience. I caught Michelle's eye, as I wanted to give her a "knowing nod," but she pulled her gaze away too quickly. I was sure she was still mad at me.

"No one will ever love you as much as your dad and I do." Mother smiled as if this was the best news a parent could bestow upon their child: "Hey, you've won the lottery by being my child! No, not monetarily, but by having all my love and no one else's love ever. Isn't that great?"

I grew up believing that violence was love.

5

What Can I Buy You?

I looked forward to our shopping trips with my mother and sisters. At least twice a year, some combination of my mother and sisters and me would make a day of it and replenish our closets for the new season, replacing clothes that no longer fit, often scoring an extra four or five dresses and outfits reflecting the current fashion trends.

Of course, our father knew nothing of this day, and Mother would make sure we'd sneak our polyester and cotton goods inside so he'd never find out. But the bill came later and so did the argument, so it didn't matter if we were successful in hiding our clothes or not. Money was the source of many of the arguments between my parents. My mother was a spender, shopping her seasonal sport, and my father was a saver, a man of no hobbies. They had completely different views on money.

I usually didn't mind the hour-and-a-half drive to Cumberland Mall or Lenox Square where we'd spend hours and Mother would hold nothing back, especially for Easter. The frilliest, laciest, puffiest dresses in an array of pastels ended up in our shopping bags; then came the black or white patent leather shoes and gloves. To round out the look, Mother usually bought us a hat.

"Carol, your girls are just adorable! Those dresses! Where do you find them?" her church friends would croon.

"Well, sometimes I make their dresses, but this year, we were lucky enough to find these at Davison's. Aren't they cute?"

"You've outdone yourself. Your three girls could be models for that store! *They* should pay *you*!" And they'd laugh and fall onto each other's arms, and Mother's pride would shine like the bright morning sun.

When Mother announced it was time to go shopping, Michelle, Chelsea, and I would run to the car to get the best spot in the back.

But I couldn't even think about shopping because of our arguing that started about a mile down the road.

I said, "Michelle, move over, you're hoggin' the whole back seat and I don't have anywhere to sit!"

"No, I'm not! You have plenty of room."

"Move, Michelle! Mother, make her move! I don't have any room!" I pleaded.

Chelsea, wanting to be a part of the action, said, "You have room, Savannah!"

The three of us were screaming at each other at the same time, and Michelle refused to move one inch. Mother looked in the rearview mirror, her voice rising above us all. "Shut up! Just shut up!" She never told us to shut up; so we shut up, our eyes as large as little fawns. In the quiet of the car, she said through tears, "Sometimes, I wish I had never had you kids."

Her words made me shrink, making me smaller than I already was, and then there was plenty of room for me to slide back into the seat next to Michelle. Her words punched me in the gut, and I wondered, *Does Mother mean that? She wishes we were never born?* Michelle and Chelsea were quiet, staring straight ahead. The rest of the drive was wordless, and we sat, each of us, in our own little spaces in the back seat, not daring to let a thread of clothing rub up against anyone.

Later that night, at dinner, I asked Mother to pass the fried chicken. She didn't move, she kept on eating, not making eye contact with me. She stabbed at her mashed potatoes, and Daddy asked her, "How was your day, Carol?"

Mother sat with her head down, lips puckered, put down her fork, got up from the table, and went upstairs to her bedroom. Their bedroom door shut, and Daddy's mouth turned down. He asked, "What happened today, girls?"

"Nothin'," all three of us said in unison.

Daddy said, "Now, I know somethin' must have happened for your mother to leave the dinner table like that." He gritted his teeth and his nostrils flared. "She does so much for you girls—y'all need to be more helpful around here. She can't do everything. I don't know what happened, but I expect all three of y'all to clean this kitchen spick-and-span, do you hear me?" His eyes gleamed as he pointed them like a laser at each of us. We all agreed to clean the kitchen, but deep inside, I knew it was a bad idea to have us all try to work together without an argument.

I also knew it wouldn't be a good idea to tell him that Mother said she wished we were never born. I knew on a cellular level that it would be our fault that she said that; that we had pushed her to that point. Maybe we shouldn't have been born.

Sure enough, the arguing started when I told Michelle that I wanted to dry the dishes, not wash, that I had washed the last time we cleaned the kitchen together.

"No, you didn't, you liar! You're washing tonight. I'll wipe off the counters while you wash, and then I'll dry."

"I did it last time, Michelle! You always think you can tell me what to do, and then you lie about everything!"

We went back and forth like that for a few more seconds, and then, without warning, Daddy rushed into the kitchen and shouted, "You two will stop your yelling this instant! Just clean the damn kitchen! If I hear one more word out of you two, you're both going to bed."

Michelle said, "It's only seven—I can't go to bed!"

"Well, then stop the arguing and clean the kitchen!"

Michelle mumbled something, and then she slipped out, "So stupid."

Daddy jerked his head toward her. "What did you say?" He got up closer to Michelle. "I said, *what did you say*?" His big eyes and red face dared her to repeat it.

She stood up and said, "Nothing!"

Michelle had no idea how much I admired her for her bravery, but I also wished she'd just be quiet. She made things worse when she talked back.

"Get up to your room right now!" He was already taking off his belt. "Not only are you grounded, but I'm going to spank you so hard you can't sit down for a week!"

He was swinging, and Michelle was running. Even though Daddy was unleashing his anger on Michelle, I was scared to death. I wanted to stop it somehow, but it was too late for one of my impersonations to make him laugh, so I started washing dishes.

My heart ached for Michelle; it sounded scary what was happening. Big tears started falling down my cheeks because I loved my sister and I wanted the fighting and yelling and belt-swinging to stop. I hated it when Daddy acted like that. I wished we could all just get along.

I went to my room to be alone. I picked out my favorite *Frog and Toad* book and read. I loved these books because they made me want to have that kind of close friendship with someone. The yelling died down, and I kept reading and wondered what Michelle was doing, if she was hurting or crying or cussing, and then I got sleepy. I fell asleep with my clothes on, which was unusual because my parents always made us say good night to them after we put on our pajamas.

The next day, Mother came in my room to wake me for school. "Savannah, Chelsea, get up! Y'all are gonna be late." She left our room, leaving the door open. That was weird, because she liked to hug us when we woke up.

I popped right up in bed, because I didn't like being late for school. I changed my clothes and brushed my hair and ran downstairs for breakfast, which Mother always cooked for us.

"What's for breakfast, Mother?"

Silence. "Mother?" She was ignoring me. She was cleaning out her purse.

When my parents were angry with me, or when my mother ignored me, I got a feeling like a rock was sitting in the bottom of my stomach. I went back upstairs to finish getting ready for school. It was raining, and lightning struck through the clouds, so my mother drove me to school. I slid in the front seat and remembered that I was going to ask her if my friend Tracy could come over and play that afternoon. I didn't want to make her angrier, so I sat speechless, never asking about Tracy.

When she pulled the car up to the school, I got out and said, "Bye, Mother. I love you." She kept her eyes forward on the parking lot in front of her. No response from her, so I shut the car door. The rock moved, and my stomach hurt more until I got inside the school where I was distracted with schoolwork and my friends. It was a temporary escape, because as soon as I got home, the rock came back again.

The rain dried up, and Chelsea and I walked home together. We threw our books on the floor, and Mother sat at the kitchen table while Daddy paced, talking to someone on the phone. He was never home that early! *Something must be wrong*, I thought. He yelled, "I know that! She never made it to school today, and I want to know who I can talk to to find her!"

Mother was crying. I walked into the kitchen, feeling

very scared. What happened?

"Where is Michelle?" Chelsea asked.

Michelle didn't walk home with us, but sometimes she walked with her friends. Chelsea and I always walked together.

Daddy hung up the phone and said, "Well, it turns out that Michelle is with Kathy and her family."

Mother slammed her hand down on the table and said, "That trashy friend Kathy? I never liked that girl. I knew she was trouble from the beginning." And then, as if Kathy were in the other room, Mother whispered, "Kathy got pregnant out of wedlock and gave the baby up."

"She gave her baby up? What did she do with it?" Chelsea asked.

I said, "She gave it to people who wanted a baby," I said as an eight-year-old who understood adoption as a simple transaction.

Mother said, "People shouldn't have babies before they're married—that's wrong. So, they give them up for adoption." Mother, putting a negative moral spin on things.

"Kathy gave her baby to a nice couple who will take good care of it," Daddy added.

"I thought you liked Kathy, Mother? You were always nice to her when she was here," I said.

"Well, I'm not going to be rude to someone in my own home. That's not what you do. I just never trusted Kathy. Michelle told her too many bad things about us too. Untrue things, of course, but still I think Kathy believed them. She never acted very friendly around me. I don't know, I just didn't like her."

Michelle fought a lot with my parents, which generally ended up with her screaming that she was going to run away and that she hated living with us. After what happened yesterday, I guess she finally decided it was enough and actually did what she always threatened to do.

That afternoon, my parents picked Michelle up. My dad asked Kathy's parents not to tell Michelle that they were coming, but to send her outside, to trick her somehow, so he could get her into the car. When she came outside, he grabbed her and threw her into the car. Knowing my sister, there was lots of screaming and crying, I'm sure. Still, I was glad she was home because I missed her.

It had been a few days since Daddy dragged Michelle back home, and Mother wanted to have one of her "talks" with Chelsea and me.

Mother told Chelsea and me to sit on the sofa. We did, and my feet hung over the side, dangling. She said, "I want you girls to know that your dad and I love you both very much, I hope you know that. And everything we do, we do out of love for you. We're a good family, we go to church, we love the Lord, Dad works hard for us to provide and give us a nice house and go on nice vacations and buy nice clothes, so we need to be thankful for that." She paused, and I wondered what in the world was going on. Why was she telling us these things?

"Michelle has made some bad choices, and she has told some lies about your dad and me. We're sending her to a Christian school so she'll start getting her life turned around and follow the Lord. Your Dad and I love you so much, and no one will ever love you as much as we do." She held out her arms, and we hugged her and told her we loved her.

Chelsea hopped off the couch to go get a snack in the kitchen, but Mother and I stayed longer in the living room, talking.

"Mother, will Michelle still live here with us?"

"Oh, yes, it's a regular school. They just teach the students about the Lord and the Bible and how to live like a Christian. That's what we want for Michelle."

"Does she want to go to the school?"

"She doesn't have a choice at this point. Michelle is using drugs. Drugs are bad for you, and I hope you never, ever do drugs. Drugs are like pills that get people high, and they become addicted."

I imagined people lying on the floor laughing uncontrollably and never being able to stop. "I'll never do drugs, I promise, Mother."

All was right in my world, as I had my mother's attention again. She was confiding in me, and it made me feel happy. She became my lifeline, and when she squeezed the relational hose by refusing to interact with me, it felt like I wasn't getting any air into my lungs, and I'd panic, searching out ways to get her approval, just so I could breathe her in again, just to have her smile at me, laugh at my jokes, tell me I'm pretty and smart and talented. I lived for her approval and her love.

Michelle didn't make it a full school year at the Christian school and was kicked out for smoking on school grounds. She went back to public school, and the disagreements with my parents just got worse.

Michelle ran away again, and this time, my parents called the police and they put her in juvenile detention. She stayed there for a week, and this did nothing to help the relationship between Michelle and Mother and Daddy. Michelle called herself the black sheep of the family, and I thought it was a cool thing to be a black sheep; I thought they were unique and stood out. I loved black sheep, but Michelle didn't mean it in a good way.

I began to wonder why being a Christian didn't make our family happier. Why were we so miserable? My friends who weren't Christians, or who didn't go to church like we did, were so much nicer and their families got along. How could that be? My mother and the church convinced me that only lovers of God were truly happy, that it was because of Jesus that people had joy, but I didn't see the evidence of that in my own family.

6

The Good Daughter

In the earliest morning hours on a school day, I was abruptly awakened by an upset stomach. I ran to the toilet, but one heave and dinner ended up all over the carpet in the hallway, just outside the bathroom.

My mother was up and at my side before I could cry out her name. She walked me into the bathroom to clean me up, saying, "Oh, bless your heart, honey," over my crying. It was the only time I didn't fear her anger. When we kids were sick, she transformed into a nurse with the capacity to endlessly give of herself.

Mother's sweetness on the outside made it easy for her to make lots of friends. Everyone loved her, so even though we lived in Boston for one year, the year I was born, Mom made a best friend, Ava, and she was on her way to visit us in Atlanta in two days. It had been eight years since they'd seen each other, and it was important to Mom that our house was cleaner than usual when Ava came to visit. This we knew, but as children, we didn't feel the same urgency she did.

I stayed home from school that day, and Mother brought me saltines and ginger ale; she'd let me sleep and then take my temperature when I woke. By 5 P.M., I was ready to eat and Mother brought me a bowl of chicken noodle soup to my bedroom. She set it on a TV tray and fluffed my pillows so I could eat in bed. My fever was gone, and I was able to keep my food down too. My illness was a short-lived one, and I went to school the next day.

Ava was to arrive that evening, and Mother gave us girls instructions that we were to clean the house after school. By the time I got home from school, I had forgotten about cleaning altogether. Instead of cleaning, I was in my room changing my dolls' clothes for the umpteenth time.

Mom pulled her car into the garage and walked through the side door. She threw her keys onto the kitchen table and screamed, "Michelle! Savannah! Get down here!"

We ran as fast as we could to the kitchen. Mother paced and threw dirty dishes into the dishwasher. "Why isn't this kitchen clean? I told you to have this house clean when I got home! Now I have to do everything! I work all day and come home to this pig sty."

She was crying and screaming and throwing things at this point. I started to pick things up, but she yelled at me, "I can do this myself! Go do something else! Ava gave you your first bath, Savannah, when I brought you home from the hospital—you of all people could have made the house presentable for her! How could you be so selfish? Bunch of ungrateful kids!"

The two sides of my mother always showed up when

she wanted to impress people. To us, her family, she ranted and raged, or used stone-cold silence to get her way. But to her closest friends, she was as sweet as pie, the perfect southern belle, because she wanted to be the queen of the ball, the one they adored.

I had learned not to defend myself to Mother. I didn't have a good reason why I didn't clean the house, and I'm pretty sure it wouldn't have mattered if I did. All that mattered was that her house was immaculate for Ava.

After about an hour of scurrying and scouring the house, the doorbell rang. Mother shouted, "Pick up those skates in the garage, right now! And then come meet Ava."

Mother floated to the front door as if she were Zsa Zsa Gabor, opened the door, and said, "Ava!" and wrapped her arms around her friend. "Come in, come in, you must be exhausted from the flight. Are you hungry? Can I get you anything?"

Ava sat down on one of our floral wingback chairs and said, "Oh my Gawd, Carol, I'll just sit here in the pahlah for a minute. No thank you on the food, but I would love a drink. Watah is fine. You didn't warn me how humid it gets here. My hair is a great big frizz ball."

"No, you look wonderful! I'm so happy you're here. Girls! Come here and meet one of my dearest friends in the world," Mother hollered. She sashayed into the kitchen to get Ava a glass of water.

All three of us scampered through the house and found our way to the living room where Ava and Mother sat on the couch. Ava was a thin woman with brown curly hair cut above her shoulders. She had pretty brown eyes that squinted when she smiled. Ava stood up and said, "Oh my Gawd, Carol, the girls are just adorable! Okay, this must be Michelle. Oh, honey, aren't you just the cutest—and I love your glasses. And, now, is this Savannah? What a pretty little thing she is! And you, Chelsea, what a sweet little girl. Come here, let me hug you! Let me hug all of you!"

We gathered around her like puppies, and she wrapped her arms around us and pulled us in to a huddle. We started giggling and liked Ava immediately.

"Yes, Michelle and Chelsea both take after Bob's side of the family. They have those short little legs. Savannah takes after my side of the family," Mother said as she stood smiling down at me. "Maybe later she can play some of her piano pieces for you."

Mother humiliated us in ways that would haunt me for a lifetime.

Not that my daddy was much better. I remember a hot June Saturday morning, when we were headed to Gatlinburg, Tennessee, on a family vacation. I brought one of my suitcases out to Daddy, and I found him grumbling in front of the open trunk of the brown Chevy Caprice.

"Here ya go, Daddy," I said as I hoisted my blue hard suitcase onto the bumper.

"No, no, no, you're gonna scratch the car!" He pushed the suitcase away, causing me to stumble, and he brushed his hand over the bumper for scratches and dents as if it were a priceless work of art. "I'm not ready for that yet. I've gotta figure out how we're gonna put all our junk in here.

I try to tell your mom that, but she never listens," he said, clearly irritated.

"What time are we leaving?"

"I don't know!" he snapped. "Get back inside and get all your things out here. Tell your sisters too." Daddy put his hands on his hips and turned back to the car to make a trunk-packing game plan.

I ran back in the house, feeling that rock in the pit of my stomach. I didn't like being around my dad when he was angry and short-tempered.

About an hour later, we loaded into the car and drove awhile before Michelle said the words most driving dads dislike to hear: "I'm hungry." There was a long pause, and then she repeated it a little louder. "I'm hungry."

"Didn't you eat breakfast?" Dad inquired. He kept staring straight ahead, hands firmly set at ten and two, with no outward intentions of slowing down for the next exit.

"Yes, but I'm hungry again," Michelle said.

"Me too," Chelsea piped in.

"Me three," I said, thinking I was funny. No one laughed, though. My mom started digging in her purse and said, "I might have some crackers in here." At every restaurant, she dropped the leftover oyster crackers in her purse.

Chelsea whined, "I don't want crackers!"

Daddy sighed a heavy breath and said to Mother, "Help me look for the next McDonald's. We'll stop there real quick and then get back on the road."

We walked into the fast-food restaurant and stared up at the huge menu hanging above us.

Daddy said, "Okay. Chelsea. Savannah. Michelle. What do you want to eat?" He seemed angry, and I hadn't done anything wrong. Yet.

None of us said anything. We stood wide-eyed trying to read the looming menu.

"Come on, now! People are waiting behind us. You can't take all day!" Daddy waited a few seconds.

Michelle pushed up her black cat-eye glasses and said, "I don't know what I want yet."

"I just want a ham—" I started to say but was cut off by my marine daddy.

"They'll all have regular hamburgers!" he said loudly, pushing our tiny frames forward toward the counter, our feet shuffling across the orange tile to keep up. My face turned red as people stared at us. And to the teenager behind the counter, he said, "I don't know why they're so shy." Daddy shook his head as if he couldn't understand how we got that way. "Carol, go take the kids and find a place to sit," he commanded.

Despite the traumatizing lunch as a family, that trip was one of my favorites and where my love for Native Americans was solidified. I craved being one of the people of the earth. That's how I saw them; they lived, not off the land, but *with* the land. They were a part of the earth and sky. They respected nature and were one with her. Even as a little girl, I wanted the connection they had with nature. I wished I were an Indian. I begged my parents to take us to a Cherokee Indian reservation, to see tribal people, to talk to them and see how they lived. I wanted to walk into a tepee and feel the cool earth beneath my feet, smell the food they ate, and touch the furs of the animals they wore to keep them warm. My parents obliged my request and bought a tomahawk for me and headdresses for both Chelsea and me. Michelle wasn't interested in those toys, so my parents bought her a pretty beaded necklace.

The minute we got home from vacation, I got out of the car and ran fast to see if my friends were outside. I wanted to show them my cool new Indian things. They weren't home, but I put on my headdress anyway and got right into character. My little sister came out, and I made her Squanto, the Indian who helped the pilgrims. I, of course, was the chief of this little tribe and I lifted my head and hands up to the beautiful Georgia summer sky with the puffy marshmallow clouds and aptly chose the name Chief White Cloud.

We played for at least an hour before I noticed my dad bringing long wooden poles out from the garage to the backyard. He laid them on the ground in a specific way and tied the tops together. My spirits raised up as he lifted his homemade tepee. It was a large, six-feet-tall tepee standing in the middle of our backyard. My daddy, the man who couldn't hold in his temper for the life of him, whipped us too hard, worked too much, didn't go to church, cursed and smoked and drank, was making me a tepee because he knew that would make me happy.

7

Double Standards

The next summer, Mother came into my bedroom early one June morning when I was ten. "Savannah," she said, "you and Chelsea wake up. It's time to get ready for Fripp Island. Daddy's getting the car ready, and you girls need to pack your bags. Come on now, sleepy heads, get up! It's going to be a great week! Michelle's already up and eating breakfast."

I yawned and stretched, then jumped out of bed. "Chelsea, get up, get up! We're going to the beach!" We were already tan from the Georgia sunshine, but after this week, we'd return with a deeper, darker tan. Mother made us matching shorts and shirts sets and maxi dresses. We loved the clothes she made for us. She allowed us to pick out the fabric and she made sure the fit was just right on us. We thought we were princesses in our beach apparel.

Chelsea and I got our things together that we'd need for a week in South Carolina, and we ran downstairs to get some breakfast. "Girls, did you pack your dresses? And the sunscreen and sunglasses? And your hats?"

"Yes, ma'am," Chelsea said.

I said, "Yes, ma'am, and I packed my purple shorts with the flowers on them too. I love those!" Bits of bacon fell out of my mouth and onto the floor.

"Savannah, pick that up! And stop talking with your mouth full!" Mother reprimanded.

"Sorry. Will Uncle Mike and Aunt Louise and Mary and Bobby be at Fripp Island when we get there?" I asked.

"Yes, Savannah, for the umpteenth time, they are meeting us there and we're renting a house together on the island. The house is big enough for all of us to stay in. Now, hurry up and finish packing." As I ran past her, she said, "Bring your bags down for Daddy to put them in the car!"

I was smart enough this time to simply give my daddy the bags instead of helping him. Not too long after that, we were on the road for the four-and-a-half-hour drive from Atlanta to Beaufort. I don't know how I did it, but I got a seat next to the window and didn't have to sit in between Michelle and Chelsea.

With my window partly down, I breathed in the ocean's saltiness as the breeze tickled my face entering the low country. The palm trees swayed with the whim of the wind as we drove over island after island, until we came to our beloved Fripp. On this day, it was sunny and a breeze softly sang through the palms that surrounded our rental house at the very tip of the island. My aunt and uncle's car was parked in the gravel driveway of the house, and Michelle, Chelsea, and I couldn't get out of the car fast enough to see our cousins. Daddy told us to grab our bags first before racing down to the beach; otherwise, he knew he wouldn't see us until dinner.

After we threw our bags into our bedrooms, we ran full-on down to the water. The sand was cool under the trees and hot in the sun. It was midday, so the sun was high in the sky, just about ready to fall slowly back down to earth. I took in every element that I could. The hum of the sea. The slow rhythm of waves coming and going. Feeling the gritty, raw sand on my feet, wedged between my toes. I watched as the water rushed toward me and then took everything back it had just brought to me, making me dizzy as the sand under my feet tried to stay put. I took deep breaths to take in the smell of the ocean—fishy and salty, foamy and fresh—and I licked my arm to taste the saltiness on my skin. I threw my head back, closed my eyes, and let its beauty wrap itself around me like a warm hug.

My dad seemed to change into a different person when he was around Uncle Mike. My mother's sister, Mary, married a man who loved alcohol and sex. My dad was never a prude, but in our own home, we weren't allowed to watch certain television shows, go to certain movies, or tell sexual jokes. Anything sexual was considered off-limits to us and considered as bad, especially by my mother. But my uncle Mike told inappropriate jokes, had sexual comic books in his house that we kids sneaked sometimes, and drank a lot of alcohol. When my dad was around Uncle Mike, he drank and laughed wholeheartedly at my uncle's gross sexual jokes. On one occasion, I caught them, my dad and uncle, feasting on a pornographic magazine at the convenience store.

I had rounded the corner of an aisle when I saw my uncle holding a magazine up for my dad to see. The cover of the magazine showed a woman in a sheer top, leaving nothing to the imagination. There was something else in the middle of the magazine that resulted in my uncle's mouth gaping open and saying in a low voice, "Oh, wow."

My dad licked his lips and said, "Oh, yeah, that's real nice." Inside, I recoiled and then backed away to peek around the corner. I was stunned that my Christian father would engage in this kind of behavior, ogling at women in this way. Anything sex-related was forbidden in our home and considered to be the ultimate evidence of moral decay. I walked away with my lips curled. I tried to put the disturbing image out of my mind, but I kept thinking, *What a hypocrite!*

One night, Michelle and I were watching a movie and there was a kissing scene playing when my mother walked in the room. She stopped, and somewhere between a scream and a holler, said, "What are you two watching? Turn that off this instant! You are not allowed to watch that kind of trash in my house! Go up to your room and think about what you've done!"

We walked to our rooms in silence. I lay on my bed and thought about sex for a long time. I thought about the cute boy at school I liked and wondered if he liked me. I thought about the book my cousin Mary showed me at her house that had drawings of cartoon-like characters of naked men chasing naked women. And I thought about how sex made my mom scrunch up her face in an ugly, disgusted way. I wondered if that's the way I was supposed to feel. Was I not supposed to wonder what it would be like to kiss the cute boy in school? Was I to abstain from any thoughts of this foul, disgusting act called sex?

The year my little sister and I went bathing suit shopping with our mother, after I had just turned eleven, was a game changer as far as what was considered appropriate beachwear.

Although I'd started my period, my body hadn't changed much from the year before; no curves, and I still wore a training bra. My mother had purchased two-piece bathing suits for me before, and I didn't think this year would be any different.

"Mother, I love this one." I held it up high, a two-piece with pink and purple flowers. I smiled and waited for her to join me in my excitement.

"Now, why would a nice girl want a bathing suit like that? Only sluts wear suits like that!" I pulled the bathing suit close to me, and the upward line of my mouth fell. She went on: "You're a Christian girl and you'll wear a one-piece. It's so skimpy! It barely covers anything, Savannah!" She shook her head and walked away as a woman walked by and her eyes traveled down from my head to my toes, then she made a "humph" noise. My shoulders rounded, and I put the bathing suit on the nearest rack.

I wanted to run and live with another family, but as

usual, the fight in me died down and I became as limp as a dead bird. I agreed to whatever Mother suggested the rest of the shopping trip and stuffed any ideas or desires I had away. *Can someone please explain life's rules to me?* I ended up feeling like there was something very wrong with me, the three-legged dog.

I left the store with an ugly one-piece bathing suit. I don't think I went swimming at all that summer, and that ended my enjoyment of bathing suit shopping and began my personal body shaming.

8

A Firstborn

B ryce seemed happiest when he was coaching the young boys on his football team.

He became a mentor to a little boy, Manuel, who was eleven years old and had no father figure in his life. His mother and grandmother raised him, and I thought he was one of the sweetest boys I had ever met.

Bryce often picked him up for football practice, took him home afterward, and treated him to dinner, occasionally bringing him to our apartment for short visits. Bryce treated Manuel as if he were his own son. He taught Manuel how to use a computer and how to change the oil in a car, and they'd occasionally wrestle in the living room. Once I actually talked Bryce in to letting Manuel play a board game with me. Manuel and I laughed a lot, and I adored it when his changing voice squeaked out sheer happiness.

"This is fun, Miss Savannah! I think I'm winning." We were playing Battleship, a childhood favorite game of mine.

"Well, I think you are, Manuel. But you'd better watch out, I'm pretty competitive, and I don't like losing."

I winked at him and smiled. He ended up winning that game, and I challenged him to another board game night that he promised he'd come back for.

That night, after Bryce took Manuel home, he came home in a good mood and said, "Hey, thanks for supporting me. I know I don't always show it, but I do love you." He came over and put his arms around me, and we kissed. He then moved his lips and kissed me up and down my neck.

We only had sex a few times in the year and a half we'd been married, and each time, it lacked spark for me. I was so confused because I wanted a loving relationship with my husband, but the chemistry between us was missing.

He continued kissing me, and I shivered as he pulled me in closer and whispered, "Why don't you go put something more comfortable on?" I was excited by the suggestion and moved my hands slowly down his arms and turned to walk to our bedroom. I picked a silky nighty that flowed over my body like water. I hadn't worn it yet for him, and I felt irresistible in it. *Maybe tonight will be different. He's got to be turned on by* this. When I came back out to the living room, he had turned off the lights, lit a few candles, and put on soft R&B music, which he knew wasn't my favorite style of music.

I wanted him to feast on my body with his eyes, but instead he turned toward the pile of blankets that he'd laid out on the floor and sat down. He patted the covers for me to come over, and I did. *Do you find me attractive, Bryce? Why aren't your eyes roaming over me?* We lay down and started kissing. It felt very much like an evening he had orchestrated in his mind, but it lacked passion and desire. I didn't resist or say anything, however, as I was ready for a baby. We had sex, and I'm sure that's the night I became pregnant with our son, Nicholas.

Bryce picked me up and swung me around when I told him I was pregnant. He involved himself in every part of my pregnancy from what I ate to the colors of the baby's room. We laughed more together than we had in a long time, and he seemed genuinely content.

Nine months later, I went to the doctor and I was two centimeters dilated! I was so tired at work and I couldn't wait to have this baby. A little boy. I wondered what it would be like to have a son. I grew up with only sisters but always wanted an older brother, someone to protect me. I promised to be my son's protector.

My parents were excited about the baby too. They bought us a beautiful crib, which Bryce wasn't excited about, because he wasn't in control of which crib to purchase. But when he saw how expensive they were, he relented and accepted their generous gift.

We chose a jungle theme for our little boy. One day, I came home from the store and I couldn't find Bryce anywhere. I peeked out the window, and he was out in a tiny wooded area near the complex. He was chopping down a small dead tree.

"Bryce, what in the world?"

Sweat poured down his forehead and into his eyes. He wiped his face with his shirt and said, "I'm going to take this dead tree, clean it up, make sure no bugs are in it, and then put it in the baby's room. I'll drill holes, and you can put some artificial leaves in it, and then we can hang some stuffed animals in it—ya know, for the jungle theme." He grinned and went back to preparing the wood and cutting it down to size and letting it dry out and sealing it before he attached it safely to the wall in the baby's room.

We brought Nicholas home from the hospital on May 12, 1995, and from the many baby showers, there were plenty of baby clothes and diapers, I was sure, for the first few years of his life. I would soon find out, however, that babies poop a lot and grow fast.

Having Nicholas transformed me. The focus went from me to him in an instant. When they laid him in my arms, tears welled up in my eyes and I said, "Oh, my baby." I kissed him a hundred times. I was lost in love, crazy in it. I would have stood in front of a train for him; I could have *stopped* the train with the strength of my love and feelings of protection for him. I took in every inch of his face and caressed his soft cheeks with my fingers. I never wanted to let him go.

I took eight weeks off of work to be with Nicholas and loved every minute of it. I was tired every minute of it too, but I knew these were priceless times that I'd never get back. I savored them. I spent hours talking to him, smiling at him, reading to him, and gazing at him while he slept. I couldn't get enough of him, although I did have my moments when I'd rock him and wonder if I had what it took to meet his needs for the next eighteen years. I thought of him every minute I was awake, and only slept very lightly so that I could hear any movement of his during the night.

One night, he was fussy. I couldn't understand why; I hadn't eaten anything spicy or anything that I knew of that would have upset his stomach from my breast milk. Little I did comforted him, so finally I had to lay him down in bed to see if he'd fall asleep on his own. I went back to our bed and lay there for just a few minutes. Bryce threw the covers off, complaining about the baby crying as he rushed into Nicholas's bedroom. I, of course, was right behind him.

"Bryce, what are you doing? I'll take him!"

"Get out of here! I've got him!" And he grabbed my precious four-month-old baby, held him up, and gave him one shake. "Stop that crying! Stop it right now!" Bryce yelled at our infant son.

Through my own tears now, I screamed, "Bryce! You stop it! He's just a baby! You're hurting him! Babies cry, and you're making it worse. Let me have him. I'll rock him to sleep." Tears streamed down my baby's tiny cheeks, and he made little fists while his body shook. I felt like I had left my own body and was standing beside myself.

Bryce finally put Nicholas back in his crib and left the bedroom. I picked up my crying and now frightened child and held him tight and kissed his teary cheeks. "It's okay, Mommy's here. Mommy's here. You're okay, buddy. You're okay." My breathing slowed down, and I rocked back and forth, holding him as close to my heart as I could, which seemed to help. He started to quiet down until he cried himself to sleep. But I didn't put him down. I held him for the rest of the night, sitting in the rocking chair in his bedroom.

I'm never letting go of my baby.

9

Fight with a Monster

Fifteen months later, I was only days away from giving birth to my second child, a baby girl. Charcoal clouds stirred the sky, and thunder rumbled in the distance, getting closer every minute. I pinched the skin at my throat as I watched streaks of lightning threaten to take out every light in the city. *Where is Bryce?* I was used to him being late, but he should have been home by now. Nicholas was asleep in his crib, which I made sure was not near a window, so he was safe.

I backed away from the sliding door and knew that a batch of my grandmother's buttery chocolate chip cookies would settle me.

I mixed the ingredients and plopped sugary tablespoon-size clumps of creamy dough onto cookie sheets, avoiding the temptation of eating any and risking salmonella for my incubating baby. I filled two cookie sheets and my cast iron skillet for one large cookie. I slid the cookie sheets in the oven, along with the skillet, and waited for them to bake to a beautiful golden brown. This process of measuring flour and sugar and cracking eggs and stirring distracted me from the impending storm breathing down on me. As I stood with my face peering into the oven, the front door of our apartment burst open and Bryce came in, soaking wet from the rain.

"Hi! Wow! It's really raining out there! You're soaking wet!" I said, realizing I was stating the obvious, but hoping some of my cheerfulness would rub off on him.

"Yeah, you're keenly observant," Bryce replied as he wiped his face with his wet hand. He didn't smile and kept his gaze downward. He yanked his dripping coat off and threw it on the floor, took his shoes off, and walked into our bedroom. Although I had come to expect this kind of irritable response from Bryce, it was like a knife shredding my flesh and breaking my bones as it made its way to my heart. He was a cruel husband, but I always held out a flicker of hope that he'd have a change of heart, especially after becoming a parent, and be kind or lighthearted or romantic or even friendly toward me like he used to be when I first met him.

I caught my reflection in the oven window. I had pulled my dirty-blond hair into a ponytail, but wisps of hair framed my face. I stared at myself for a moment, noticing how much older I looked, and I thought, *Maybe I need a highlight*. I then opened the oven door and took the sheet cookies out; they were perfectly baked. I put them on the cooling rack and started another batch and shoved them into the oven along with the skillet cookie, as it wasn't a warm golden brown yet.

Our only phone rang once, then twice. I wondered why Bryce wasn't answering it, as it was in our bedroom where he was. I ran to answer it because Bryce didn't like it when the phone rang for too long. When I went into our room, the light was on, but Bryce was on the bed, sound asleep. I grabbed the phone, hoping not to wake Bryce, but unfortunately, the phone only had a six-foot cord, so I was tethered to the bedroom. "Hello?" I said softly.

A tiny, gravelly voice said, "Hi, Savannah. It's Grandma Eunice. How are you, honey?"

Grandma Eunice was Bryce's paternal grandma, whom he adored. She was a sweet old woman who lived alone, except for her oldest son who never kept a job for more than six months, so he moved in the last time he got fired and never left. Her other children worried that he was taking advantage of her financially, but she insisted she was fine and resented the implication that she couldn't handle everything by herself. Whenever she called, we always knew it would be a long conversation because she had a lot to say and liked to talk. She also couldn't hear anything you were saying, so she just kept on talking. In conversations with her, I could never get a word in between her run-on sentences, so I simply listened and, when I could, inserted "uh-huh" or "yes."

The lightning and thunder hadn't stopped, and I was nervous about being on the phone, but instead of telling her I should get off, I said, "Oh, hi, Grandma! I'm fine! How are you? It's been so long since we've talked!" I really did love her and wanted to make her feel special.

Grandma told me all about her garden, her grown children, all the friends at her church and the surgeries they had, and how she needed to replace the toilet in one of her bathrooms because it kept backing up. After a good ten minutes, it hit me that I had cookies in the oven that needed to be taken out. Bryce just lay there. How could he sleep like that?

"Grandma, I need to—" I attempted to interrupt Grandma, letting her know about the cookies.

"Well, I can tell you right now, I'm not paying Don to fix my toilet when he lives here for free!" Grandma didn't hear me at all and kept on talking.

"That's good, but Grandma, I have burning—" I tried again, but she didn't hear me.

She went on about Don and how little he did around the house. My heart rate picked up, and I stopped listening because all I could think of was the burning cookies and the fire department being called and me standing there, still talking to Grandma, as the apartment complex burned to the ground. I bit the inside of my mouth and twisted the phone cord so tightly around my hand that the blood flow was cut off. I knew that Bryce hated being woken up. I unwrapped my hand and took a small step in his direction.

"Bryce!" I whispered as I held my hand over the phone receiver. Grandma didn't seem to notice, as she kept on chatting. He didn't move. "Bryce!" I said a little louder. I moved his foot with my free hand. He squirmed a little, and I said, "I need you to take the cookies out of the oven, please. I'm talking to your grandma." I said all this quietly, hoping Grandma wouldn't hear me. I didn't want to be unkind to this lonely woman who needed to talk.

Bryce sat up like I had just called him a nasty name. He stomped through the apartment into the kitchen. I knew I'd be in trouble when I got off the phone, but I put that aside and said, "Uh-huh, Grandma, that's nice," to something she said about her tomato plants yielding some of the best-tasting tomatoes she's ever had.

Suddenly there was a terrible crashing sound, like twenty baking pans hitting the floor, but worse than that. I stretched the cord on the receiver as far as it would go but still couldn't see down the narrow hallway into the kitchen. Not really listening or hearing anything Grandma was saying, I continued adding a "yes" here and there, praying that she'd grow tired and say goodbye.

After about ten more minutes, she finally said goodbye. As I passed Nicholas's bedroom, I peeked in on him; he was still sleeping but moving around restlessly. I shut his door quietly and said a quick prayer that he'd stay asleep, then I approached the kitchen like one might look in on a crime scene. Bryce had yanked the oven door off its hinges and hurled it across the room. He'd thrown the baking sheets, and cookies had flown all over the counter and the floor. My cast iron pan still sat in the oven, holding an overbaked cookie.

"You dumb bitch." I turned, and Bryce sat on the edge of the couch with his elbows on his knees and his hands hanging between his legs, emphasizing each word as if he were reading them written in bold. "The next time you need cookies taken out of the oven, do it your damn self. Do you understand me?" I stood still like a child terrified of speaking, and he shook his head and spewed, mostly to himself, "Why the hell did I marry you?"

I knew that I needed to be careful with my tone of voice, because any hint of blame or hostility on my part might set off a physical assault. In a gentle, almost whispery voice, I said, "I was on the phone with your grandma, and I didn't want to be impolite, so I thought you wouldn't"—I took a breath—"mind taking the cookies out. I didn't want them to burn." My hands were shaking, and I was holding them so he wouldn't notice. I paused before asking him, with a tone of concern, "Was something wrong when you got home? Did everything go okay with Manuel?"

He stood up slowly and then walked toward me. His eyes were ice cold and stared right through me. I walked backward into the wall, not knowing what he was going to do. At his worst, he had punched and slapped me, ripped the phone out of my hand as I tried to phone for help, but this time he swept past me into the kitchen and fought with the oven door to get it back on.

I checked on Nicholas, and he was sleeping soundly to the gentle purring of the fan. I decided to go sit in our room on the bed to wait out the storm, the one happening in our apartment. After several minutes and some banging in the kitchen, the latch on the apartment door clicked, and when I peeked into the kitchen, he was gone. I walked out to see if Bryce was in the living room, and I was more than relieved when I discovered his coat was gone and the oven door was fixed.

I put the salvageable cookies in my cookie jar, threw the rest away, and cleaned up the crumbs that were on the floor and on the counter. Then I put away the flour, sugar, and butter and washed the pans. I took a couple of cookies from the cookie jar and headed for the couch, but I only took a couple of bites because a swell of nausea hit my throat. I laid back on the couch to calm my stomach. *I want out. But how? How do I leave? I can't. I have a son with him, and another baby about to be born. He'd never let us leave. I'm such an idiot! And a loser. No one would want me.*

I decided to sleep on the couch, so I grabbed a blanket and my pillow from the bed. My baby belly was getting so big that it was getting difficult to breathe, especially when I tried to put on socks or tie my shoes. I lay down, and my eyes became heavy. With only a hall light on, I fell asleep fast.

It was a fitful sleep. In the fuzzy darkness of my mind, the shape of a man formed. He wore a white suit and he stood at the bottom of the stairs in my house. It was all white inside—white walls, white staircase. The man walked up slowly, almost gliding, yet deliberate and scowled at me as he did. When he got to the top of the stairs where I was standing, he grabbed my wrist, tight, and pulled me into a room. I tried to pull away and scream, but I had no strength and no voice. Gradually, my mind came back to consciousness and I opened my eyes to a man standing in the middle of my living room.

I said, "Oh my God, Bryce!" I rubbed my eyes and

breathed in a quick, short breath. "You scared me half to death. What are you doing?"

He said nothing, but his flared nostrils and laser-beam eyes made me shiver. I sat up, tearing the blanket away from my swollen feet and sat on the edge of the couch.

"What's going on, Bryce?"

"We need to talk about what happened earlier," he said, his jaw tight.

"Okay." I waited for him to start, but he didn't. "How about you go first." I swallowed hard.

"Do you know what it's like to be married to you?" He sneered. "I thought I married a woman, not a *child*."

I cocked my head to one side and said, "What are you talking about?"

His expression was flat. "You know exactly what I'm talking about. Making cookies when it's storming, talking on the phone when I'm trying to sleep, asking me stupid-ass questions all the time," he said through gritted teeth.

Something told me to lower my eyes, as if in submission, but our eyes were bolted together. There was a long silence. He bared his teeth and lunged at me. Before I could jump away, he grabbed me by my hair and threw me. My pregnant middle hit the floor hard. I held my stomach, praying to God she wasn't hurt in any way. *Oh my God, what's happening?* I screeched out, "Bryce, stop! The baby!" I caught my breath between sobs.

Bryce stood over me with a smirk on his face, watching me struggle to sit up.

He got on his hands and knees and pushed me back,

causing me to hit my head on the couch. He started with my breasts, moving his hands all over them, and then he moved to every part of my body in mock enjoyment. His sickening tone: "Ooh, yeah, baby."

I screamed, "Stop! No! Stop!" My throat burned as I tried to push his hands away.

His hand went up my dress and grabbed my underwear, and he yanked so violently that he ripped them in two. His hand remained between my legs, violating me. He licked his lips and leaned in close to my face. With hot breath and spit flying at me, he turned his head back and forth and said, "Come on, baby. I know you like it." He drew out every word in a voice so low I barely recognized it.

I was wailing sounds that were nonhuman—deafening screams—and begging him to stop. My arms and legs were so heavy, much like I felt in my nightmares when trying to move or run, but I can't. With lead in my veins, I kicked, scratched, and pushed, but all my efforts did nothing to protect me and my baby from the assault of this man I called my husband. Every inch I gained in getting him off me, he'd come back toward me with greater force. He slammed his lips onto mine, then he grabbed the top of my head and pulled my hair as hard as he could.

I curled my fingers into a fist and gave him a blow to his face. The flesh and bones in his cheek smashed together, but he acted as if I hadn't hit him and he kept feeling me and grunting, making noises like some sort of night creature.

How can I get him to stop? How will this night end? My heart was beating fast, and I was sweating. I was in for the fight of my life. I pleaded with God to help me get out of this alive and to protect us, for a guardian angel to swoop down and rescue us, my baby and me.

He morphed into the monster I suspected he was—but a monster I never could've imagined. His face disfigured, his eyes red and watery, and his arms popped with veins and muscles that seemed to grow before me. Drops of sweat fell from his forehead as he growled at me.

I prayed a simple prayer: *God, help me.*

Then, for reasons I'll never know, he let go of me and the madness ended. The last thing I remember was Bryce walking out of the apartment.

10

A Girl's Work

Daddy was at work, and I wanted to go outside to see if there were eggs in the nest I'd found on our porch. I changed into my shorts, T-shirt, and tennis shoes and walked down the stairs to run to the front door, but before I could get there, Mother yelled, "Savannah! Get in here and help me clean the kitchen. And after that, I want you to vacuum the living room."

"I want to go outside for just a minute! I'll come right back in to do the stupid inside chores!"

Mother almost ran out of the living room and grabbed my arm, digging her nails into my skin. "Get in here this minute and don't you dare talk back to me."

Her grasp hurt, but I didn't let her know it. I waited for her to walk away before I rubbed my arm. As fast as I could, without getting caught for doing a poor job, I cleaned the kitchen and the living room. Mother also wanted Chelsea and I to clean our rooms and our bathroom. The garage door opened while I was vacuuming.

I ran into the garage and, with bright eyes, asked, "Hey,

Daddy, can I cut the grass for you today?"

He studied my face for a second or two and said, "Well, I'll have to show you how to use the push mower. You're eleven now, and I think you're old enough."

I jumped up and down and clapped. "Yay, thank you! I know I'll do a good job! I can't wait! When can I do it? Can we start now, right this minute?"

"Slow down, now, I've got to get changed and do a few things first. While you wait, you can go see if there are weeds to pull."

I finished vacuuming the living room and ran outside into the front lawn and started weeding. I thought the Boxwood hedges needed trimming too, as they were a little uneven. I loved running my hands over the little leaves of the boxwood and sometimes grabbing a stem a few inches down and pulling up, snatching all the leaves off and then sprinkling them around like glitter.

Daddy got the mower out and put gas in it. He showed me where to put gas and oil, and where the gears were. "Now, Savannah, pull this string here, and the engine should start."

I grabbed the string and pulled as hard as I could, but nothing happened. I did that four or five times and I couldn't get it started. I said, "I think something's wrong with it."

Daddy laughed and said, "No, I just need to prime it." He pushed a little squishy button a few times. "Okay, go ahead and pull it again."

I pulled again, with all of my might, and the engine

rumbled to life. I smiled at my accomplishment and rubbed my shoulder because it felt like I had pulled my arm out of its socket.

Our front and back yards weren't that big, so it took me about an hour to do both. Dad was always nearby, just in case I had a problem. He was the acting "yard supervisor" and helped me the first few times I had to empty the bag of the grass cuttings. I didn't realize I would have to do that part, but it was worth it just to have my dad say, "Good job."

"Okay, now your lines are gettin' a little crooked. Keep your eyes a few feet in front of the mower, and that should help you cut straight lines."

"Daddy, I guess I'm the son you always wanted," I joked.

My mother told me that Daddy had wished I were a boy when I was born. After having three daughters, she wanted another child, but my dad said no because he didn't want to risk having a fourth daughter. It stung to hear that, but I kept those feelings to myself.

The smells of cigarette smoke and gasoline clung to his clothes, and I felt safe with my dad outside. He was calm, unlike being inside the house, caged up with an angry bear. Working in the yard with him was the only time I had him all to myself and he wasn't scary. I think it was a bit of a sacrifice for him to let me help because he would have rather been alone and done the work himself.

"Okay, Savannah, we're all done." He wiped his brow with the back of his hand. "I'm going inside now."

"All right, I'm coming too." I followed him in like a puppy. He went right to his corduroy recliner and asked me to turn on the television and put it on football for him, which I did. He also wanted me to get him a beer, which I did. I would have carved him a statue of himself if he'd asked me.

I sat on the couch across from my dad and watched him watch football. "Daddy, why did they call a flag on that play?"

"The defensive lineman crossed the line of scrimmage before the ball snapped," he explained without taking his eyes off the TV. He taught me all about quarterback sweeps, touchbacks, and scoring. I became a fan of the University of Georgia and the Atlanta Falcons and Steve Bartkowski (oh, those dimples), and dreamed about being an NFL star myself, throwing a Hail Mary–winning touchdown to Alfred Jenkins.

After one particularly long game and "sudden death" flashed across the screen, through tears, I started praying for the person who died and the family that was heartbroken over their loss. Daddy noticed and asked, "Now what in the tarnation are you upset about, Savannah?" When I told him, he threw his head back and laughed and explained that no one died on the field. We laughed off and on the rest of the night about that. My dad always had a good sense of humor.

A few weeks later, Daddy came in the house and said, "Savannah, come outside. I want to show you something."

I was reading in my room, and he had shouted from

the bottom of the stairs. I quickly shut my book and bounded down the stairs, Michelle and Chelsea tailing me. We went outside to see a shiny red riding lawn mower on our front lawn.

Mother came out too and started laughing. "Do you think we need this monstrosity to cut *our* tiny little yard?" She demonstrated how tiny our little yard was by putting her index finger and thumb close together, like the size of a postage stamp. She was still chuckling as she shook her head in dismay. *Why is she making fun of Daddy?*

Daddy's face got red, and his eyes shot daggers at her. He turned to me. "I'll have to teach you, but you can use it to cut the grass on Saturdays if you want to."

I clapped and shouted, "Yes! Yes, I want to! Thank you, Daddy! I'm so excited! Can I try right now?" It was as if he'd just given me my first car.

"Can I too? I want to do it!" Chelsea chimed in.

Michelle was bored already and said, "Are you serious? This is what you brought us out here to see?" She went back inside, and Mother followed her. I couldn't understand how they weren't thrilled like Chelsea and I were.

I was elated that Daddy trusted me and that he and I could spend time together doing yard work. This became our routine, Daddy and I working in the yard on Saturdays.

My cousin Bobby called at the end of that summer. He wanted to talk to my dad. We were eating breakfast, and I had my eye on a hummingbird whizzing its wings outside the kitchen window when Dad took the call.

"Oh, hey, Bobby, how are you? Oh? Well, sure, sure. I think we could do that. Plan on next Saturday. One o'clock, okay?" My dad hung up the phone and came back to the table to finish his coffee.

Mother asked, "What did Bobby want?"

"He asked if he could cut the grass for me. I thought it'd be good for him, to learn some responsibility. I told him he could start next week. And of course, I'll pay him something," Daddy explained.

Suddenly the hummingbird flew away and my heart sank to the bottom of my body. *That's my job—my time with my dad! You can't just barge in on my space, Bobby!* Bobby was one of my favorite cousins, but I think I hated him right then. *Won't you miss our special time together, Daddy?*

I lost my appetite and asked to be excused from the table. I was released only after my mother commented on how much food I hadn't eaten.

As it turned out, my cousin Bobby wasn't that motivated; he only cut the grass for a few weeks, and then I got the job back. I never got paid, but that didn't matter too much to me. I just wanted to hang out with my dad.

Dad always seemed pleased with my work by saying, "Okay, good, good, that's good. You're getting better at this, and there is still more to do, but this will do for now." That was my dad's way of saying thank you and that he liked the progress. To him, there was always room for improvement in everything. We can never rest on our laurels, he'd say.

11

My Southern Roots

I waved goodbye to my last year of elementary school where I'd outgrown my pants, snack time, and recess. I talked to my friends about changing classes and carrying books to our very own lockers, which made us feel important and so grown-up.

My best school buddies—Tracy, Lori, Vicki, and Stacy—and I had every class together, ate lunch as a pack, and talked about how creepy our new public school sixth-grade teacher was, Mr. Richards. He had a fat mustache and stared at the girls and made comments about their outfits, such as "You look so nice," especially if the girl wore a dress. We gossiped about the popular kids, and we giggled about which boys we wanted to kiss. This was a group that would always be my friends, ones that I could count on, the girls I'd go through high school with. My confidence was on the rise, and I thought nothing could stop me.

Until cheerleading tryouts.

I'd never taken gymnastics or dance classes, although I'd asked my mother many times, but it didn't seem too difficult to be a cheerleader. I did cartwheels, roundoffs, and summersaults in my yard for hours, and my friends and I had built our own human pyramid a few times; I stood on top, albeit shaking and for no more than two seconds, but how hard could this cheerleading gig be?

After the pep rally, a couple of the cheerleaders went to each classroom and invited the girls to try out for this year's team. Stacy and I were wide-eyed, and we talked after class and decided that a few days of practice that weekend would suffice. We promised each other that we'd go to tryouts together the following Thursday. Every day after school, I ran down to our basement and worked on my cheerleading jump, the herky, and my splits. I called Chelsea down to watch me.

"You're so good, Savannah! You'll make the team for sure." Her eyes were filled with pride for her eleven-and-a-half-year-old sister. She had no idea if I was any good or not, but she thought I was, so when I showed her my splits, it didn't matter that I couldn't quite get down all the way. My fourth-grade sister thought I would be the best cheerleader the middle school ever had.

Tryouts came, and Stacy became pale and pulled me aside. "I-I can't do it. I'm not going in there. I'm riding the bus home. Sorry! Gotta go, bye!" She jogged down the hall to her bus.

She left me standing there, my mouth wide open, ready to either cry or scream at her. I'd worked so hard all weekend! My heart pumped faster at the thought of doing it alone, but I wasn't a quitter, even when all the evidence screamed at me to stop. So, in my flappy little shorts and loose-fitting T-shirt and flat Keds, I got in line to wait for the perky cheerleader helpers to call me into the gymnasium.

As I waited, I scanned the other girls around me. They had hired professionals to prepare for this day, I was sure of it. They had on tight shorts and glittery form-fitting tops, and their hair was pulled up high in ponytails. Their legs were long and lean and smooth, and mine were splotchy. I'd forgotten a comb, so my hair was stringy and unbrushed. I tucked it behind my ears as best as I could. I wasn't allowed to wear makeup, but my cohorts had on foundation, blush, and lipstick—and beauty pageant smiles to match. There were even some mothers there to support their future cheerers. I wasn't sure my mother even remembered I was trying out today, and my confidence plummeted.

With only a few girls left waiting in the hall, my name was finally called, along with four other girls, one of whom wore a maxi skirt. We filed in as if we were signing up for chemistry. The judges asked us to perform the cheer that we had been given the week prior, and we did; it went okay, except for the girl on the end was offbeat a little and the maxi-skirt girl ended after the rest of us saying an extra "fight!" with such force that she farted. We all jumped up and down and cheered, like good cheerleaders do, but I kept my arms close to my side so my shirt wouldn't fly up.

When it came time to do our cheerleading jumps, we each were asked to come to the middle of the circle and do our best jump, the herky. My stomach churned, being on display like that. *Oh, God, I think I'm going to be sick.* I mustered up all my courage and bent my knees and jumped as high as I could, concentrating on contorting my body in all the right places. I was flying, and I just knew I'd jumped two feet in the air, executing the perfect herky. I landed, but my ankle twisted and I swayed, my arms flying about. I took a step backward to regain my balance. One of the judges lifted her head up from her clipboard and said, "Okay, you can do your jump now."

"Oh, um, I-I just did it," I said with a shaky voice.

She pulled her glasses down her nose at the judge sitting next to her. The other judge squished her brows together and puckered her mouth. She shook her head, waving a hand. She said under her breath, "Yeah, she did, but it's okay, you don't need to see it."

I remembered that I forgot to do my military clap, so I did that quick. The judges held back smiles, even one excusing herself as she held her hand over her mouth.

"Thank you," the blond judge said. "You may leave the gym now."

"Oh, I worked on my splits too, if you want to see."

"No. No, thank you, that's okay. You can leave," she said again. Then she lowered her head back down at her clipboard.

The next day at school, even though tryouts didn't go as well as I'd hoped, I couldn't concentrate on anything other than fantasizing about getting a uniform and meeting some really cool girls on the squad. After my last class of the day, I ran down the hall, my heart racing, to see if my name was on the list. I scanned the list. I didn't see my name. My eyes darting about, I scanned it again, still not seeing my name. My neck and face grew warm and red. *Doggone it! It's because they didn't see my splits!*

"Hey, Savannah, did you make it?" Stacy asked behind me.

"No, it was stupid, anyway. I really didn't want to be a cheerleader." My face still crimson, I shook my head and wrinkled my nose. My nose prickled, and I blinked back tears.

Stacy grabbed my elbow and said, "Come on, let's get out of here."

Walking down the hall, arm in arm, she said, "Yeah, cheerleading is for prissy girls, and we are not those kinds of girls!" We laughed, and I felt the weight of the cheerleading world lift off me. We made fun of the cheerleaders all the way down the hall until we got on our bus.

We decided we'd try out for the volleyball team, and Stacy promised me she wouldn't quit at the last minute. We swore we'd practice together, and then when it was time for basketball, we'd try out for that too. I ran off the bus and skipped a few times through our garage and into the house. With my friend beside me, it didn't matter anymore that I didn't make the cheerleading team and I knew I could face anything.

Later that night, my mother called me into her bedroom. She sipped iced tea as she tapped the bedside next to her. I took a hesitant step closer to her as she rarely called us into her bedroom. I hopped up near the end of the bed and stared at my feet. She said, "Savannah, I've been thinking a lot about this, and I'd like you to go to a Christian school this coming fall. A different one than Michelle went to, but I think you'll love it."

My head jerked toward her, and I said, "But I don't want to change schools, Mother. All my friends are going to Centerville, and that's where I want to go."

Mother sighed and said, "You will make good Christian friends and learn about the Bible." Her mouth gaped open as she placed her hand on her copy of the Bible lying open next to her. "Don't you want to learn about the Bible?"

"No, Mother, I don't want to switch schools. I like where I'm going. All my friends are there. I *don't* want to go," I pleaded. I knew I didn't have much of a chance once my mother made up her mind, but I wanted to at least try to persuade her.

"Savannah, just give it one year, and if you don't like it after that, then you can go back to your school." I knew in my heart that was a lie. The only way I would go back to public school was if Mother wanted it.

I felt sweaty and I jumped off the bed. I crossed my arms, defiant. "I don't want to! I like where I am! I like my friends, and if I change schools, I'll lose my friends."

"Savannah, you'll make good Christian friends at this new school. God wants us to have good friends, ones that love Him, and you'll make those kinds of friends there. Trust me. Plus, if your friends are truly your friends now, they'll be your friends even if you change schools. I'll sign you up for one year."

You have no idea what you're talking about, lady. My friends are true friends, and if I change schools, we won't see each other and we'll all make different friends. Changing schools would be the end of a good thing I had going on at my public school. All the plans Stacy and I had just worked through on the bus ride home, the excitement for our athletic future, and all the happiness immediately drained from me.

I lowered my head and let my arms fall loosely by my side. The tickling in my nose made it hard to hold back the tears that were developing in my eyes.

She talked more about "bad influences" in public schools, but I knew the "discussion" was over, especially when she inadvertently revealed that she had already enrolled me at the little Christian school for the following school year, my seventh grade.

Near the end of that summer, Mother called me into the kitchen and said the one thing I dreaded: "It's time to color your hair again. You want it to be nice and blond when you start your new school, don't you?" Even though my hair was as golden blond as it could be from the penetrating Georgia sun, it wasn't as light as my mother liked it to be.

"Mother, I hate coloring my hair. It grows out, and then the roots show, and we never cover them soon enough. I don't want to."

"Well, I want you to. I've got all the stuff. Sit down right here, and we'll get started. It always looks so pretty when we're done. I know you'll like it." When I started to talk back to her, she grabbed my face, pinching my mouth, and said, "It's either a coloring or a perm! And I know you don't like the smell of the permanent, so sit down and put this towel around you."

My sisters never had to endure my mother's hair tampering. They had gorgeous, thick chestnut-brown hair, while mine was a cross between dirty blond and strawberry blond, depending on the time of year, but either way, not blond enough for my mother's tastes. My hair was a few inches past my shoulders, fine and straight. For a while, she gave me perms that made me look like Shirley Temple, but not in a cute way. She started out using the smallest rollers, then at my begging, moved to the larger rollers, as I hoped the curls would fall out sooner. For three whole days, I couldn't wash my hair, so I put my hair up in a ponytail to try to hide the evidence, but you can't, I discovered, hide the horrendous smell of a 1976 store-bought permanent. It stays with you and follows you down the halls and sits with you in art class. Oh, how many times a classmate said, "What is that smell?" I wanted to dig a hole in the tile floor of my school, stick my head in, and die.

My quintessential southern belle Mother didn't care what it was like for me to have her change my hair to suit her, and my anger bubbled up inside me. I pulled away from her and shouted out, "No! I'm sick of you doing things to my hair!"

Mother slapped me across the face so hard that it burned like a million stings to my skin, the pain lasting for the next ten minutes. My heartbeat and breathing seemed to stop, and with wide eyes and a mixture of disbelief and venom, I glared at her. The skin where she hit me was on fire, but I refused to touch it, refused to bring my hand up to my face.

Mom, catching the hatred in my eyes, said with equal venom and tighter lips, "Don't you dare look at me that way. I'll slap you into next week!"

Gritting my teeth, I lowered my eyes to the box of hair coloring, with an urge to slap *her*, or at least shout back at her, "I hate you!" but I started breathing again and came to my right mind. To make it through the night with what was left of my dignity, I turned to walk upstairs to my bedroom, but she grabbed me by the arm and said, "Sit down! We're coloring your hair!"

I pulled my arm away and plopped down in the chair, stared at the floor, and became motionless and tried to see how long I could hold my breath. She put an old bath towel around my shoulders and began pouring the pungent coloring solution on my roots. When she was finished, I sat alone in the kitchen as I waited for my hair to process. I rubbed my cheek as soon as I knew she was out of sight.

Forty-five minutes later, Mother checked my hair and it was ready to rinse. I leaned over the sink and closed my eyes tight with the towel over my eyes. Still, water got into my eyes and poured down my shirt too. When the rinsing was over, she washed and conditioned my hair, and then I stood up and wrapped my hair in a new towel. I started to go up to my room again.

"Where do you think you're going? Help me clean this up," Mother demanded.

She was determined to keep me a prisoner. I picked up the empty box of color, the plastic bottle, and the newspaper underneath, crumpled it all up, and threw it in the trash, with a look of scorn on my face. The bitterness for this woman was growing in me. I refused to speak to her. I hated her.

I stood in the middle of the kitchen and saw that the table was clean, so I took another chance and turned to go upstairs. This time, she let me go.

I shut and locked my bedroom door. Chelsea was in her pajamas and in bed reading.

I looked in the mirror and saw the shape of my mother's hand on my cheek. My tears had dried up, but I lay on my bed and buried my face into my cool pillow.

I was Mother's favorite, her confidante. She had spent hours telling me how horrible my dad was to her, as if we had this common bond, something that kept us close and together. I lay motionless, finding it difficult to form complete thoughts in my head.

As I lay there, a heavy darkness covered me like a quilt. *How could I be so stupid to trust her?* My room seemed soundless, or maybe it was my own inner silence; I listened for footsteps, for Mother to come running up the stairs and say she was sorry, that she should have never slapped me and that she'll never do it again. But there were no footsteps. No one came to check on me to see if I was okay. I let out a heavy sigh as the loneliness crept up to me. My mind raced trying to find a way out of this isolation. What would it take for me to feel loved? I couldn't go to my dad; I never went to him for love or tenderness. I didn't trust him. And now I couldn't trust Mom. She had isolated me from everyone in this family; Michelle hated me, or as Mother said, she was "jealous" of me, and Chelsea was too young to talk to about anything.

I started to wonder if there was something wrong with me. I couldn't see it, as it wasn't an outward handicap or defect, but was there something deep within me that was flawed? My mother, the one who gave birth to me, the one who loved Jesus so much that she was at church at least three times a week, the one who had friends and seemed so outgoing and friendly, wouldn't hit me or withhold her love from me if I didn't somehow deserve it.

12

Grooming a "Christian" Daughter

My first day of Christian school, and I thought my heart was going to jump out of my chest. I had to keep wiping my hands on my dress because they were so sweaty, and I had developed a spasm in my left eye.

I didn't know anyone at the school, and I was intimidated by the strange rules that were laid out for me during orientation. For example, girls had to wear dresses every day and culottes for sports and swimming.

The idea of the school being Christian triggered my need to be "good" and to please God by obeying my superiors, so I chose my favorite new white dress for school, possibly subconsciously thinking white represented goodness. I hadn't developed physically in any way to show for, so like usual, I wore my training bra and a half-slip underneath to school. My mother approved of my outfit, and off I went to a small new school.

I didn't realize how strict this school was, however,

until my first encounter with my homeroom teacher. She displayed not one inkling of warmth or friendliness. Her skin was smooth but pasty white, and I thought she looked like an angry funeral director. She pointed to an empty chair and told me to sit down, all without a smile. Soon after, each student was called up to her desk to order lunch for the day. I was confused, because at my public school, we had a cafeteria that we'd go to at lunchtime and get our lunch through the line around noon. But this morning, it was 8:30 A.M. and I was supposed to tell this teacher what I wanted for lunch. I shuffled up to her desk, only hearing my own heartbeat, and stood there because I wasn't sure what to say. She pointed to a piece of paper with a list of food choices and asked in an annoyed voice, "Would you like this hamburger?"

Staring at the menu, I cleared my throat and replied, "Yes."

I chewed on my lip and waited for my next set of instructions, but nothing came. It seemed my teacher had become a mannequin, so without moving my head, my eyes met hers and she was glaring at me. Her lips quivered and one of her eyes narrowed. She took off her glasses and bellowed for all to hear, "That's yes *ma'am*! You will always address me as ma'am, do you hear me?" Her eyes never left mine, and her scowl put me in some sort of trance until I repeated, "Yes ma'am," which I did with a quiet, squeaky voice. Then she told me to sit down. The classroom grew as quiet as a church library on a Friday night.

I walked back to my desk, which was in the front

row, and all the eyes in the classroom seared through me, and I grew redder by the minute. I willed my face to stop blushing, but the harder I tried to stop it, the redder it got. I grew so warm that I'm certain I developed a fever right there in her classroom.

It was an enormous relief when she asked us to get our books out and start reading chapter one. At least I could distract myself with the words on the page. I had learned a huge lesson: Never speak to your elders in this school without including *ma'am* or *sir*. I spoke those words around my family, to my mother and my daddy, but they weren't militants about it. Here, at this school, it was mandatory.

The humiliation of first hour moved to the back of my mind and was replaced with walking all alone, no friend or acquaintance with whom to saunter in to my next class. Right then, a gregarious girl named Telly walked up next to me and said, "Miss Lubbard sure was in a mood this morning! What a freak!" She rolled her eyes and shook her head and laughed. Telly had frizzy brown hair that she somehow had put on top of her head in a conch-shell shape, and I wanted to touch it. It was so large that I wondered if something could live in it.

I laughed and said, "Yeah, she was weird! I didn't know what she was talking about." And then we both laughed, and my anxiety melted as we walked down the hall together to math class. And that's how our friendship started, based on a mutual intense dislike for Miss Lubbard, and my keen interest in Telly's hair and how she got it to stay on the top of her head like that.

We were miraculously seated near each other. I had to concentrate hard because math didn't come easy for me.

Halfway through class, like an African cat hunting her prey, the dean of women sneaked up on me and whispered in my ear, "Please come out in the hall with me."

I jumped as if I'd fallen asleep and had been jolted awake, and thought, *Who are you and why do you want me in the hall?* Telly widened her eyes and gave me a nod, so, without question, I went.

Then, other disturbing thoughts came: *Oh no, what if both my parents have been killed in a flaming car crash and I'll have to raise my little sister because Michelle is on drugs? We'll be shipped off to Aunt Louise's house to finish school. I'll change schools again. Maybe I'll get to go back to my other school.* No one was in the hall but Miss Davis and me. I searched her eyes and waited for what she was going to say.

"My name is Miss Davis, and I'm the assistant principal here at Summit Christian Academy. You might remember me from orientation?" She didn't wait for me to reply. "Well, I've talked with your mother."

Oh, thank God, she's alive! What about Dad?

"She's coming to pick you up." She paused, tilted her head, crossed her arms, and rested her chin in her hand, like she was trying to figure out a complex story problem. "Do you have a full slip?"

For what? The funeral? For my dad's funeral?

I stammered, "U-Uh, a whole slip? Yes, um, no, I mean, I'm not sure. I just wore what I had."

"Your dress is too uh . . . how can I say it?" Her eyes

darted around the hallway and then right at mine as she said, "*Revealing*. The boys can see your bra, Savannah, and here at this school, we promote modesty. Young women must dress with discretion and purity. They must, at all times, cover their bodies, never tempting anyone to sin." She pursed her lips, like my mom does when she disapproves of something, and blew air through her nose. "Your dress is out of school parameters, and so your mother is on her way to pick you up and take you home so you can put on something more appropriate for our school."

I blinked. *So, my dad's okay?*

Miss Davis was a single woman of about forty years old. She may have been twenty-three; I wouldn't know, because her dress went below her knees and was buttoned all the way up to her chin. Her round face wasn't smiling. *Do these people smile around here?* She wore no makeup, and her brown hair was cut short in the shape of a bowl. She had pretty brown eyes but with dark veiny circles underneath. She was the appointed disciplinarian for the girls in our school. Any out-of-line female issues went straight to her where she dealt firmly and swiftly with the girl. No shenanigans were allowed, and no girl was going to cast a shadow on the lily-white reputation of Summit Christian Academy. Rightness, not empathy, was a shared value between Miss Davis and the academy.

When it registered with me what she was talking about, I pulled at the front of my dress. I couldn't wait for my mother to come rescue me. *How could I have gone out like this? I've been walking the school halls in this sheer smock? But my mother dressed me! She bought me this outfit! How could she have been so wrong about it?* I was horrified to think of all the boys who had seen me and what they must think of me.

I asked, on the verge of a meltdown, "Can I go wait for my mom in your office?" I was hoping she'd offer to go get my things in the classroom. I'd rather die than go back in there, considering I was walking around half naked in the school and causing who knows how many boys to think ungodly things. She agreed to that and offered to get my books for me.

When I got in the car with my mother, she let loose. "I can't believe this! They sent you home because of your dress? Your dress is fine. I can't believe I had to leave work for this. Ridiculous!" What would I tell the kids tomorrow when they asked where I went? I'd just tell them I had a doctor's appointment I'd forgotten about. "And I'm not taking you back today—you can stay home," Mother added.

Later, with red puffy eyes as I rested on my bed, something started bothering me. I thought, *Why are the boys looking at my dress and my body like that? And why aren't they getting in trouble?* And besides, my goodness, there was really nothing to see! But I knew I couldn't stand against this authoritative regime, so the fight in me died down and my desire to please my elders grew.

I accepted the premise that not only was I responsible for my own sexual purity, but I was responsible for not provoking all the boys in my school—and all the boys in the world—to notice me, to lust after me. How in the world could a boy be held responsible to control his thoughts if

I wore a dress that's a little bit see-through and he notices my bra, even a training one, and has an impure thought? *I must take better care for how I portray myself.*

The teaching that the female was and is the sexually responsible gender was as fundamental a teaching as the rapture. Pressure was put on girls to be pure, or a virgin, to wear white on her wedding day, to be modest, sexually uncertain, and shy, while the male counterpart was fully expected to be assertive, sexual, animalistic, carnal, and sensual. However, his strong and vile desires were to be restrained, tempered, and tamed through the untainted and chaste portals of a "good woman." If he didn't have a good woman in his life, any exploits he may have had would be understood and explained away as "in his nature." Throughout my adolescent and teen years, I, too, accepted this weight of responsibility upon my shoulders, although I didn't understand all the implications or the problematic thinking or the incorrect biblical teaching behind it. It would take decades for me to understand the faulty foundation upon which my life of "faith" had been built.

The next day in school, only one person asked me about leaving early; it was Telly, and I told her I had a doctor's appointment I'd forgotten about. I couldn't make eye contact with her when I lied to her. I liked her and thought we might become good friends.

Months later, I sat in Bible class drawing my favorite doodle: a house near a pond with a smiling sun. The back of my neck was clammy, just like my underarms, because our school didn't have any air-conditioning and it was ninety-eight degrees outside. I wore a navy-blue polyester dress with pantyhose that day, which did nothing to help me stay clean and fresh.

I added trees to encircle the house and pond and thought, *I'd love to live in a house like this someday*, when Mr. Dayton broke into my daydream saying something about heaven. As if he'd personally been there, he said, "Young people, there will be streets of gold and pearly gates and angels singing—now doesn't that sound beautiful?" I kept drawing, but he'd caught my attention.

He went on: "In heaven, we will have transformed bodies. They will go back to what they were intended to look like, the way *God* created us." He paused, and the class was silently waiting for him to say more. *Where is he going with this?*

I stopped moving my pencil and looked up; he was staring directly at me. With a grin, he cocked his head to one side and said, "Isn't that right, Savannah?" Immediately, kids turned around in their seats to gawk at me, some of them snickering.

He looked around at the students and drove his point home. "So if you have fake blond hair, if your hair is *bleached*, your hair will go back to its natural color that God gave you—brown." His gaze ended on me, and his shoulders bounced up and down as he laughed.

My heart pumped feverishly in my chest, and I squirmed in my chair. Spinters exploded in my gut, and a rush of heat traveled to my face and ears, making them glow purplish red. *My roots! My two-inch dark roots are showing! I'm such an idiot. I should have asked Mother to color my hair sooner!* When the laughter didn't die down, I let out a chortle too, pretending not to be humiliated. I rested my elbows on my desk and then rubbed my forehead. *I never want to come back to this school. I hate Mr. Dayton!*

When I got home from school that day, on the kitchen table sat a hair-frosting kit. Did Mother hear about what happened at school?

She walked up behind me and said, "Instead of coloring, we'll pull your hair through a cap, and that will help with the roots."

"How soon can we do it?"

"I can do it tonight." Mother sighed. "That's why I bought it."

It was Wednesday, and I had two more days of possible mockery at school. But what if I hated it and the kids and my teacher mocked me for my new frosted hair? At least with my current dark-roots situation, that's what everyone expected to see, so I said, "Let's wait till Friday just in case I don't like it. At least that will give me Saturday and Sunday to do something to cover it up."

Friday night came, and on went the cap. Mother jabbed a plastic hook through tiny holes all over my head, sometimes going too far and jabbing my scalp. "Ouch! That hurt!" I'd say.

"Oh, sorry," Mother said. She poured terrible-smelling bleach over my capped skull, and the skin on my head started tingling. We waited for the longest possible time, about sixty minutes, so Mother could be assured I had the blondest hair on the block. *What is it with her and blond hair?* After rinsing and drying my hair, the dark roots were gone, but now my hair had a grayish tint. All I wanted was to go back to my natural hair color, which was blond anyway, but she refused to take me to a salon so a professional could fix my hair. She went to her hairdresser every six weeks, but for me, it was an at-home Clairol coloring or frosting kit. At this point, I started wearing my hair in tight ponytails. I figured the less of my hair that was showing, the better.

I was finally beginning to make a few friends at Summit Academy and was tolerating the rules a little better.

One of my new friends, Teresa, and I talked all during study hall where Miss Davis monitored. We made a game of it to see who could talk the most without her finding out who was doing all the talking. We buried our heads in our books as if we were enveloped into our studies, all the while talking to each other, but "throwing" our voices across the room when she was looking the other way. It was great fun for us, even when we got caught, which was often. Even though I cowered when Miss Davis walked into a room, if I could make Tessa throw her head back and laugh uncontrollably, then it was worth it when Miss Davis glared at me over her glasses.

One day in study hall, as I was pulling my chair out to sit down, I accidentally bumped Teresa's arm. "Ouch!" She winced and held her arm.

"Oh, I'm sorry, are you okay?" I cupped my hand over my mouth.

"Yeah, it's nothing." She rubbed her arm, and I caught sight of a black-and-purple mark.

I leaned in close to her and asked, "What happened?" I drew my eyebrows together and nodded toward her arm.

"Oh, my stupid brother hit me," she whispered. She rolled her eyes and shook her head.

Miss Davis walked close by our table, and I sat up and popped open my social studies book. When she passed and headed in the other direction, I said, "He *hit* you?!"

Teresa said, "Yeah, but swear you won't tell a soul, okay?"

I nodded. "I swear."

"Danny, my brother, drinks a lot and he was goofing around with a baseball bat and swung it and he accidentally hit me. He apologized and kept asking me if I was okay, but I can't tell anyone because he was wasted and my parents would kill him."

Images of my drunk and high sister Michelle flashed in my mind. I'd never seen her wasted, so I imagined her screaming and hollering, swinging a bat around too. I wondered if Danny and Michelle knew each other. Was there a partying circuit of older teens in the greater Atlanta area and did they run into each other?

I reached over and softly touched her hand. "I'm sorry that happened. I hope the bruise goes away soon."

Teresa smiled weakly and said, "Thanks." She flipped

through a notebook and said, "You should come over some time. We have rabbits, and one of them just had babies. Would your parents let you have a rabbit?"

I shook my head and said in a deeper voice, "Never! They hardly let us have a dog. But I'd love to come over and see the rabbits!"

Teresa said, "Okay, maybe this weekend. And maybe you can spend the night! I'll ask my mom." It felt amazing to make a new friend, one who understood me.

Miss Davis rounded the corner before either of us saw her and pointed to me and commanded, "Savannah, bring your books and move to this seat over here." She moved me two tables away from Teresa, and we weren't able to finish our conversation at all that day.

The next day, I looked forward to talking more with Teresa, but the bell for the start of first period rang and the eighth-grade students piled into their homerooms. There was a distinct change in the atmosphere of Mr. Stoddard's classroom. People were quieter, some of the kids weren't talking, a couple of the girls were crying, and the teachers seemed to have more than their usual somber faces. I began to get out my first-hour social studies book and notebook when Mr. Stoddard asked the class to close our books. His eyes were swollen, and his voice was weak.

"Class, I have some very bad news. Teresa Rogers was killed in a car accident last night."

What?! I gasped and put my hand over my mouth. I stared at him in disbelief, but as the news sunk in, my breath quickened and I shook my head slowly at first, but then faster. *She was just here yesterday. I just talked to her.* I got lightheaded so I rested my head in the crook of my arms and began to cry.

Someone handed me a tissue, I'm not sure who, and I wiped my eyes and nose and sat up again. Tears kept streaming down my face, and I could barely see as Mr. Dayton walked up to the front of the class and said, "Teresa was in a car with kids who were drinking. The driver was drunk." He clasped his hands together and added, "Class, be sure your sins will find you out."

I sniffled and took a few deep breaths to stop crying. My classmates were stunned and quiet. Before I knew it, my hands had fallen to my lap and I was staring at my bare desk, not blinking. Mr. Dayton's words were fading away, and I didn't notice when he left our classroom or when Mr. Stoddard asked us to open our books. My thoughts tumbled. *How can Teresa be gone? She was just here yesterday. This can't be true. How can we just go on like this as if our friend didn't just die?*

13

Black Dog and Teen Angst

Another year had gone by, and just as I thought would happen, I lost contact with my public school friends. After Teresa died, Telly and I did a few things together, and we were forming a friendship, so even though I hated the "Christian" school, I at least had a friend. I didn't even try to talk to my mother about switching schools again.

As destiny would have it, changing schools became an issue anyway when my dad informed us that he had taken a job up in northern Indiana and that we were moving the summer following my freshman year. I didn't want to move and leave Michelle, her new baby, David, and my other family members and the life I knew in Georgia. It wasn't a perfect life, but it was my life and I knew what it was all about there. And I definitely didn't want to go through the struggles of going to a new school and meeting new people all over again. I had just started feeling like I could belong at Summit, but now I was being torn away again. I wanted to stay in one place and feel like I fit in somewhere.

My ninth-grade year wasn't my best year. I was obsessed

with worrying about moving and I was having trouble with my friendships. Telly was the only friend I had, but I pulled away from her because I thought, *Why bother having friends when I'll never see them again in a few months?* Plus, when some of the kids found out where I was moving, they didn't like that I was moving north.

"Hey, Savannah, so you're a Yankee now?" Lance asked one day after math. He asked me in front of three other guys and a couple of girls as I was getting my books out of my locker. The other kids laughed.

"A Yankee? What are you talking about?" My face got red, naturally.

"Yeah, you remember about a little war called the Civil War, don't you? Well, anyone north of here is a damn Yankee, and now you're one!" He pushed passed me, knocking me into the lockers, and the kids followed him like he was their gang leader.

I don't want to be a damn Yankee!

I tried to talk to my parents that night.

"Do we have to move? I don't want to. I could live with Aunt Louise," I begged.

"No, you can't live with them. They have enough on their plates right now, and they don't need to add raising another child to their list. Plus, I'd miss you. Wouldn't you miss us?" Mother said.

I wanted to scream, "No!" but I lifted my chin and almost shouted, "But I don't want to leave my friends here. I really don't want to go!"

"You're going with us, and that's the end of this discussion, Savannah," Dad said, pointing his finger at me.

My parents were making me go no matter what kind of other options I came up with. I had developed a hatred toward my parents, and I let them know it. My dad moved up to Elkhart six months before we did, and the tension between my mother and me grew. Mother yelled at us every day, and I yelled right back. One day, she couldn't take my back talk anymore, so she called my dad at work. She handed me the phone.

"Hello?"

"Savannah, I will not have you disrespecting your mother. Now, do what she says, do you understand me?"

"Yes sir."

"Give the phone back to your mother."

With a heated glare that could have seared meat, I handed the phone back to Mother. I hated her. I was losing everything, and all she cared about was if I had cleaned my room or if I'd done my homework or if my hair was blond enough.

"Bob, if you could have just seen the look Savannah just gave me, you'd have knocked her into next week!" Mother started whimpering. "I just don't think I can keep doing this anymore."

I was halfway through the kitchen to go to my room when she called for me. "Savannah, get in here. Your father wants to talk to you!" She had such a piercing voice that I thought my ears would bleed.

I grabbed the phone out of her hand and sighed into the phone. "Yes?"

"Savannah, if I have to, I will come down there and make you mind your mother, do you understand me?" Dad punched each word. "I will not tolerate your attitude. You are a selfish and ungrateful little brat!" His voice escalated, and he went into a coughing fit. I waited for him to recover. "You think this is hard on you? Think about how hard this is on your mother! Now go upstairs and clean your room and do your homework!"

I put the phone down and stomped my way up the stairs into my room. I didn't quite slam the door because I didn't want to hear my dad's voice again that night, nor did I want him to show up at the house, but I did shut it loud enough for it to feel good to me. I sat on my bed and just stared at the floor. I turned on my radio and picked a hard rock station. Led Zeppelin was playing "Black Dog." That wasn't my normal strain of music, but tonight I wanted something darker, angrier, something I could get lost in. Michelle had introduced me to a new genre of music that gave me a place to let my adolescent emotion run wild and free.

I lay back on the bed and stared at the ceiling. The music took my anger and let it float away, and my limbs went numb. When the beginnings of something started tickling my nose or eyes, I held my breath and pushed the feelings down, way down, so far down that I wasn't sure I'd find them again.

I was a southerner through and through, and I was proud of that. I was nervous to move up to Indiana, because I had never been anywhere north of the Mason–Dixon

Line. I imagined New York City: tall buildings, taxis, tons of traffic, people walking everywhere, and everyone loud and rude. My parents got whatever they wanted regardless of how it affected me and my sisters. *Dad wants us to move to God knows where? Okay then, no questions asked, let's pack up the family and head there. We're going to leave Michelle and David? Okay, sure, no problem. Mother wants me to leave all my friends, never developing any close bonds and join a Jesus cult? Okay, I'll sign up right away and do it with a smile.*

14

Time for a Change

After ten years in Georgia, at the end of May 1981, Mother, Chelsea, and I made the long trip north. I continuously played the song "Hot Child in the City" by Nick Gilder on my cassette tape player while images of skyscrapers, overcrowded sidewalks, and traffic jams ran through my mind, but I was surprised, maybe a little disappointed, to find that quiet neighborhoods also exist in Yankee territory.

I wore flip-flops, jeans, and a short-sleeved shirt, but thankfully I also brought along a windbreaker, because I shivered in the balmy 72 degrees in Indiana. I opened the door to the rental house, and a stale odor filled my nose. I muttered, "Disgusting." Chelsea smelled it too, scrunching up her nose. I held my nose and was now even more angry at the life my parents were forcing upon me. *Great, an old musty house.* I stomped up the winding staircase to see the bedrooms and pick one. The entire house was carpeted in pink.

After Chelsea and I happily agreed to our bedrooms,

we started unpacking. The moving truck arrived and set up our beds and dressers, and we started filling them with our Georgia life. Sadness lurked around my heart all day, and I finally went into Chelsea's room and sat on her unmade bed. "I miss Georgia and I want to go back home." I fell back, staring at the ceiling fan.

Chelsea agreed. "Me too. It feels weird here, not like home." She lay down beside me on her side. "I never thought we'd move away from our family and friends."

"I know. I keep thinking this is a bad dream and that we'll move back. I miss everybody and I don't like how cold and gray it is here."

A few days after moving into our house, the doorbell rang. I ran to answer the door, and there stood a guy and a girl, about my age, with the goofiest grins on their faces. The girl had curly brown hair, eyeglasses, and braces. She stood with her shoulders round, and her arms hanging loosely by her side. The boy was cute, no glasses or braces, but he stood there with a ridiculous grin and laughed when I said, "Hi."

The girl said, "Hi, my name's Carol, and this is my brother, Ben. We were wondering if you could come out and play."

I stood there for what seemed like forty-five seconds, lobbing my eyes from Carol to Ben, waiting for one or both of them to start cackling. They were around my age, fifteen years old. No one asks to "play" at our ages. No one. So, I waited. And then I chuckled to let them know that I knew I was on to their little joke. They were trying to embarrass the new little southern girl. The "Yankees" were apparently going to try to beat the southerners again and make them feel inferior or something like that. *Yeah, yeah, I get it, we lost the war.* I said with the widest grin I could achieve, "Why, sure, I can play! What y'all wanna play?"

Without missing a beat, Ben said, "Well, I see you have a basketball hoop. We could shoot some hoops."

Dadgummit if he wasn't serious! They literally wanted to play. Basketball was fine with me because I wanted to try out for the team here. I loved the game, and even though I wasn't tall, I worked hard and practiced at being a point guard. I said, "Sure, I love basketball. I play every day. Come on, my ball is over here." I took them around to the side of the house, and we played a simple game of H-O-R-S-E to get started. I still couldn't get over that they asked me to play. How strange. Is this how kids in Indiana talk? *Oh, God, this is going to be weird. I'll never fit in here.*

The summer continued on, and Ben, Carol, Chelsea, and I hung out all summer playing basketball and board games and watching television. They said we had a funny accent, but Chelsea and I thought they did, but it was okay. We liked them and we were having fun, and it beat sitting around with our mother all day.

I wanted to go to the public school, but I had mixed feelings. Hours of biblical teaching against sex, drugs, and rock and roll had me convinced that every student in public school was participating in one or more of these evils and were damned to hell; if I were to associate with these people, I, too, would be caught in the grips of the devil's schemes. On the other hand, I knew inside me that the strange Christian school philosophies couldn't be right; God was supposed to love all His children, and the awful rules and punishments they imposed on us didn't mesh with who they said God was.

But Mother was praying her heart out that Chelsea and I could go to the Christian school in town. Dad didn't start the application process at any point during that six months he was in Indiana before we arrived as Mother asked him to do. Therefore, when Mother inquired about enrolling Chelsea and me, there were no openings; they said we would be put on the waiting list in case something became available. The day before school started, the Lord must have heard her prayers because the principal called and told her that two openings had become available and that we were able to attend this Christian academy. "Praise the Lord," my mother said every time she told this story.

I soon found out that Grace Baptist Academy was not like the other school. The students were like my public school friends, and the teachers were caring. The academy had some rules, but they weren't odd rules such as girls wearing culottes to play sports or swim in. They offered a Bible class that was taught by a kindhearted man who didn't try to embarrass the students. None of the teachers did that.

One of the teachers took an interest in me because I liked her classes, English and drama. I started the school year shy, but by the time she worked with me and helped pull me out of my protective shell, I was able to try out for the school play and sing a solo. One day, though, as I was walking into rehearsal, my teacher said, "Okay, everyone, gather around and sit here on the floor in a circle."

We all sat with our legs crossed on the hard gym floor. She turned the lights down low and said, "Savannah, I want you to come up here. Stand here and sing your solo for everyone. Come on."

I was seated on the floor next to my friend Susan. The big gymnasium suddenly became tiny, and my mouth and throat dried up. I was speechless. I wasn't expecting this, and I wanted to run out as fast as I could, but finally I sputtered, "D-Do I have to?"

Mrs. Elling smiled warmly and said, "Yes, you have to. Come on up here. Everyone wants to hear your song." She clapped her hands.

And all my actor friends joined her and clapped and said, "Come on Savannah!" and "You can do it!"

My knees were shaking as I stood up and walked to the center of the circle. I cleared my throat at least ten times and held my hands clasped in front of me. The music for my solo started and so did my giggling, purely out of nervous energy, but when it was my time to sing, I found my note and out came my voice, on pitch, angelic. I sang the entire song from memory, jittery, and couldn't make eye contact with anyone, but the rush of satisfaction and happiness warmed my body and I couldn't stop smiling. I had tapped into something life-giving. I was truly alive when I was acting and singing, and I wondered if it was the reason I was put here on earth. My desire to be a psychologist fell to the background, and my newfound singing and acting gig took the spotlight. I started singing in choirs and acting in the school and church plays and even a few community theater productions, playing the role of Mayella in *To Kill a Mockingbird*.

Mother came to every performance whether it was acting, a piano rehearsal, or singing in church. She bragged about me to her friends near and far. Mother and Dad discussed my future many times; Mother wanted me to continue in an acting and singing career, while Dad thought it was a waste of time and thought I needed to focus on a more practical career such as business or psychology.

After living in the rental house for a year, we moved and my parents bought a more updated, cleaner, fresher house about five miles away. It had about a half-acre front yard, and it was covered in weeds.

School was out for the summer, and I remembered the days in Georgia when I helped Daddy take care of the yard, so I decided I'd spend some time in the front yard weeding. I got the wheelbarrow out, put on gardening gloves, and started pulling. I bent over and pulled and tossed for about five minutes, then stood up to see my progress. *My gosh, this is going to take me forever!* But I kept at it, even when I got hot and sweaty. I ran inside and drank a glass of water, and then I went right back out to the dirt and weeds. I pulled weeds for five hours straight.

I was bent over, the blood rushing to my head, and Dad's car tires rolled over a few acorns driving up. I stood up too fast and got a headache and had to hold my head for a minute. But I ran fast and said, "Dad! Dad, come out here! I want to show you the yard." He came around the corner, and I said, "See what I've been doing all day?" I had more to do, but the yard had at least seventy-five percent less weeds than yesterday.

"Wow, you've been busy. This is good," he said, nodding in appreciation. "There's a lot more work I've got to do, though." He sighed and went back inside.

I thought Dad was happy that I was working on the yard, and I was determined to finish the job. The connection with him was like when I'd cut the grass for him as a young girl.

At dinner, I said, "One of my goals for this summer is to work on softball. I want to make the team next year."

"That will be nice," Dad said as he continued reading the front page of the folded newspaper. He was a baseball star on his high school team.

I loved talking with my dad about sports and just being with him. "Will you throw the softball with me after I help clean up from dinner?"

"Savannah, no, I'm tired. I just don't feel like it tonight. I'm going to sit in my chair and read the paper. Maybe tomorrow."

Tomorrow came, and his answer was the same as the night before. I asked a few more times before it became apparent that he would not be teaching me the art of throwing the ball. I took the two gloves I was keeping in my bedroom—one was Dad's old baseball glove from his high school days, and the other one was mine—and threw them in the garage and left them there.

15

A Cloudy Life

I lay on my side, motionless, holding my belly for what seemed like an hour before I rolled onto my back on the living room floor. I bent my knees and tried to comfort my unborn child from Bryce's attack. I was in a fog, floating away, staring at nothing.

My stomach churned, but I swallowed and breathed deeply to fight the urge to vomit. My eyes were full of burning tears, and they rolled down my red, raw cheeks. *How could this have happened to me?* I moaned as I took in each breath, my lungs and throat scorched.

I needed to gather my thoughts and my strength; I needed to collect myself. I didn't know where to start. I didn't feel capable of getting off the floor. *Can I stay here all day? Can I die right here? Why did I fight Bryce so hard to live, only to want to die?*

Nicholas was crying. *My baby! Oh my God, he heard all of this.* I pushed my body up from the floor, and my head was pounding, every muscle in my body searing with pain. Nicholas's little face was red and wet with tears. I picked him up, wincing in pain. His mouth shivered as he cried, and I held him close in the rocking chair, rubbing and patting his back until he fell back asleep.

I considered gathering up my baby and all our things and leaving Bryce forever, but every time I tried to grab on to the idea, it became a drop of color in a pool of water; I reached for the thought, but the idea instantly dissolved. *Where would I go? I'd have to tell everyone about the violence.* I couldn't carry the tremendous weight of what just happened. I was retreating deeper into a dark cave within myself, into a place where no one would ever find me. I wanted someone to rescue me and my babies, but I feared no one was coming and I didn't have the strength or courage or whatever it was I needed to walk out the door.

The idea of leaving Bryce caused such anxiety that my mind shut down. I could think of no options, no one to call, no shelter, no police; my parents, sister, and best friend weren't possibilities to me at that time. It seemed easier to stay, to sit in the shame, rather than face my greatest fears and leave. The lights of imagination and choice were shutting down in my brain, and my mind was as blank as a white sheet of paper. Nothing was coming to me but to stay. I believed I had nowhere to go.

I knew, however, that I had to go forward, prepare to give birth, and maneuver around life without giving any hint of living with an abusive monster. I resolved to make my current life work. What continued to propel me was this: *I can't let anyone find out about what's really going on. I must keep this façade up so that people believe I have a good life, because that's what my parents raised me to do: to either have the perfect life, or make it appear to others that I have a perfect life—at all costs. If I fail, they fail, the family fails, and the entire charade falls apart, and then God knows what will happen.*

Come on, Savannah, you can do this. You've done this all your life. You can keep pretending. I put Nicholas back in his crib and I became aware of how much my head pounded and tingled. I stumbled to the bathroom and threw my shredded underwear away, and when I saw the violent remains of the night—my strewn-about hair, red marks on my face and neck, and my bloodshot eyes—I flopped down on the toilet and held my head in my hands.

I finally stood up and turned on the shower. The warm water flowed over my body and soothed my chills. To steady myself, I put both hands on the shower wall as the water washed a significant amount of my hair down the drain. My neck was aching, and my headache pressurized into a migraine, which there was little medicine I could take because of my baby. After showering and dressing, I used a heating pad and lay down in bed. It was close to 5 A.M., and I knew I only had a few hours before Bryce would return.

Like wild horses, my mind raced. Sleep eluded me. *How did I get here? What's wrong with me? I must deserve this life. Oh, God, where did I go wrong? I tried so hard to get life right. I screwed this up badly. I can't imagine the next ten, twenty, thirty years like this. And yet I can't imagine what getting out of this would be like, either.* I pulled the covers up closer around me as a thousand prickles crawled up my back.

While in bed, my mind floated back to when I was a little girl, lying on the grass in the summertime, taking in the millions of stars, twinkling and winking so far away, and I knew God was with me. But tonight, from the window in my bedroom, the sky was black and forsaken.

16

Love Soothes

Miraculously, Samantha Joy was born completely healthy two weeks after the assault, although I worried about how much she suffered that night of terror.

Love overcame me like an avalanche when I first held each of my babies. The old me died, and I rose up and was reborn a mother. I couldn't believe how much I didn't know about love until they were born. I took one look at their sweet, round perfect faces, and I was crazy about them, upside down in love with my son and daughter. They gave me a reason to live.

I learned how to read Bryce like an FBI special agent in forensics. I could pick up his most negligible facial alterations, detect the slightest exhale or inhale, the change in his body language, the movement of his hands as he spoke, the way his eyes turned ice blue when he was manipulating and midnight blue when angry and ready to pounce. My mind was like a computer categorizing the data, determining my level of risk.

I lived in such a way that he'd have no reason to have a

problem with me, although that didn't always matter—he could always find a reason to lash out at me. Still, I did what my mother did and what her mother and her mother's mother did: kept the house spotless, worked a full-time job, paid the bills on time, and put on a happy face to the outside world. Keeping the children safe, avoiding divorce, and appearing normal were my life's goals.

Inside, however, I felt anything but normal. I had divided like a cell and become two people. The outside me wore a mask, reading faces and situations so I'd know how to respond, making sure no one would see the real me; then there was the inside me: scared, lonely, sad, insecure, confused, sick.

Unfortunately, I also did a good job of hiding my life from my best friend. We didn't see each other very often, so it was easy to put on the smile and pretend everything was okay when we'd occasionally visit. She was always a ray of sunshine in my life, though, ever since I'd met her back in college.

One day, we met for lunch. I got to the restaurant a little early, so I got a booth near the back. I sat by the window and watched her drive up in her Mercedes-Benz. She quickly found me, waving and smiling so brightly, and walked over with her perfectly highlighted hair. She wore a black leather jacket, a black tank top, and black jeans with red boots. I stood up and threw my arms around her, and we both squealed in delight. I said, "Kay, you look amazing as always. Where'd you get this? I love it!" I touched the arm of her expensive jacket.

"Oh, girl, I got it when we were out in San Francisco at this little boutique. Cutest place ever, and I just had to have it. Isn't it amazing?" She sat in the booth and situated her Gucci bag on the seat beside her.

I was painfully aware of our socioeconomic discrepancies. She came from a wealthy family and spent more time and money on her nails, hair, and makeup than most people spent on groceries. I grew up in an upper-middle-class home, but since my marriage to Bryce, I had gone down a peg or two financially and didn't have extra income for trips to the nail salon. My wardrobe consisted of throwing a top or a skirt into my grocery cart, but never the two at once and only once a month, if I was lucky to have a few extra dollars.

"So how *are* you, Savannah? Is married life going well? How are the kids? Tell me everything!"

"Things are fine. I mean, I'm tired, of course—keeping up with two children, but they are so much fun. What about you, any trips planned for the near future?" I asked, trying to divert the conversation away from my marriage. I fidgeted a little in my seat, hoping she would stay on herself and keep the spotlight off me.

It worked. We talked about her trip to Fiji coming up and how she had been preparing for that. We laughed at old memories, and she invited me, Bryce, and the kids over for a family cookout. I already knew Bryce wouldn't want to go and I'd have to come up with an excuse.

Our time together ended, and we hugged goodbye; she held on longer than normal, and it seemed like she didn't want to let me go. Then she put her hand to her chest and said, "Oh, gosh, I almost forgot! I have three trash bags full of clothes for you."

My heart leaped in my chest because it was like Christmas when she gave me her clothes. Her hand-me-downs weren't the typical faded, worn clothes you'd get as a child. No, this was more like if Saks Fifth Avenue called and said, "We have a few extra clothes here. Would you be interested?" Um, yes, please!

"Kay, are you sure you want to give me all these clothes?" I called her when I got home. I had a couple of hours before Bryce would be home, so I opened the bags and pulled out each item as if it were my birthday. About halfway through the second bag, I pulled out a black silk top with pink and yellow embroidery on the edges of the neckline. It was from Neiman Marcus and had a tag on it. "Some of them still have tags on them!" I said. It wasn't uncommon for her to give me never-before-worn clothes with Versace and Fendi labels.

"Yes, I'm absolutely positive. They're yours if you want them, and if you want to share some with Chelsea, you can do that too. I need them out of my closet, because, as you know, I've purchased more clothes, so those can't come back to me. Take them and enjoy!"

"Oh, I'll enjoy them, all right! Thank you so much. You're too good to me, ya know?"

"Oh, don't be silly. You deserve it. I love you. You're like a sister to me!"

Her love for me was startling at times. I had a hard time

wrapping my mind around how much she seemed to love me. I mean, why me? *Am I worth all this? Do I deserve nice things?* She bought me my first and only cashmere sweater for my thirtieth birthday and she was always doing the most generous things for me and others. I watched her over the years do for herself things that I'd never even think to do for myself. I didn't think I deserved it. But Kay, she didn't think twice about buying herself an entire outfit, shoes included, and then getting a full-body massage—all in the same day. She worked hard too, though. She worked a full-time job, had a little girl, and on the weekends was busy cooking delicious meals for her family. She was an inspiration to me, and I'd often think, *Could I live the kind of life she lives?* After a while, her kindness began to sink in, and I started to believe, just a little bit, that if she thought that highly of me, maybe I could think that highly of myself.

I knew Bryce would be angry if he saw all my new clothes, so I packed the items I didn't keep and hauled the bulky black bags out to my trunk. Bryce had me convinced that regardless of the fact that the clothes were free, it was too materialistic to have those nicer things. I planned on taking them over to Chelsea later that week to see what she wanted, and then I'd share the rest with friends at work. Any leftovers, which was rare, were donated to charity.

Much of my personal fulfillment came from my job. I worked for an organization that taught the Bible through radio, television, and print media. I worked in the counseling department, and our job was to respond to letters and emails from those who wrote the organization with personal questions or stories about their lives. I loved my work; my coworkers were kind and caring, and I got immersed in learning how to apply biblical principles to daily life and helping others do the same.

The counseling department was small, just four people, and I was the only female on the team, but I loved being around the guys. They seemed to value my opinion and treated me as an equal. Jim, the team leader, would stop by my cubical to say good morning every day as he arrived with his large cup of coffee in hand.

"Good morning, Savannah, how are you?"

I was writing a letter and didn't hear him approach, so I jumped a little and my knee hit my desk. I laughed and said, "Besides my knee, I'm good!"

"I'm sorry! I didn't mean to startle you. Would you have a minute some time today to talk about a letter?" He took a big gulp of coffee.

"Sure, can I finish up this letter first? Would you like to meet in your office?"

"Yeah, that would be great, thank you."

He left, and I finished writing, printing, and signing my letter. I took great care with this letter, as it was from an eighty-one-year-old woman whose husband had passed away the prior year. She needed to hear about God's comfort and love, so I answered her as thoroughly and as warmly as I could. When I showed up at Jim's office, he waved me in and said, "Sit down." He took papers and books out of one of the office chairs.

"I have a letter from a woman who's trapped in an

abusive marriage, but she's afraid God will be disappointed in her if she leaves him," Jim said. I was more interested in what Jim thought than sharing what I had to say. I sat down and waited for him to explain more.

He went on: "I guess this letter kind of hits a nerve with me, because when I was a new Christian, I was afraid that God was disappointed with me for the way I behaved at times. Even after I'd confessed my sin, I didn't feel forgiven. I had to work through those emotions of letting God down. I thought He was like my earthly dad. My dad was—*is*—distant and very hard to get close to, and I often thought I was a big disappointment to him."

I tilted my head and asked, "How did you feel like a disappointment? From things you've told me before, you were a good kid."

He nodded and said, "I was a good kid, but that didn't seem like enough to get my dad to spend time with me. I wanted him to know me and to want to be with me, not for what I could do to make him look good, but for just being his son. He treated me more like a trophy than a child."

Trophy? "Do you mean, he liked showing you off? Like a trophy?" The bells were going off in my head. Connections were made for me and my life story. It rang true for me too, but with my mother. I was her trophy child. The daughter who reflected well upon her. My heart jumped around because Jim was telling *my* story. I wanted to hear more.

"Yes, exactly! He never wanted to spend time with me unless I was doing something that made him appear as though he was dad of the year. For example, I always wanted him to shoot hoops with me in the driveway, just to be with him, ya know? But I don't remember one time that he said yes. He was always too busy or too tired. He came to my championship games, though. And I appreciated that, but I wanted more from him. I just wanted to talk like father and son."

My eyes started to water, so I blinked a lot and fiddled with my pen on my lap.

He noticed and paused before he said, "Looks like you might know what it feels like."

I swallowed and took a deep breath. "Well, some of the things you said about you and your dad are true for me too, except it's with my mother and me." I bounced my knee. "She has always put pressure on me to do and be things that aren't for me but for her. I don't think she cares how it affects me as long as I do it for her."

Jim said, "I don't think you can get close to a person like that."

I turned my head because more tears filled my eyes until the salty tears fell down my cheeks. My throat was closing tight, but I swallowed and somehow choked out in a voice that didn't sound like my own, "I'm sorry. I don't know why I'm crying. That was a long time ago."

Jim grabbed the box of tissues on his desk and offered them to me. "I'm sorry, I didn't mean to bring up something so painful."

"That's okay. I really don't know where this is coming from." I shook my head and waved, as if what I felt were as important as a housefly.

Jim squinted his eyes and lowered his voice. "May I ask you, does she still do that to you?"

I wiped more tears away and knew that she did it to me still. Not as much because I was married and had children, but the same feelings I had as a child remained in my relationship with her. I nodded. "She still does it from time to time."

His voice was soft when he said, "I'm not surprised. It's hard for people like that to stop manipulating. And it's hard to notice that pattern, especially when you were raised with it." He waited a second before he asked, "Do you sometimes find yourself doing things for others that you don't want to do? I struggle with that and I wondered if you do too."

I was trying to take deep breaths. I breathed out slowly. I still was turned away from Jim so that he couldn't see my face. I rubbed my neck. How did I get into a therapy session?

"All the time." My face was red, and I decided I couldn't continue this conversation anymore. I had a full day's work in front of me, and there was no way I was going to be able to write caring, warm letters in this state of heart and mind. I added, "I don't want to take up too much of your time, Jim, and I should get back to work, but I appreciate your talking with me."

He said, "Of course, it's no problem. I care about how you're doing, and if you ever want to talk, I'm here."

My stomach fluttered, and I said, "Thanks." I turned to leave but remembered the letter that started this whole conversation and said, "Oh, about the woman in your letter?

I think she should take her chances with God and leave the asshole." I walked out of his office and covered my mouth to hide the slow smile that was spreading across my face.

I went to the bathroom, and for the first time in months, my eyes were bright. I wished Bryce would talk to me like this. *Did Jim have feelings for me? Were we flirting? Was this inappropriate?* I wanted his friendship; it was like a cold drink of water on a hot day. But I didn't know how much I should share with him. I wasn't ready to tell him about Bryce and me just yet. I had hidden my past bruises and had never shared any of the abuse with anyone before.

17

A Major Life Change

I was twenty-three when one morning, around 5 A.M., I woke up feeling nauseated. I ran upstairs to get to the bathroom just in time. I threw up five or six times that morning. I called in sick and I never got any relief from the nausea. Instead of running up and down the stairs all day, I just left a trash can by my bed. The next day, I tried eating saltine crackers, but I couldn't hold those down, either. I thought about calling my mom. My mother was a lot of things, but when we were sick as children, she was the best. I missed her and wished she could help me.

I hadn't spoken to my parents for about a month; they had kicked me out of the house for staying out too late with my boyfriend, Raymond.

The night they threw me out, I came home late to find Mom sitting at the kitchen table in her robe, her head in her hands, and Dad leaning against the counter with his arms crossed.

Dad's eyes were wide, and his voice was deep when he said, "Mom and I are not going to tolerate your disrespect

and disobedience any longer. You're staying out late partying, and we won't have any of that in our house." He waved
his arms around the spotless kitchen and said, "Plus, you
never do anything around here. You're lazy and you don't
help your mother with the housework. You have to move
out. Tonight." He pointed his finger at me as he said this.

"Tonight?" I asked. It was true I had been out with
Ray drinking that night, and many other nights, but my
stomach lurched forward as I thought about where I'd go.
"How can I leave tonight? I don't have anywhere to go."

"Well, that's not our problem," Dad said with finality.

I was motionless as it sunk in what my parents were
saying and doing, and I knew they meant it. I blinked slowly and shuffled off to throw a few things in a bag. *Where
would I shower? How could I afford an apartment on my own?
Don't I need a deposit and to fill out an application?* I needed
to leave that night, so I packed a few things and drove my
car down the street to sleep in it. Thankfully, it was a warm
night. The next day, I went to Lisa's house (my coworker)
and asked her if I could stay with her and her husband until
I found a place to live. She and her husband welcomed
me in and insisted that I stay on the couch for as long as
I needed. That's how I ended up in her basement, because
my stay was longer than I had anticipated and I felt guilty
sleeping on their couch every night, even though they never
once complained.

By the time the first week of sickness was over, I must
have weighed about ninety-five pounds. I still was nauseated every day, but I had to get back to work. One day

I wore a pair of pants with an elastic waist and a sleeveless top tucked in. All day the pants were slipping off my hips and the shirt was untucking, and I was constantly pushing it back in. I remember a woman at work walked by me and said, "Wow, you look like you need to eat something." Barb, the woman with her, said, "Oh my God, Charlotte, shut up. That is so mean!" I remember my laugh sounded tinny and fake, not at all like myself.

After two weeks of feeling this nausea that wouldn't go away, the unthinkable dawned on me: *Oh my God. No, please, no. What if . . . what if I'm . . . pregnant? I can't be! What will people think? What will they say? They'll know what I've been doing. They'll know I'm not the good Christian girl they've always seen me as. What will I do? I can't face that.*

After work, I drove to a drug store, alone. It didn't even occur to me to call Raymond. I turned off the ignition and sat in the car for a few minutes, not believing what I had to do. I watched a woman with two children walk into the store. I thought, *She probably has a nice life and a good husband to provide for her and their children. Here I am alone and afraid. How do I get what she has?* A pit in my stomach had become so apparent that I couldn't ignore it anymore. It was a pit of loneliness.

The creak of my car door was earsplitting as I got out and walked up to the drug store. When I opened the door, it had a bell attached to it, which rang and announced to everyone that I had entered. My heart beat loud and fast. My eyes darted back and forth, trying not to make eye contact with anyone but scoping out the joint nonetheless.

I walked down the cosmetics aisle pretending to pick out a lipstick color. I had never purchased a pregnancy kit before and I wondered where they kept them. *Did I need to show them personal identification? I don't have to give them my name, do I?*

I wound my way around to the pharmacy area, where I decided pregnancy kits would be. I found them on a shelf near the KY jelly and condoms. I hesitated before taking a box, but then I rushed toward the register, keeping my head low. I handed the cashier my money and almost left without getting my change. On top of my anxiety about someone seeing me, I was also feeling nauseated again and needed to lie down and eat more crackers.

I drove to the duplex, and I was relieved to find no one home. Before I could take the pregnancy test, I had to lie down for a few minutes until my nausea subsided. When it did, I grabbed the kit and ripped open the box and read the pamphlet inside, my hands shaking the entire time. I went into the bathroom, followed the instructions, and waited on the edge of the tub. Then I stood up, stared blankly at myself in the mirror, and sat back down. After the time limit, my heart beating like a drum, I took the stick and a positive plus symbol had developed like a neon sign. Panic poured into my throat—*Oh my God! No. No, no, no, no, no, no.*

I was terrified of my parents. If they found out I was having sex—and was now pregnant—they wouldn't want to have anything to do with me ever again. A pregnancy stood in the way of this ravenous hunger for parental love that

I might be fed one day. I couldn't face the possibility of that love not ever being given. *No, this just can't be real. This can't be happening. No, not to me.*

My heart dropped. Dark, dizzying confusion settled into my brain, and I wasn't breathing normally—I could manage only small short breaths. *There is no way. I'm trapped. How can I take care of a baby while living in Lisa's basement?* I had hoped I was wrong. I didn't want to be pregnant. I *couldn't* be pregnant. I slid down to the bathroom floor and leaned on the edge of the bathtub, rocking back and forth. I closed my eyes at the thought of anyone seeing my exposed sin. That's all I cared about: getting through this without anyone ever knowing. No one could ever find out. *There is no way I can be pregnant. No one must ever find out. No one must ever know. No one. Not ever.*

I called Raymond and asked him to come over, that it was important. He sighed when he told me that he'd have to cancel his plans to play basketball with his friends. Maybe I was imagining it, but he seemed a little distant the last few days. But today I needed him to be present with me so he could help me figure out what we were going to do. My pulse raced when I thought about telling him; I had no idea how he would react. What if he was excited and wanted to have the baby? I tried to imagine that happening. I played that out in my mind, but I still couldn't visualize us telling my parents. That picture couldn't materialize in my mind. It just couldn't happen.

Yes, there was a part of me that hoped he would respond with excitement and courage and say something like,

"We're having a baby! Isn't that wonderful? I'll be by your side through it all." But even if he had, I think it would have taken a miracle to get me to be able to tell my parents and face the horror that would have resulted. I wasn't ready to be a mother.

When Ray drove up, I opened the front door before he got out of his car. I said hi, and he kissed me briefly, but neither of us smiled. Since we had the duplex to ourselves, we sat upstairs on the pink flowered couch facing each other. I pulled out the pregnancy test stick and laid it on the fabric between us.

His face turned pale, and he mumbled, "Oh, shit." He slumped down on the couch and rested his head on the back of the sofa, closed his eyes, and blew out a long breath of air.

I said to him, "I-I-I can't be pregnant." I turned away from him and was nauseated again. I ran into the bathroom, but nothing came out. On the way back to the living room, I grabbed my sleeve of saltines and a ginger ale and curled up on the couch, still a few feet away from Ray.

I wasn't really saying I "can't" be pregnant; obviously, I was. I was saying, "I'm scared I can't face being pregnant alone. Will you please help me?" But I could not get in touch with that. When he didn't say anything, I shook my head vigorously and repeated, "I can't be pregnant."

He was silent for the longest time. He asked, "You weren't on the pill?"

"No, I'm pretty sure I told you that. And you could have worn a condom. God, are you blaming me?"

"No, no. I just don't know what we're going to do! What do we do?"

My breathing quickened, and I pulled my knees up close to my chest and whined, "I don't know." I had hoped he had some answers, a way out of this. I rested my head on my knees and realized Raymond wasn't any closer to his paternal feelings than I was to my motherly ones.

He glanced around the room as if it contained the secret solution to our problem, and then he said softly, "I mean, I hate to be the one to say it, but what about an abortion?"

I continued staring at him, and he at me. Our eyes told a story of two people, terrified, knowing there was only one option, one chilling choice to rescue us from the frightening and distressing reality of becoming ill-equipped parents.

"Well, I don't want an abortion." I let my head fall back and closed my eyes, breathing out a quiet "Oh, God." The religious teachings on sex before marriage were so ingrained in me and so strong that, in my mind, it was the worst sin a person could commit. I had seen how Christians treated sinners of the worst kind. I convinced myself that if I could hide this sin, it was less bad than a sin that was out there for all to see. And a pregnancy outside of marriage was definitely out there for all to see. If I were to have this pregnancy come to full term, my child would forever be described as Tommy or Sally, born "out of wedlock." I said after a minute, "But what other way is there? I can't be pregnant." There it was again, that sentence that wasn't describing what I wanted or needed. It's simply declaring a state of being that I can't be. A statement of denial.

"Yeah." He offered me an understanding nod. We were silent for a while. "I'll pay for it," he said as he reached over and touched my leg. He paused and then added, "The abortion."

This was the conversation that was to affect one of the most critical decisions of our lives, and it lasted about fifteen minutes. Neither of us was prepared to face this life event, together or alone. For us, it wasn't a matter of "facing the consequences of our choices." We couldn't put it in a moral category, nor could we relax and enjoy that we were going to have a child. My cognitive faculties had shut down, and no amount of reasoning could jolt me into making a rationally sound or morally right decision.

Early on a cold November morning, I drove to meet with a female counselor in our local Planned Parenthood to discuss my options. When she brought up abortion, she explained that the procedure was quick and painless and that I might have minor cramping and bleeding for a few hours afterward. She explained that the "tissue" was just a tiny glob, about a quarter of an inch long, and since I was coming so early in the pregnancy, the tissue would feel no pain.

The entire time the counselor was talking, I kept seeing a vision, be it ever so slight and murky, of someone rushing in to rescue me from my life, someone to run in and grab me and say, "No, Savannah, don't do this. I'll be with you. We will do this together. You *can* be pregnant. It's not the worst thing in the world. We will stand together against anyone, your parents especially, who might judge you or shun you. Be strong and be brave. You can do this." But no one came. No knight in shining armor. No rescuer. No savior. It was just me, and I couldn't do this alone.

I signed all the forms like a robot and set up the date for the procedure the following week.

A week went by, and neither Raymond nor I were deterred from our decision. We knew we weren't ready to be parents. We spoke little, our phone conversations brief. We wanted out of this situation as quickly as possible.

Raymond arrived that cold morning after a light dusting of snow with his jacket zipped up to his chin. He hugged me and asked, "Are you ready?"

"I think so," I said, shakily putting on my gloves. We drove the fifteen-minute drive in silence. He drove to the back of the parking lot and parked. We stole glances at each other, and then hand in hand, walked into the facility. I signed in, he paid, and then we sat down and waited to be called back.

A woman wearing a white medical coat and holding a clipboard opened the door to a hallway and said, "Savannah Young?"

"Will you watch my purse?" I asked Raymond, assuming he'd wait for me in the waiting area. He nodded.

I was taken back to a consulting room. The woman asked if I had any questions, and I didn't know what to ask, so I said no. *I'm scared to death, I don't know what to say, and I just want to get this over with*, I thought.

A nurse led me into a corridor where the halls were white—everyone, it seemed, wore white—and the hospital bed and sheets were white. If white had a smell, the place smelled "white." There was no personality; it was lifeless. *Ironic*. They took me back into a small room and told me to put on the white hospital gown. I never once believed that I truly had a choice or that I was making a choice. To me, there was no other way. This was it, and it was too late to do anything else.

I was taken into a larger room but separated into sections only by a curtain with, I'm assuming, other women having abortions. My legs were put in stirrups, and the doctor came in and asked me how I was feeling, to which I replied, "Fine." All I remember after that is a sensation of something going inside me, and then cramps. My hands gripped the sides of the bed as I held my breath and as tears rolled down the sides of my eyes and into my ears and down my neck. I imagined sitting up and screaming bloody murder, but I didn't do that; I was paralyzed with shame and didn't move to wipe my tears away.

I don't remember how long I had to wait before I could go find Raymond in the waiting room, but I walked in a daze until he caught my arm and wrapped his arms around me. I melted into the warmth of his embrace. He drove me, again silently, back to the duplex, and I wrapped myself in a blanket and sat on the couch. Mark and Lisa were at work, so I had the place to myself. I didn't know what to do. What does one do after an abortion?

The counselor told me to expect some cramping and bleeding and to rest and drink lots of water. She said I should be back to normal activities by tomorrow or the next day. She also recommended that I start on the pill if I was planning on being sexually active, and she gave me a prescription for my first month and told me that I could continue getting them there or see my doctor for a prescription.

Ray brought me a tall glass of water and sat beside me for a while. I lay my head in his lap, and as he rubbed my back, a sense of relief washed over me. I wasn't pregnant, no one would ever know (besides Raymond and me), and I didn't have to raise a child in a basement. I wanted to enjoy this freedom and relax, but my guilt wouldn't allow that. The church's teachings of "murdering a baby" ran through my head along with the term "baby killer."

After about an hour, Raymond left to go play basketball with his friends. I didn't want him to go and yet I didn't need him to stay; at least that's what I told myself. In dark, chilly silence, for hours, I went back and forth between staring out into the deserted street and dozing off. It was cold with low light-gray clouds outside, their presence thick and threatening to forever censor the sun. Snow flurried about, but none accumulated; it just swirled around like a turned-about snow globe. As the sun set and people came home from work, a profound sense of isolation hit me.

I tried to get back to my normal routine; it brought some comfort. Work gave me a place to be and people to see. It gave me a distraction from my inner life, which was filled with confusion and darkness. My entire body was a heavy weight, and breathing was an effort.

I'm not pregnant anymore, I thought. *My problem is*

solved. I can go on with my life, thank God. I didn't have to explain anything to anyone and I could move on as if nothing happened. It's what I wanted all along. Release, almost a high, surged in my heart and mind that I was no longer pregnant. What I couldn't seem to eradicate, though, was the sadness that engulfed me.

Raymond and I continued to date, and I spent more time at his parents' house. He wasn't a big fan of my parents because of how they treated me. Every morning I checked my phone to see if my mom had called and I had missed it. I checked at my lunch hour—maybe she had called to check on me then. No, she didn't call me. Of all people, I wanted my mother to reach out to me and help me, and yet, deep down, I knew she would not lower herself to my level of depravity.

18

The Darkest Night

I had started a new job working as a receptionist at a loan company. As usual, it was a busy day, and I was drowning in papers and phone calls. I was putting one call through when two others rang in.

After I took care of the last call, there was a short reprieve from the ringing.

"Hello, Savannah."

Oh, God, I recognize that voice. My mouth dropped at the woman with professionally teased hair and immaculate makeup: my mother. Her lips were tight, and before I could say anything, she said, "I've come to take you to lunch."

I caught my breath and stumbled over my words. "I, uh, well, I'm pretty busy." I shook my head slightly, and we stared at one another. Then to fill the silence, I put my arms out to show her my desk full of forms and messages. "As you can see." Just then, the phone rang again.

"Good morning! Home America Loan Company, this is Savannah, how may I direct your call?"

Out of my peripheral vision, I could see my mother still

standing in front of my tall reception desk. "One moment, please," I said in a sing-song voice, then I sent the call off to underwriting.

"I'm sorry, Mom, but you'll have to wait." Someone walked into the building and was headed toward my desk. "My relief person doesn't show up for another twenty minutes." I played with my pen and averted my gaze.

She turned her head and said, "Fine. I'll wait." Then she proceeded to sit on one of the couches in the lobby. She picked up a magazine and flipped through it as I assisted the next client and continued answering the phones.

Twenty-five minutes later, we drove separately to the restaurant of her choice. When we sat down at our table, she said, "I don't know why we couldn't drive together."

"It's easier for me. I have to go back to work."

"Well, so do I," she said, her voice raised.

I took a deep breath and scanned the menu. *Is this how she's going to be?* I glanced at my watch, counting the minutes until it was time to leave. *I've wanted this meeting to happen for so long, but now that I'm here with her, I want to bolt out the door.* I pushed my food around on the plate, and when I felt her watching me, I took a small bite.

"Savannah, I'm sorry for whatever I may have done to hurt your feelings. You know how your dad is. He just gets so angry and gets out of control."

"Okay. Well, thank you." I played with my food and took a small bite of a french fry.

"Your dad was the one who kicked you out, not me, so I didn't understand why you weren't calling me."

What? Are you kidding me? You were complicit in this. You and Dad are so sick and twisted. Honestly, you two need help. I swallowed the dry potato and took a drink of water; it almost went down the wrong pipe, since my throat was so closed off.

I said, "I didn't think you wanted to hear from me. And I thought maybe you'd call first. I mean, I was the one who was kicked out." I moved from her eyes to a sign in the restaurant that read, No one makes burgers like we do!

Mom started tearing up and said, "Well, maybe I should have. I just wanted to apologize for anything I may have done."

"Well, you could have stood up to Dad. You could have defended me." I ached to hear her admit she should have at least defended me that night.

She was quiet for a minute, then said, "It's harder than you think to stand up to your dad."

I let out a chortle, louder than I meant to, and shook my head. "I know very well what it's like living with him."

Silence again. She wiped her eyes with her napkin. "All I want is for us to be a family again. I want you to come home for Christmas and visit us and I want to be able to talk to you."

"You're free to talk to me anytime. Does Dad know you're here talking to me about this?"

"No, I'll tell him tonight."

Most likely, his anger had died down and we'd never speak of it again.

We finished our lunch, and Mother called a few days

later telling me that she'd talked to Dad. He said it was fine with him if I came over.

"What do you mean 'it's fine with him' if I come over?" I asked, frustrated. "Does he want me to or not?"

"He wants you to, but just don't expect an apology from him."

"God forbid," I said, rolling my eyes.

I talked Raymond in to going over to my parents' house for a short visit on Christmas Day. Ray, even though he had resisted going, walked up to my mother and hugged her and said, "Merry Christmas." Even so, she had her lips puckered the entire time, because I told her we weren't staying for dinner. She tossed my gift my way when it came time to open gifts. I must have walked the mall ten times before I decided on an air popper and a new blanket for Mom and Dad. Mom didn't say much. She said, "Oh, okay. I think we already have an air popper," when she opened her gift, but Dad offered a hearty "thank you!"

After the holidays, Raymond and I talked about someday getting married and thought we should take our relationship to the next level and buy a house together. On the weekends, we went to open houses during the day and parties at night, as church became a distant memory.

19

The Happiest Two Years

Raymond and I spent every waking minute together. We both loved being active and playing tennis and going on long hikes.

Ray's sister was a real estate agent, and she helped us find a cute little two-bedroom house situated on a busy street. Even though it didn't have a garage, we decided it had to be ours! We put in an offer, and they accepted. It was my first house, and since it was 1991, I couldn't wait to start decorating in puffy mauve and green valences and big silk flower arrangements.

My hand rested on the telephone before I nervously called my mother to tell her the news. We had patched up our relationship as best as we could, but I knew she'd have questions and criticisms.

"Mom, Raymond and I found a house that we're going to buy together. It's a two-bedroom, one-bath, and it's only twenty minutes away from you and Dad." I forced a smile as I spoke into the phone.

Mom hesitated at first. "You're buying a house together? Before getting married? Back in my day, that would have been frowned upon. It's not right, Savannah."

"We're twenty-four years old, Mom, and plus we're planning on a fall wedding." I anxiously waited for her response.

"*This* fall? Already? That's only seven or eight months away! Do you have enough time to plan everything?"

"I think so. We're getting married at a park, and I have that reserved already."

"A *park*? What about a church? Maybe I can get my church for you," Mother suggested.

"We really want to get married outside, but thank you."

Mother wasn't done. "What if it rains, Savannah? What would you do then?"

The questions came at a rapid pace. "Did you have the house surveyed and inspected? Do you even know what I'm talking about? Did you have a reputable realtor?" She said these more as accusations than as questions.

"Yes, Mom, we had a good realtor who helped us, and the house has passed all the inspections. Raymond's sister is our realtor. You remember her, don't you?"

I heard a *humph* come from the other end of the phone. Then she said, "Raymond doesn't have a college degree, and you're working on your master's in counseling psychology. How do you think you two are going to complement one another with you being more educated than he is? Men like to feel smart and feel like they are in charge of things. A husband wants to earn more money than his wife. I think that's going to be a problem later in your married life. Trust me, I know how small things now can become big problems later in your marriage."

"Mom, we love each other, and that's all that matters to us. He makes me feel good and he appreciates me. Isn't that all that really counts? I love being with him and I don't think a difference in education levels should matter."

Little did my mother know, she had lost all credibility with me. She and my father couldn't get it together and have a loving and respectful marriage, even given all their talk about Jesus and the church and God. Why, then, should I take her advice? How would she know what it would take to make a strong marriage?

Planning our wedding was stressful because my parents wanted to control it all and they did it through the money channel. Anything I wanted, I got the furrowed face of my mother and my dad saying, "That's too expensive." When I'd ask for a budget, neither parent would give me one. My mother acted as if she wanted to be a part of the wedding planning, but every time I came to her, she seemed angry with me, so I stopped asking her for things and stopped asking her to be a part of the planning.

Raymond and I planned our wedding anyway. My parents came through, surprisingly, with the money we needed, and our wedding was beautiful and fun. We had all our friends with us, and Michelle, Chelsea, Lisa, and Kay were bridesmaids, while Raymond's brother and three friends were groomsmen. I wore a white mermaid-style dress that hugged my curves, and he wore a white tuxedo with a purple tie. We stood under an arbor delicately wrapped in drum roses, vines, and berries as Raymond looked down at me with his sweet dimpled smile and took both of my hands in his and kissed them. It was my dream wedding, and he was my dream man.

After the reception, we took off to spend our first night in Chicago. Raymond booked a room with a view of Lake Michigan in the Drake Hotel where we got lost in the cloudy soft sheets and explored each other's bodies through the night. The rest of the honeymoon was spent in Florida. We slept in and had late breakfasts and spent long afternoons in the sun. We walked the white sandy beach, holding hands during orange sunsets, and got to know one another deeper as husband and wife. Several times, Raymond would suddenly turn toward me and put his arms around me and say, "My beautiful wife." I'd never been happier, and it seemed that these exquisite times of connection could forever wash away the previous dark winter blues.

On our honeymoon and when we got back home, we talked about our dreams of building a house and growing old together. I shared with him my desire to finish my degree and start my practice, but that I'd like to have children, maybe four someday. He thought those were great plans and he seemed excited about them too. He also had career plans that he wanted to accomplish, and I supported him in those.

We settled into being a married couple; we went to work, then I'd make dinner and he'd tinker around with his car or have friends over to play basketball on his new hoop I'd given him as a wedding gift. We were like magnets, always drawn to one another, especially in the bedroom. When our lips were pressed together, or when his fingers tickled my skin, or even if he swiped his body next to mine, sparks made my hair stand up on end.

A year and a half into our marriage, I started talking to Ray about children. Raymond said he wasn't ready for fatherhood and began staying out later with his friends and was coming home drunk and even high at times. He was never mean, though; he'd come home very jovial and either want to have sex or he'd fall asleep with a smile on his face, making some silly, nonsensical joke. While I was thinking of a future with children and going to church together, he was thinking of partying and playing tournament basketball. We weren't heading in the same direction at all.

I was feeling more disconnected from my husband, and that old feeling of loneliness crept up again and grabbed me by the throat. I tried to talk to Raymond about it, but he simply said he wanted more freedom and for me to get off his back about things. I'd get angry and yell at him, and he'd leave the house, slamming the door behind him. We tried counseling a few times, but then he stopped going.

I was losing my husband. More and more, he was hanging out with his friends, and he was leaving me out of his life. To revive our relationship, I joined him at the parties he and his friends went to, but I didn't feel any deep connection with Raymond there. There was lots of beer and drinking to excess and pot. I hated these parties, and they made me feel even more disengaged from Raymond.

One Friday night, I asked Ray if we could stay in and

not go out to the parties. I was tired from the week and not in a mood to see people I barely knew, but he was pumped and wanted to go, so he went without me. I tried watching television, but then after about thirty minutes, I'd stand up abruptly and walk into the kitchen, trying to imagine what he was doing at the party. I opened the refrigerator, but nothing looked appetizing, so I got a spoon and peanut butter and sat back down on the couch to watch more television. I finally went to bed, dozing off, then waking up wondering where Ray was. I bounced around from worry to anger. Around six that morning, the back door creaked opened and closed. Ray walked into the kitchen and poured himself a glass of water. I gripped the covers up around my chin, hoping he'd come crawling back and apologize, but he stayed where he was. I jerked the covers off and stomped into the kitchen. He was staring out the window at the sink, and when he turned around, his eyes were bloodshot and his skin was pale. I asked with my hands on my hips, "Where have you been? Why didn't you come home?"

Raymond offered a strained but dimpled smile. "I didn't want to drive because I'd been drinking, so I stayed at Steve's house."

I stared at him. *Was he lying? Did he cheat on me?* "Well, the next time that happens, call me and I'll pick you up," I said, irritated. I swallowed and I crossed my arms, waiting for him to respond.

"It's no big deal. I just stayed at Steve's for the night," he repeated as if I hadn't heard him the first time.

"It's a big deal to me." I uncrossed my arms and held

my hands open. "I didn't know where you were. I was worried that something might have happened to you." I walked closer to him and leaned on the butcher block between us. "I would have appreciated a phone call."

Raymond averted his eyes. "Yeah, okay, whatever." He scratched his head and turned to walk back out the door.

"Wait, we're not done talking. Raymond, we're married, and you can't just not come home." I was growing in my intensity as he seemed to be minimizing the situation.

His face turned pink, and he licked his lips. "You just need to back off. I can do what I want, and if I want to sleep at Steve's house, then that's what I'll do."

Raymond had never acted this way before, so defiant and rude. I didn't understand what was going on. My blood pressure was rising, and my neck was hot.

"So, I'm supposed to just sit at home and worry about you? Is that what you're saying?" I stood glaring at him.

"I don't care what you do, to be honest," Raymond mumbled.

The heat from my neck traveled up to my face, and my eyes began to burn. I blinked several times, my voice shaking. "Well, I care about what you do. And what you did was shitty." My chin trembled.

Raymond ran his hands through his hair. "Look, I'm sorry, but it seems like you're always unhappy with me. I can't do anything right."

"What are you talking about? I'm happy. I mean, not this very minute, but I'm happy most of the time." My voice was hard, stern.

"Last week, you complained three times that I was working on my car too much." He held up three fingers. "You don't seem very happy to me."

"I can't help it if I'd like to spend some time with my husband! What's so wrong with that?" I said loudly.

He threw his hands in the air and said, "Oh my God, I can't spend every minute with you!" He moved closer to the door. "Sometimes I wish I'd never m . . ." He trailed off, but I knew what he was going to say.

Heat rushed up again, and that familiar rock in my stomach returned. "What? You wished you'd never what? *Married* me?" Raymond turned to walk away again, but I grabbed his arm. I yelled, "Don't you dare leave!"

He yanked his arm away and said, "Let go of me!" and he left. He sped out of our driveway, and I stood at the door trying to process everything. I was breathing so fast that I got light-headed. I backed up against the wall and sobbed.

I don't know where he went, but he didn't come home for three days. One the third day, while I was at work, Raymond left me a three-page handwritten note telling me that he was in love with someone else and that he was leaving me.

I sat alone on our bed, holding the letter, my hands shaking as I read it. He explained how he thought he was ready for marriage, but he wasn't. He wanted more freedom; he couldn't stand being suffocated by me anymore. He said he cared about me, but he couldn't take the burdens of married life. "We want different things," he wrote. He didn't come home that night, either. He didn't call and he didn't answer when I tried to call him.

I sat on my bed for hours, off and on, staring at nothing, and then curled up like a baby. I jumped up and moved around, picking things up, cleaning, doing anything to get my mind off his desertion. Then, I sat down on the bed again, my mind searching endlessly for a clue as to how we got here. *We were so happy. What happened? He can't leave me. What will I do without him?* The heaviness in my chest made it hurt to breathe and to think, even to try to dream. I had no dreams anymore.

I took the next day off work and lay in bed all day. I had no will to move, much less to get out of bed and interact with people. I cried, then the tears dried up, and then I'd stare at the ceiling and cry more. I called Chelsea, then I called Kay, who said things like, "You're a gem, and he's an idiot for not seeing that" and "You're a strong, smart, and beautiful woman. You'll get through this." It helped hearing her messages of positivity and love. It helped because even though I didn't always believe the messages, she did, and if she did, then maybe they were true and I could start to believe in them.

I dreaded the call to my mother. I stared at the phone on my kitchen wall. I backed away from it and poured a glass of water; my mouth was so dry. I washed the last of the few dishes I had in the sink, aware of the task I needed to do. I dried my hands and took another drink of water. I swallowed several times and grabbed the phone, quickly punching in the numbers. It rang three times before I tasted blood in my mouth. I'd been chewing on the inside of my cheek.

"Hello?"

"Hi, Dad, how are you?" I said flatly.

"Oh, fine, fine." He rarely answered the telephone, but when he did, he always sounded jovial. "You probably called to talk to your mother. Let me get her for you."

She answered, and I told her the basics—but not everything. I told her he left me a letter and that he wanted a divorce. I didn't tell her about our fight.

"What? He wants a *divorce*? I never knew you were having any problems!" Her voice was rising. "Now, tell me, why does Ray want a divorce, Savannah?"

I closed my eyes and said through tight lips, "I don't know, Mom." I swallowed. "I guess he doesn't love me anymore."

Without missing a beat, she asked, "Well, is there someone else?"

I chafed at the question and lied. "I don't know." I wanted to hang up, but I shriveled up inside and listened to her lecture me for the next few minutes. I finally told her I needed to get off the phone. She ended by saying, "If you need to talk, I'm here for you."

It took every ounce of pure grit I had left in me to get up every morning and fulfill my duties to complete my counseling practicum, which included helping people who struggled with depression, anxiety, or self-esteem. Every morning when the alarm went off, I pushed the snooze button two or three times so that by the time I pulled myself out of bed, I was rushing around to make it in time to my first client.

Staring into the eyes of the person across from me, I tried to ignore the knot in my stomach and my fast-beating heart. My lips parted slightly, and my eyebrows wrinkled at the woman who talked about her husband and what a slob he was. I clenched onto the arms of my chair to avoid punching the man in his forties confessing the affair he was having with his secretary. And the client who came in complaining of the emptiness she felt inside. I rubbed my chin as if deep in thought, my eyes darting around the room, praying somewhere in there would be an answer for both of us.

I had made it this far, and I wasn't quitting now. If it killed me, I was going to make it to the end of this program and was going to get my degree and my license. I marched through my life like a soldier on a mission, and the same year that my husband served me divorce papers, I walked across the stage to receive my master's.

My parents drove me to the ceremony. I sat in the back seat alone, wishing Ray was beside me, but also enjoying my own accomplishment. As I was in my own thoughts, my mother said, "Savannah, wouldn't it be nice to get your PhD?"

I stared at the back of her head, disbelieving her nerve to dismiss all the work I had just completed. I watched her head bob back and forth as she talked about all of her friends' children who'd received their PhDs. I wanted to scream at her to shut up, to tell her that all I had done was amazing and I was proud of myself and that she should be too. I wanted to tell her that I would never be able to live up to her unrealistic expectations, that she herself couldn't live up to those kinds of standards. I wanted to cry and have someone hold me and comfort me and tell me it was going to be okay. But I didn't. I sat silently in the back seat, like I did when I was a child.

20

From Purgatory to Hell

After I completed my practicum, life consisted mainly of working in a marketing job, putting out résumés for jobs in my field, and going to interviews. It had only been eight months since Raymond and I divorced, and I spent most of my downtime staring off into space wondering what he was doing that very minute. After work, I'd take one of his shirts that I'd packed right before I moved out of the house and I'd curl up on my bed and hold it tight, right up to my nose. When I'd breathe in his smell, it took me back to the days when his touch would give me tingles all over.

A friend from college, Maggie, called to invite me to her church. I wasn't sure I wanted to go, but I figured I could use a little Jesus about now, so I dragged myself out of bed and moved like a sloth. I couldn't do anything with my hair, and I had circles under my eyes that even my makeup wouldn't cover, but I told myself my appearance didn't matter. I met Maggie in the parking lot, we embraced, and she said, "I'm glad you came. I think it's good to get out and meet new people. I hope you like it here."

Meet new people? I took a deep breath and followed her up the stairs to the front lobby. *I came to listen to music and hear a sermon, not make new friends.* We stood in the sanctuary talking before the service started, but I had to work hard to hold eye contact with her and keep my eyes from falling to the floor. Then she waved someone over, and I thought, *Oh, here we go.* I slipped my hands into my coat pockets and lowered my head, trying to hide my eye-rolling. A guy walked up to me, not waiting for Maggie to introduce us.

My heart skipped a little. He had the bluest eyes I'd ever seen, like aquamarine blue. He held out his hand and said, "Hi, I'm Bryce."

Maggie had a wide smile on her face, which clearly meant she had invited him to church too, hoping we'd meet. Had I known, I would have made more of an effort to appear bright-eyed. The three of us chatted only for a minute or two before the service started, then as the music played, we filed into a row of chairs and Bryce ended up beside me. I stole glances at his legs when we sat down; his tight jeans covered legs that were lean and strong. After the service, Bryce asked if he could walk me to my car. At first, I wanted to refuse, but then I acquiesced because I thought it might be rude if I didn't accept his offer. Plus, his beautiful eyes.

"So, what is it that you do?" I asked Bryce. He was carrying a black notebook.

"Well, I work for a delivery company, and then I also have a ministry that I developed for inner-city kids. We train adults to mentor older elementary and junior high kids, mostly through a football league I started." He pointed to his black notebook as if it contained the secrets to the football league.

"Oh, wow, that sounds interesting." I fought back a yawn. "So, it's mostly young boys?"

"Yeah. I attend an inner-city church. It's an African American church, and I find that so many boys there need a positive role model in their lives."

I cocked my head to one side and asked, "You're going to a black church? How did that happen? I mean, did you know someone there?"

Bryce blinked and put his notebook up against his chest, as if he were hugging it, and said, "Well, that's a long story. I can tell you about it some other time. Maybe over coffee?"

A small voice inside me told me, *No, don't get involved.* But as I was used to doing, I turned down the volume of that voice, because I was more concerned about his feelings than my own. I turned toward my car and said, "Um, sure. I'd love to hear more." My hands shook as we exchanged phone numbers.

I drove home thinking, *What am I doing? He's cute, but I'm not ready for a relationship.* My mind floated to Ray again, and my chest started to burn.

Several days went by before Bryce called and invited me out to coffee. I accepted the invitation because I didn't have anything else going on.

He told me about his passion for helping children

whose parents couldn't be there for them and how he wanted to continue being a football coach to the inner-city boys. He loved that part of his ministry. I told him about my divorce, and he listened and didn't react with judgment. He said he'd dated one or two girls since college, and that one of them was a really hard breakup for him, but that he hadn't married yet. He made me laugh too. He had a good sense of humor, and I really liked that.

Even with all the doubts swirling about in my head, I started spending more time with Bryce and he started to grow on me. One night, we were sitting around in his apartment and his phone rang. "Yes, I'll be right there," he said.

"What's going on?"

"One of the boys on my team, his dad's car broke down on Jefferson Street, and they need a jump. Do you mind if I go do that? You're welcome to come, or you can wait here. I won't be too long."

I waited for him at his apartment, and forty minutes later, he was back with two milkshakes in hand. "I hope you like chocolate." He smiled, offering me the shake.

"You can never go wrong with chocolate," I said, smiling back as I took the shake. It tasted delicious.

After a few months of seeing each other, Bryce and I decided that we were in a relationship. I wanted to introduce him to my parents, so I arranged a dinner at their house.

That night, I stood in their kitchen with sweaty palms. "Hi, Mom, Dad." I took a deep breath. "This is Bryce." You'd have thought *I* was the one on display.

Mom walked over and shook his hand. "Nice to meet

you, Bryce."

Dad was next. He set down his newspaper and stood to shake his hand. "Savannah tells me you're a football coach?"

Bryce nodded and was about to respond, but Mother interrupted, "And what is it that you do, Bryce? For a living, I mean?"

When Bryce explained his part-time work and working on his ministry with the kids, my dad made a low, guttural groan. It was barely audible, but I could pick up that sound of disapproval from standing outside in the front yard.

Dad cleared his throat and shifted in his chair. "Now, tell me, how long have you worked at your current job? Do you plan to stay there?" His lips pressed together.

Before Bryce could answer, Mother asked, "Is that your career, Bryce, or a transition job to your real career?" Mother's smile faded away as she turned around to chop tomatoes for the salad.

It was a long night of inquisition. My neck was hot, and I didn't eat much, as I'd lost my appetite, which of course my mother pointed out to everyone. "Savannah, you only ate a small amount of lasagna and you didn't even touch your salad."

And that's how the night went: my parents asking Bryce twenty thousand questions, and he answered each one without hesitation.

On the way home, Bryce started laughing and shaking his head. "I don't think your parents like me very much."

I knew he was right, but I shook my head too and said, "No, I don't think it's that. They just want me to be happy and secure financially."

I turned my head and gazed out the window. It was more than that, though. When Bryce explained that he lived in an apartment with another guy and didn't own a house or a decent car, my dad's expression fell flat and he ever so slightly moved his head back and forth in dismay.

The heat rose in my belly when I saw him do that. *Who is he to judge Bryce? Clearly money and status don't bring you and Mom any happiness or closeness, so why should that be something I attain to?* I thought both my parents were hypocrites.

Bryce said, "Money just isn't that important to me." I had no idea if it was that important to me or not. I slouched in my seat and stared out the window.

All alone that night, I took Ray's shirt and breathed it in like I always did, but this time, the smell was gone. I sniffed again. Nothing. No more Raymond. Just a long list of unanswered questions, ones he had refused to answer. *Did he ever love me? When did he first cheat on me? How long had he been lying to me?* The image of his arms around another woman, giving her that dimpled smile, flooded my mind. *Did he love her like he said he loved me? How could he do this to me? I thought we'd be together forever.* I remembered many nights being by myself, waiting for him to come home. He was probably with her, caressing her, when he should have been home with me. *When was the first time they had sex?* Thinking of him with her, them making love, made me sit up straight and take a big breath. *Time to get rid of this shirt!* I threw his shirt on the bed and searched for scissors. When

I found them, I cut the shirt and ripped it into shreds and then threw it in the trash.

I then gathered all my wedding photos. I held them and remembered how happy we were. Suddenly my body shivered with cold and I began to cry. I stood above the trash can where Ray's shirt was in a heap, but I continued to gaze at the photos longer. Tears poured down my cheeks as I thought about all that I'd lost. I was in such pain and just wanted it to stop. I didn't want to throw out the photos, yet I knew of no other way to get the pain to end. Seeing us together, knowing the memories were in a box somewhere, just seared my heart, so out they went—I just had to get rid of them, not knowing if I'd regret it someday. I took old love notes and ticket stubs of concerts we went to and ripped them like a shredder. I decided I was done with that part of my life and I was moving on and moving forward. I didn't want any more reminders of Raymond or what we shared.

After six months of dating, Bryce and I went out one night with a few friends to karaoke. Maggie and her husband, Chelsea and her boyfriend, and a couple of Bryce's friends from work were there.

Chelsea said, "Savannah, get up there and sing!"

I played with my hair and said, laughing, "You couldn't pay me enough to get up there. I just came to watch everyone else." My heart was beating so fast, and my hands and knees were shaking. *Why did I come? I'd rather die than get on that stage.*

We ordered pizza, and as I was eating and chatting

with Chelsea and Maggie, Chelsea's eyes looked past me, widening. I turned to see Bryce standing on the stage, mike in hand, and my chest tightened. He said into the microphone, "This is for you, Savannah." My mouth gaped open, and then I put my hand over my mouth.

He sang Rick Astley's "Together Forever." He was a little off tune at times and a little more dramatic than he needed to be, staring at me and winking at one point. During the song, I clutched my purse and subconsciously searched for the exit signs. I wanted it to be over. Maggie and Chelsea were both grinning as if they were saying, "Isn't this sweet?"

When the song ended, relief washed over me. I hated being the center of attention, and yet I thought it was a sweet gesture. My reaction made me wonder if I truly was in to him. I mean, what girl wouldn't want her boyfriend to sing a love song to her?

I noticed Bryce hadn't gotten off the stage yet; instead, he was getting down on one knee, saying into the microphone, "Will you marry me, Savannah?"

My heart stopped. I covered my mouth and was frozen to my seat. This is what I've always wanted: a man who loved me enough to embarrass himself and sing to me. How could I turn him down? He was the kind of man who would always be by my side, and we could raise our children together. Still, I sat like a statue when Maggie tapped me on the shoulder and said, "Go up there! I think he's waiting for you to go up there."

Oh my God, I'm not sure I'm ready to do this again. And

yet, I can't hurt his feelings. All I know how to do is put a smile on my face and walk up there. I pushed my chair back and walked up to the stage. Looking down at him, my voice quivered as I said, "Yes, Bryce, I'll marry you." We hugged and kissed, and while everyone applauded, I started crying, but not for the reason everyone assumed.

21

Bryce's Rage and His Things

As we ate dinner in front of the television, with plates on our laps, Bryce was so angry at how I had cooked the chicken that he threw his entire plate of food across the living room and it hit the wall, spraying mashed potatoes and gravy and meat all over. I sat there, stunned and silent, staring straight ahead, afraid Bryce was going to order me to clean up his mess. Inside, I was screaming at him to stop terrorizing us. Bryce stood up, like an angry gorilla stomping around the small living room.

He stopped in front of me, his eyes red and full of rage, his hands clenched into fists. He stared me down and said, "God, you can't do anything right. I can't swallow that chicken, it's so dry!" He started pacing again, and I had no idea what was coming next, so I sat very still. "I'm the only man who would put up with you." His lips curled upward when he said it.

Samantha, just six months old, was crying, and I willed her to be quiet. Nicholas, two years old now, normally very talkative, sat as still and quiet as he could. His eyes were wide as he twirled his Mickey Mouse spoon. Bryce finally walked over and picked up his plate and threw it in the sink. I was surprised later to see that it didn't shatter. I prayed so hard that he wouldn't notice when I picked up Sami to comfort her. I moved slowly to her, quietly got her out of her bouncy seat, and held her close to me. I sat close to Nicholas and rubbed his back.

While Bryce cleaned up his dinner mess, I fed the children and then took them back into their bedroom to play for a while before getting them ready for bed. I read to them, hugged them, and tucked them in.

Nicholas was extra sweet. "Mommy, I love you and you're a very good reader. I think you read the best."

"Oh, honey, thank you." I swallowed to calm my shaky voice. I managed to say without crying, "I love reading with you and your sister." He kissed my cheek as I pulled the covers over him. I turned out the light and closed the door but hesitated before walking into the living room.

Bryce wasn't out there, so I peeked into our bedroom. He was already asleep. I finished cleaning up the kitchen and put the kids' toys away before I climbed into bed. I wondered if what Bryce said was true. *Can I do anything right? What am I good at? I'm not extraordinarily good at anything.*

With Bryce sleeping next to me, sleep became restless and unattainable, but when he got up and left for work, I was able to put my mind at rest and sleep before the children woke up.

I was in a beautiful cloud of soft slumber when the

phone rang at 7:45 A.M. I groaned because it was a Saturday and I was exhausted and didn't want to talk to anyone, especially my mother, who I just knew was on the other end of that call. She always called at the most inconvenient times, as if she had a camera watching my life, and when it was least helpful—for example, if the baby was crying or someone was ringing my doorbell—I could count on her to call.

If I let the call go to voicemail, I'd have to call her back. I decided it was less painful to get the conversation over with now, so with a long sigh, I reluctantly said above a whisper, "Hello?"

"Hi, honey, it's Mom. How are you doing? I hope I didn't wake you."

"I'm okay," I lied. I was so far from being okay. I was still reeling from Bryce's outburst last night. I wondered if he cleaned everything, or if I would find gravy dried on the baseboards, even though that was the least of my worries.

"What's wrong? I can hear it in your voice. You don't sound okay," Mom pried.

"No, I'm fine. I'm just hot and I didn't sleep well last night," I said, hoping she'd believe me and move on to some other subject other than my emotional well-being.

"Oh, I'm sorry. I wish you could afford air-conditioning. Ya know the humidity is what's keeping you up at night." The heat of embarrassment started to rise on my face. She continued nonetheless: "Do you know when you'll ever move?"

My head started to pound. "No, Mom, I have no idea.

We're trying to save up for a down payment." My own blatant lie disturbed me. I knew I was lying, hiding, pretending, but I didn't know how to stop. I wanted to blurt out to my mom that Bryce had been hurting me for years and I wanted out of this marriage and would she please help me?

I couldn't trust my own mother. I saw how she treated Michelle, and I knew my mother would judge me. Her judgment wouldn't be blatant; it would show up in her "innocent" questions, such as, "Well, Savannah, tell me, when did the abuse start? Was it before you married him?" implying that I should have known better.

I wanted so badly to have a mother I could talk to and for her to wrap her arms around me and let me cry it out, hearing her say, "It's going to be okay. You're going to be okay. You and the babies are safe now, and he'll never hurt you again, as long as I live." Instead, she said, "Well, good. I worry about you and Samantha and Nicholas so much. Is Bryce working many hours? Ya know, he really should find a better-paying job. I just want the best for all of you, I hope you know that." Sweet-sounding words but spiked with arsenic. She added, "Did you hear that Maryann's son, Josh, landed a great job in DC as a prosecuting attorney? They'll be moving there soon and probably will be able to buy a nice house."

"That's great, Mom." I yawned. "Well, I need to go. I've got a million things to do today." Lie, lie, lie.

Mom hesitated and then said, "Okay, sweetheart, just please let me know what I can do to help. You know you can always talk to me." She paused, and I tried to say my goodbye, but she spoke over me and said, "Oh, I almost forgot, the real reason I called is to ask if you're going to your sister's this Friday night for your dad's birthday party? And if you are, what are you bringing for dinner?"

"Of course we are. We wouldn't miss it," I said with no emotion in my voice. "I have no idea what I'm bringing. I haven't had a chance to think about it yet. But I can let you know," I conceded.

"Oh, good, yes, let me know. I don't want to duplicate anything. It's so sweet of her to have his birthday at her house. I think your dad is looking forward to it."

I was so relieved to hang up with her. I put on some coffee and finished folding the laundry I had started yesterday. I put it away and went in to check on Sami and Nicholas, who were still sleeping. I walked into their room, and my foot bumped a yellow, plastic star-shaped toy that played "Twinkle, Twinkle, Little Star." I flinched and swore under my breath but smiled when my daughter's eyes blinked open. I scooped her up in my arms and whispered, "I love my little pumpkin." I held her as close as I possibly could.

I walked out into the living room with Samantha clutched onto me. "Hi, sweet baby girl, how was your sleep?" I kissed her on the cheek, again and again. Oh, how I loved this sweet little girl, my joy in life, my sunshine girl. No matter what was happening in my day, I could just stop and think about my son and daughter, and it would fill me with overwhelming love—my eyes would water, and I'd have to blink away the tears. I put Sami down in the bouncy seat, and she giggled.

I went back into the kids' bedroom to see if Nicholas had woken up yet; he was stirring around a little. I picked him up and snuggled his little two-year-old body, warm and sweet. I kissed him too and told him how much I loved him. He smiled at me and said, "G'morning, Mommy." My heart skipped a beat. He wiggled out of my arms to see what was new in our apartment.

We played for a short while. Samantha cooed and smiled at her big brother and me. Nicholas played with his blocks and Hot Wheels cars, organizing them by size and color.

Bryce spent our marriage making sure I respected "his" things. And I was never to touch "his" things. I learned about this rule when two years ago I found a key on his desk that I didn't recognize. I remember I picked it up and walked into the living room where he was watching football. I held it up to him and asked him what it was for.

Roughly grabbing the key out of my hand, he said, "It's my key to my post office box."

"Your post office box? Why do you have a post office box?" I asked incredulously. My stomach started churning.

"I've always had one. I had one before we got married and I plan on keeping it," Bryce said adamantly.

That old sense of powerlessness came over me; there wasn't anything I could do. He was going to keep the PO box no matter what I said or how I felt. "Well, can I have a key too?" I asked, feeling foolish, like I was a child asking for permission. I don't know why I asked that; having a copy of the key was not what I wanted. I wanted to know why Bryce didn't treat me like a partner, a wife, or even someone he trusted. It seemed like the safest thing to say at that point. Justifying my request for a key, as if helpfulness was my motivation, I added, "I could go and pick up your mail for you from time to time."

His eyes were still glued to the television, but when I offered to pick up his mail, he said in a high-pitched voice, "I could go and pick up your mail from time to time." His eyes narrowed, and the contempt poured out of him. I was standing next to him as he remained on the couch, but he was close enough to grab my wrist tightly and said through clenched teeth, "No, you don't need a key. It's my stuff. You need to stay out of my personal things."

He pushed my arm away. I lowered my eyes, held my aching wrist, and walked away. On the inside, my stomach and throat tightened. My head was pounding. It was another thing in my life I had to keep hidden. I wondered if a person had a limit as to how many things they could hide. Like a cedar chest has a space limit, do our heads and our hearts have a space limit? Had I reached mine?

22

The Birthday Clash

Friday night finally came, and it was my dad's birthday party. I made a macaroni and cheese casserole that everyone loved, even Mom. We drove up to Chelsea and Spencer's house, a craftsman-style home built in 1968 with a cozy front porch, stone columns, and a low-pitch gable roof dressing the front. They bought the house five years ago after Spencer got a job as an accountant.

As we walked into the house, Bryce carried Samantha in her car seat and I held Nicholas's hand, helping him navigate the stairs. Bryce set Samantha down in the doorway like a bag of groceries and left her there in the maze of gifts and purses and shoes sitting in the foyer that he easily stepped over.

Right away, my mom noticed Sami and she rushed over, giving Bryce a glare, unbuckled her, scooped her up, and gave her hugs and kisses all over. Sami giggled and loved on her nanna. Both Sami and Nicholas loved her and my dad so much. My parents enjoyed being grandparents. Chelsea and I talked about it and thought that our children gave our parents the unconditional love they craved and weren't able to give us.

Chelsea had made a big banner that read HAPPY 65TH BIRTHDAY, DAD! on it. My dad laughed and hugged her, and jealousy twisted my heart in two. I quickly pushed the jealousy down, not wanting to feel that toward my sister. But it wouldn't seem to go down to that place where I put all my negative feelings.

The jealousy lingered. I noticed her new couches, her beautiful woodwork in her home, the way my mom was gazing over Chelsea's artwork, asking Spencer a million questions about his job. Bryce sat on the couch alone with the same scowl he'd had all week. His anger was boiling just below the surface, and one blunder could bring it exploding to the top.

I walked over to the oriental rug and made sure the kids were settled in nicely and playing with their cousins, my sister's children, twins Charlie and Tyler, who were one year old. The oldest of the bunch was three-year-old Allie. She was the mama bear. It was hilarious to watch her try to direct the younger ones. Allie's twin brothers and Samantha stared at each other or put toy cars on one another's heads or sat on each other's laps or shared their pacifiers with each other; they didn't truly understand the concept of "the other" quite yet. Nicholas adored his cousin Allie and tried his best to do all she wanted him to do, but he was also a firstborn and had his own ideas about what was fun. It was so cute to watch and gave me something pleasant to think about.

My dad came over, and I gave him a hug and wished him a happy birthday. He hugged me back and thanked me, saying to the kids, "Hey, I think Grandpa needs more hugs!" Nicholas, Sami, Allie, and the twins all wanted to be picked up at the same time to give him hugs, so Dad, who was still in good shape, sat on the floor with all of them, but not without a grunt and a groan as they crawled and drooled on him. He just laughed and enjoyed every second of it.

Out of nowhere it seemed, my eyes were full of water and I rushed to the bathroom and shut the door. I put the lid down on the toilet and sat. I let the tears come and couldn't believe I was crying at my dad's birthday party. I wish I'd had a daddy like the one on the floor out in the living room, to feel safe and loved and enjoyed.

I threw water on my face, dried it with a towel, and searched for lotion and makeup to try to hide the redness. I flushed the toilet to make it seem like I was using the bathroom for what it was intended, not to wipe my tears. When I came out, everyone was getting ready to sit around the table and my dad was telling a story about a man from his old job who came to visit. As he was telling the story, my mom interrupted him as she frequently did.

Dad was saying, "So it's mid-February, and the door—"

"No, Bob, it was not February! You say that every time! It was mid-March when he came by!" Mom rolled her eyes.

"Well, Margaret, *you* tell the damn story if you know it so well, then!" Dad's face turned red, and his voice boomed.

I was thirty-two years old, but my heart rate quickened

just like it did when I was twelve and my parents fought.

Mom locked her eyes on me as if we had a special secret together, and then her lips puckered like she was going to cry. She got up and walked into the kitchen. It got quiet around the table, and then one of the twins spit up, so Chelsea got up to clean it. I thought she was so lucky to go clean up puke instead of sitting there at the table with our bickering parents.

I played with some of the macaroni and cheese on my plate. Then Bryce said, "Dad, you don't have to yell at Mom like that."

What? Are you kidding me? You're going to defend my mother, and yet you hit me, call me names, and belittle me constantly!

"And *you* can just stay the hell out of this, Bryce!" Dad's eyes bulged with anger when he slammed his fist down.

I got up from the table and started picking up toys and children; I was so nervous that I was moving things and babies around the room. I wasn't accomplishing anything. Then I blurted out, "Ya know, this is Dad's birthday party, for God's sake! Can we all just get along for one night?"

Bryce swung around and stared me down and sneered, "You would be the one not to take a stand." Then to my dad he said, "How did you raise a daughter so spineless?"

Dad shot back and said, "Bryce, you may think you can talk to her like that, but you sure as hell can't talk to *me* like that!"

My blood ran cold; my dad and Bryce had never had words like this before. This was different. A new level of hostility had risen. The contempt they had for each other was clear. I didn't know where this was going, and I didn't want to find out.

Chelsea was crying, and Spencer asked us to leave. My mother wasn't crying; she was standing in the doorway, arms crossed, with a scowl that said, "How dare you talk to my husband like that!" Shame overwhelmed me.

My eyes were filling with tears as I started packing up our things and rounding up the children; it took all of three minutes to get out of there. I accidentally kicked a toy, and it slid across the wood floors into the dining area. Everyone but Bryce stared at me, and my face reddened. "Oh, I'm sorry, I didn't mean to do that," I said. I wanted to stay, yet I felt betrayed by my own family. I wanted to leave, but I didn't want to leave with Bryce.

Nicholas cried, "Mommy, I don't want to leave. I want my Allie."

"I know, buddy. I'm so sorry. We have to leave, but we'll come back, I promise." I kissed his forehead and hugged him as I helped him get his coat on. I got Sami in her car seat, and she was fussy. I kissed her and gave her the pacifier, which seemed to help comfort her.

I buckled the kids into their car seats and got into the car myself, bumping my knee on the door. I cried out in pain and swore under my breath. Bryce was seething and didn't bother to help me. The thought occurred to me that we shouldn't get into the car with this maniac, but that same sense of powerlessness kept me paralyzed. I was on autopilot; like a robot, I obeyed all commands. Get the babies into the car seats. Get them out of their car seats. Get them into the house. Prepare the food. Clean the house. Cook dinner. Bathe the kids. Read bedtime stories. Take them potty. Give them a bedtime snack. Tuck them in. Go to bed. Then somehow, someway, get up in the morning and do the same thing again.

Bryce drove wordlessly back to our apartment. I glanced back at the kids, and they sat silently in their car seats. They looked back at me with big blue eyes of fear, and we all knew not to say a word.

23

How Could I Be So Selfish?

During the Christmas season, Bryce worked longer hours on Saturday mornings, so I used that time for cleaning. We had moved into another, larger apartment, closer to downtown. I pulled my tired body out of bed. The wood floor creaked, and the air was so cold that I grabbed a sweater and went into the bathroom to brush my teeth, brush my hair, and put warm water on my face to wake up. I liked to get up before the children so I could get as much done before I got busy with them. And I did: I scrubbed the kitchen counters, washed the dishes, and put them away; I swept and mopped the floor, dusted the living room and my bedroom, took my sheets off the bed, and started the laundry; I scrubbed the bathroom, top to bottom, all before 7 A.M. when three-year-old Nicholas toddled into my bedroom, all sleepy-eyed, saying, "G'morning, Mommy."

I swept him up in my arms and snuggled him, feeling his softness, his sweet baby smell, his wispy hair. "Good morning, buddy. I love you so much! Did you see all the snow outside? Let's go see." We creaked through the old apartment and through the big picture window in the living room. It looked like a winter wonderland—the snow had fallen through the night and had left a smooth white quilt on the ground. Nicholas gasped and said, "So pwetty."

We settled down for a children's show with a large purple dinosaur, but it wasn't long after that when Samantha woke up and wanted to be changed and fed. Like I did with my son, I picked her up and loved on her, feeling the softness of her skin and smiling into her sweet face. The three of us snuggled on the couch for about an hour. I loved these special times, the three of us together, on a lifeboat, saving one another from a sinking ship. I loved these babies with all of my being, as if without them, I wouldn't exist. They were my lifelines.

Nicholas stood up and sang along with the other children on TV, doing all the hand movements and dancing around, and Sami's eyes followed his every move. I could have relaxed on our pretend lifeboat all day, but I knew I had a lot to do before Bryce got home from work. He'd be upset if the house wasn't spotless and the children dressed as if they were ready for church, so after the last song, I turned off the TV and we went to finish up breakfast in the kitchen and get dressed. The children played in their bedroom while I vacuumed the living room. As I started a Crock-Pot of soup and the dough for a loaf of bread, our neighbor's car slowly crunched through the snow down our long shared driveway. I thought, *Bryce will be happy he can get into the driveway without blocking anyone.*

With me in the kitchen baking bread, and the children

216

playing with their toys, we could have been in a Norman Rockwell painting, living in one of his houses surrounded by a snow-covered neighborhood.

If my life were that painting, Bryce would've ripped it off the wall and smashed it over his knee when he got home.

Shaking me out of my daydream, he stormed into the kitchen and asked, "When did the neighbors leave?"

"About twenty minutes ago, I think. Why?"

"Goddammit! Why didn't you shovel the driveway? Now it's going to be icy!" He walked away, not giving me time to respond, slamming the bathroom door shut and then kicking it.

I walked into the children's room, and Nicholas said simply, "Mommy?"

I held them both in my lap and squeezed them and whispered that everything would be okay, that Daddy had a hard day at work, and he was tired. He just needed a nap. Bryce worked a 3:30 A.M. to 8:30 A.M. shift every day preparing trucks for mail delivery, but Saturdays during Christmas were busy and he worked until 11 A.M. It was a fine job for someone who never finished his college degree. He had full benefits even though he only worked part time. I encouraged him to get a full-time position with the company, but he wanted to use the extra time off for his work with the children's football league. Even though that was only during a few months out of the year.

Bryce finished in the bathroom and rushed past to the kitchen. I told the kids to stay put in their bedroom and that I'd be right back.

I walked down the hall into the kitchen and found him pouring coffee into a mug. "Bryce, I've been cleaning all morning and taking care of the kids. How did you expect me to also shovel the driveway? Plus, I had no idea you wanted me to do that too." I swallowed, hoping we could have a decent conversation.

"How could you *not* know? You're so fucking selfish! All you want to do is wipe a counter and play with the kids! Never mind, Savannah, I'll do it. I'll do it all." He walked out of the kitchen, leaving his coffee on the counter. He walked through the living room and out the front, slamming the door. I leaned on the doorframe of the kitchen, feeling a knot develop in my stomach.

As I washed out his coffee mug, I heard the grinding of the shovel against the cement; he was clearing the driveway. *Why didn't I think to shovel? Now that I think about it, it would have been nice for him to come home to a clean driveway.*

I held back the tears that were tickling my eyes and I tried to maintain steady breathing, but I couldn't ignore the stabbing pain in my heart. I needed to be strong for my two beautiful children, but how could I be when I felt so weak? I knew marriage was hard, but my marriage seemed harder than most.

I put a smile on my face and went back into the children's room to play with them. It was going to be a long day with Bryce around, so I decided I'd run errands later with my son and daughter, and maybe we would stop by my sister's house too. I was always relaxed with her, as she made my burdens lighter, even when she didn't know what was going on.

When Bryce finished shoveling, he showered while I put small amounts of food in snack bags for the children. They seemed to graze all day, every two hours needing food, so when we left the house, I was sure to pack crackers, cheese, carrots, grapes, and little things I knew they liked to eat. As I was shoving items in the diaper bag, Bryce came in the room and asked, "Are you going somewhere?"

Careful, I thought. *Watch what you say and how you say it. Don't offend him or make him angry.* "I thought I'd take the kids and run some errands and stop by Chelsea's for a while so they can play." I spoke in a high-pitched voice, but I avoided eye contact with him. I expected him to argue with me about my plan or challenge the way I thought or question why I'd take the children with me without inviting him. I held my breath as I waited for the bomb to go off.

"Oh, well, I'll go with you. I need to stop by the community center really quick, and it's on the way to Chelsea's." The conflict had blown over in his mind. He sounded calm and like things were okay between us.

I had mixed feelings about his sudden mood swing. I didn't trust that this was going to turn out to be a positive family outing, but I complied with his idea to join us. One wrong move on my part could turn the entire trip into a disaster. All my defenses were in place and my guard went up so that the odds of my tripping Bryce's wires and heating him up into a fiery rage were as low as they could possibly go. I did all I could to create a warm and friendly experience for us.

The day went as planned, and even the children were content, until we started on the ten-minute drive back home. Samantha started crying because, as a baby, that was her main mode of communication. My hunch was that she was hungry and tired, so I said, "Oh, sweetie, we'll be home soon!" and I reached in her diaper bag for her pacifier.

Bryce asked with an accusatory tone of which I was well acquainted, "You didn't feed her at Chelsea's?"

I bit my lip, and my stomach pain flared again. "Uh, well, I did about three o'clock, but now it's five fifteen, so she's probably hungry again. I guess I didn't plan that well," I said with a short but nervous laugh.

"Ya think? You're always putting her second. You think of Nicholas first, but you forget about Samantha."

I couldn't comprehend what he was saying. Was he saying I favored my son over my daughter? He's blamed me for a lot of things, but never this, and he knew it hurt me to the core. I became defensive. "No, I don't! I love my children equally, Bryce, you know that! How can you even say that?"

"I can say it because it's true," he spat at me. "I see it all the time. You forget to change her, feed her—you just seem to ignore her." I held on tight to my purse. *Was he saying this to provoke me?* I wanted to punch him in the face. He was toying with me and he wanted me to explode, because he knew if I did, he'd have every justification in his mind to hit me, push me, hold me down, break me.

I turned around to put the pacifier in Samantha's mouth, but Bryce grabbed my arm and stopped me. He was holding so tight that he started twisting my arm. I cried out, but he kept the pressure on my wrist, pressing down harder. Nicholas couldn't see what was happening, and Sami kept crying in the back. Nicholas said, "It's okay, Sami, it's okay." Bryce's eyes stared straight ahead. He pushed on the gas pedal and the speedometer crept up and up. He was up to eighty miles per hour. He let go of my wrist and put both hands on the shaking steering wheel. "Bryce, slow down!" I yelled. "You're going to kill us!" I was so afraid I started praying; I knew there was nothing else I could do to stop him. I just prayed and hoped someone would call 911.

We made it home, and I jumped out of the car to get the children out. Nicholas was sitting in the seat behind me, so I started with him. Bryce smirked and said, "See what I mean?"

I ignored him and continued getting the children out of the car and into the house. Thank God I stayed calm and realized that these words were coming from a manipulative and irrational man, and that arguing with him would get me beaten.

I was shaking. My arms, legs, hands—even my breathing was shaky. I couldn't calm myself down. I was on autopilot, doing everything that needed to be done—all the while, a steady stream of questions and thoughts ran through my mind, not fully in my conscious state, but enough that I knew they were there: *You're in danger. Get out, run. Something is wrong. What will your life be like in a year? Five years? What is this doing to the children? How can you all escape?*

I spent extra time snuggling with both Nicholas and Samantha that night. I read to them every night before bed, and they loved it; that night, we read *Guess How Much I Love You* three times at Nicholas's request. Maybe he knew on some level that not all was well in his world and he needed extra reassurance. Samantha enjoyed being tucked in tightly with her covers, like her own cocoon.

When I went to bed, my eyes wouldn't stay closed. I stared at the ceiling wondering if this was how my life was going to be forever. I had made mistakes, but was this God punishing me? I was overwhelmed with feelings and questions and confusion while Bryce snored into the night.

24

Domestic Violence and the Church

M y vigilance about the safety of my children became nearly hysterical. They were with me at all times unless I was working, and I signed them up in the daycare at my work. If I absolutely needed a babysitter, I'd call my mother, and though she gave no hint that she knew about the hell we were living in, she was always standing at the ready, prepared to watch my babies at a moment's call. I made sure Nicholas and Samantha were never alone with Bryce; he was too busy with the boys in the football league to notice.

The president of the organization I worked for, Mike Barnes, decided to address the issue of domestic violence in Christian homes and asked my team to be a part of this project. The plan was to address it by writing a booklet and creating a television video series. This was a historic decision for the organization, Mike said, because it was an issue that had been ignored by the church at best, and at worst, many abused wives had been instructed to return to their abusive husbands. Mike knew that to address this issue, he'd also have to address the issue of divorce, which was a controversial topic. The ultraconservative belief was that the only time a person could ever divorce was due to adultery. Mike, after years of study and collaborating with other biblical scholars, disagreed with that view. He believed that abuse was a legitimate reason to divorce a spouse.

One of the television producers, Jeff, pulled me aside one day and asked if I'd be willing to pose as a victim of domestic violence in a video they were shooting the next day. I thought, *Oh my God, can you see it on my face? Can you see it in the way I walk? How can you tell that I'm a victim?*

But I said, "Yes, I'd be glad to do that." Inside, though, I thought, *I'd better do a better job of hiding my personal life. They might fire me if they know I've been portraying a lie and that I don't have a perfect home life and marriage like the rest of the employees.* I watched the husbands and wives together at the employee picnics or coming in to have lunch; they were respectful and loving toward one another. I didn't see any hurtful glances or hear mean-spirited words. It seemed that the ministry would be disappointed in me. I needed this job and couldn't risk losing it.

The next day, the camera people, Mike, the producers, and I drove up to an old abandoned house, a perfect setting to shoot the videos. The house reminded me of Bryce's parents' house, but worse, as it had been empty for years. The wood floors were covered in dust, and the windows whispered of a time when someone cared enough to put curtains up, but now they were ancient and dirty.

I followed Jeff's instructions and stood looking out a corner window, careful not to let a spider crawl on me. He moved my shoulders this way and that, and like a photographer, asked me to turn my chin down a little, making sure the lighting was just right and that only the profile of my face showed.

As I stood still, I couldn't see Mike's face when he spoke to the camera, but his voice was soft and thick with emotion. "Domestic violence is such an important topic in the church. Christians are called to show love and mercy and to take care of the weak and the downtrodden. But we've added to the pain and suffering of abuse victims by ignoring their cries and silencing their pain when they've come to us for help." He shuffled his stance a little and said, "Their husbands are violent, and we've misused Scripture by telling wives to be more submissive." His voice cracked briefly, but he kept going. "We've wrongly given husbands authority in their homes, and it's increased the danger for their wives and children. Male privilege fuels domestic violence, and we need to change that."

I swallowed back tears; I couldn't wrap my mind around everything I was hearing—that it wasn't my fault that Bryce was so angry all the time, and his assaults were *his* responsibility. And the church's beliefs were partly to blame? I was relieved when Jeff said "Cut!" and I could move again.

Mike kept talking, though. He grabbed his water and said to one of the other producers, "My wife got a call last night from a woman in our church who was sent back to her abusive husband by one of our pastors. He told her that maybe it was because her husband had a high-stress job and she wasn't supportive enough." He paused and said, "The wife ended up in the emergency room with several broken ribs." He took a drink and shook his head. "Too many women are sent back into violent homes. They're advised to be more submissive, to have more sex, and, in general, to do more to hold their marriages together while men aren't being held accountable for how they're behaving in a cruel and violent way." He crossed his arms. "Wives go to their pastors for help, and instead of the pastor calling the husband, many pastors tell the wife to go back and try harder. I've had enough!" He walked over to his briefcase and pulled out some papers. He shuffled them about in his hands as we all watched him. He tossed the papers back into his briefcase and said with a heavy sigh, "This is wrong on so many levels, and we as a Bible-teaching ministry need to speak out against this. We men, especially the Jesus followers, need to stand up against this evil. We can't stay silent anymore. To be silent is to be complicit."

I was taken aback. Mike, this important man, cared about women. He didn't ask for or demand anything in return, nor did he hold women responsible for how violent some men were behaving—for how *Bryce* was behaving.

The cold darkness that kept me frozen for five years was beginning to wane. It was like I had been in a pitch-black room and someone lit a candle for the first time in years. I started to see things around me, able to make things out, shapes, outlines of things. And the more I listened to the truth, and engaged and connected with true Love, more candles were lit, and I saw more. The Light began to wake me, and the heat from it warmed me so I wasn't so cold and motionless. I started to see that I was worth protecting and that there were people who cared.

We went back to shooting the video, and Mike essentially repeated to the camera what he'd just said to our group. When we were done, the producers and Mike thanked me for coming and posing as a victim.

"We appreciate your coming today, Savannah. You really brought forth the emotion of an abused woman, even without saying a word," one of the producers said.

I clasped my hands together and said, "Thank you, I'm glad I could help." I couldn't speak further to tell them how badly I needed help.

For weeks after, all I could think about was Mike's words and how I might be able to tell someone I trusted about the terror my children and I were living in. But I couldn't tell anyone; I was too fearful. In addition to helping out with the video series, I was also included in the meetings with Mike and the rest of my team, where the issues surrounding abuse were discussed.

In one poignant meeting for me, Mike began, "I'm concerned about the number of wives in our churches who are living with abuse. And I'm not only talking about physical abuse. The verbal, emotional, mental, and spiritual abuse is just as, if not more, damaging. If you ask women who are abused, they say things like 'physical wounds heal, but the emotional wounds don't.' I don't believe for a minute that God would want a woman to stay in a marriage like that."

The cited Bible verse was Micah 6:8 (NIV) where it explains what God requires of us: justice and mercy. "He has shown you, O mortal, what is good. And what does the LORD require of you? To act justly and to love mercy and to walk humbly with your God."

Jim, my team leader, piped up and said, "I think God is deeply troubled when a husband is cruel to his wife. A husband is commanded to love her like Christ loves the church. What does a church do when a husband abuses his wife? Typically, nothing. They put more burden on the wife—the victim in this case—to be nicer, more submissive, to placate the abuser. And we know that giving in to the abuser feeds his appetite for power and control."

My head was circling as I took in all that was being said. The abuse wasn't my fault? I hadn't caused Bryce to lash out at me? Were they sure I didn't deserve this life of violence? I started to imagine someone holding Bryce accountable for his actions. He never listened to me and always refused counseling. Maybe he'd listen to Jim. Jim knew Bryce but didn't know about the abuse. I'd have to tell him, and I dreaded that thought.

In that meeting, I finally decided I would find the right time to tell Jim what was going on in my marriage. It wasn't the good Christian union I portrayed it to be. I owed it to myself and to my children to tell Jim that I was living the very life of hell that I had portrayed standing in the window of the broken-down house. I couldn't continue the façade any longer.

25

The Black Bag

I was finally starting to feel the gentle embrace of hope, that there was a future without shame and guilt. I had a newfound excitement to go into my office now. As I was getting Nicholas and Samantha ready for daycare and myself ready for work, my eye caught sight of Bryce's black leather backpack next to the door between a chair and a houseplant. It was so odd to see it there, startling almost, like it was an intruder. Bryce never left home without his backpack; he carried it every day to work, to meetings, everywhere he went, and was diligent about never letting me have access to it.

The kids and I went into the kitchen for breakfast, and I put Nicholas in his booster seat and Sami-girl in her high chair. I made them oatmeal, their favorite breakfast. Nicholas was pretty adept at feeding himself, but I fed Sami. As I scooped the hot cereal, there sat the black backpack, daring me to peek inside. I stared at it for a minute; I'd been curious about what he had in there, but I never dared look in. Now was my chance, and I knew this opportunity may never present itself again. The clock told me I had about three hours before Bryce was to be home. I didn't have to be at work until later that morning. However, I still wondered if he'd come rushing back for it at any moment. In spite of all that, with my heart beating loudly in my chest, I made sure the door was locked and walked over to the bag and squatted down on my knees. My stomach was in knots, as I was about to cross a line I had never dared to before. I lifted up the bag; it wasn't very heavy. Not much was in it, it seemed. Maybe it was empty.

I unzipped the bag, my hands shaking as if it might contain a bomb. I leaned over the bag and tried to make out the contents. As my eyes adjusted, Samantha started calling for me. I went to her and fed her oatmeal and gave her milk. After I kissed her sweet cheeks and tickled her and made her giggle, I ran back to the bag and continued with my search.

My heart was beating hard and fast as I imagined him finding me sorting through his things. I knew I had to act fast.

I reached into the bag and pulled out a bath towel. A bath towel? Puzzled, I reached in again and pulled out a pair of his underwear. I dug deeper and discovered petroleum jelly. *Oh my God! He's having an affair!* My arms tingled, and I dropped my head in my hands. It explained so many things: his consistently late arrivals, the all-nighters out with his "friends," the PO box, his irrational anger, our lack of intimacy. My head was spinning, and I became light-headed. *What is happening?*

I fell back on the floor next to the bag with my mouth gaping open. Yes, we've had major problems in our marriage, and I've been unhappy, so unhappy, but I never thought this could happen to me again. Blood was rushing to my head. Yes, he pushed me and called me awful names, but he was nothing like Raymond. How could he be unfaithful?

My throat tightened. My eyes watered, and I was on the floor, crying. I was not crying at the loss of Bryce, but at the loss of my dreams since I was a little girl. So many dreams gone. I didn't know what to do. Wiping my tears, I knew I didn't have the luxury of lying on the floor all day crying myself to sleep.

I put everything back in the bag like he had it, got myself up, and checked on Sami and Nicholas. They were happily eating, playing, and talking to themselves. I grabbed the cereal box to give Sami something else to eat when a car pulled up into one of the parking spaces out front. It sounded like it pulled into our spot, directly in front of our apartment. The cereal box slipped out of my hand and cereal flew all over the floor; then as I tried to run over to the window, I hopped over the backpack, but my foot got caught in one of the straps and everything came flying out of the bag. I almost fell, but I steadied myself and grabbed all I could and shoved it back into the bag.

My head started pounding again. Adrenaline rushed up through my body; my heart was beating out of my chest. Was it Bryce coming home early to find me rummaging around in his hidden, forbidden stash? The car door slammed shut. Or was that the building door? *Oh, God, he's coming!* I zipped the bag and threw it between the chair and plant and ran to the window. I yanked the sheer curtains aside.

My eyes searched the parking lot, but no sign of Bryce's car. It must have been the guy who lived above us. My breathing slowed, and a wave of relief came over me. I took a deep breath in, closed my eyes, and exhaled, feeling like I just outran the bogeyman. With the adrenaline rush over, I started shaking.

I walked back over to the bag, and there on the floor, something had flown out that I didn't see before: a zippered case shaped like an eyeglasses holder but larger, longer. I picked it up, hands shaking like crazy, and decided to open it. As I opened the case, I saw something black with lines grooved into it. I touched it, like you do if you touch the skin of a snake, pulling my hand back quickly in disgust. It was cold and like soft rubber; I reached in to pull it out and discovered it was a large black rubber penis.

Bile entered my throat, and I quickly dropped it and ran to the sink, dry-heaving. All the implications came to me at once, and I washed and rewashed my hands. I dried my hands, took deep breaths, and ran back to the bag. I used a paper towel to put all the items away as fast as I could. I held back vomiting and zipped up the bag again and put it in the same spot between the chair and the plant. I leaned against the door, trying to catch my breath.

I washed my hands another half a dozen times and then cleaned up Sami and Nicholas. I decided that it was necessary to talk to someone about my marriage, my suspicions about Bryce, the paraphernalia I found in his bag, and the horrible things he did.

The day went on as normal: going to work, taking the kids to daycare, coming home, playing with the kids, eating, cleaning, cooking. It felt anything but normal, though. When I returned home for work that evening, Bryce was not home and the bag lay in the same position I had left it. I never knew when or if Bryce would come home, but I expected him to rush into the apartment at any moment. My keen awareness of the black bag grew into obsession, making sure that it was exactly in the same spot, in the same position, where I had found it. Every few minutes, I'd rush over to it and make sure I had zipped it all the way. Or I'd wonder, *Was it really leaning toward the right like that, or was it supposed to be facing the wall?* I kept Sami and Nicholas away, and that area of the apartment became something like a roped-off crime scene, trying not to contaminate it.

His car pulled up, and I herded the kids into their room and plopped down on the floor to play with them. It was easy to get distracted with them and their funny chatter. Sami crawled into my lap, and we read books when Bryce walked into their bedroom.

We said a brief hi to one another as he leaned on the doorjamb, arms crossed, glaring down at the floor. The children didn't get excited when he walked up, and he didn't make any effort to greet them as we continued reading books. I could see that he was agitated and waiting for me to say something.

He didn't say anything, which was good, because I didn't know where the conversation would end up. He pushed off the doorway and headed into our bedroom. He was worked up, and I knew I'd better stay out of his way. I was scared, but I also began to feel a change coming, a shift in the tide, like the charade was over, or it would be soon. I'd spent the last years building a sandcastle life, and now the waves were getting close to sweeping it away, and I had no idea what would replace it.

26

Breaking Free

The next day was a bright sunny day, but I had a terrible night with Bryce. I could barely lift my head up to greet anyone when I walked in the door to work.

That night, Bryce did something that locked my decision down—not that what I discovered in his backpack shouldn't have been enough. At bedtime, he was angry because I was reading a second story to the children, so he yelled at me. Three-year-old Nicholas spoke up and said, "Don't yell at Mommy." Bryce's eyes grew dark, he turned, and he slapped my baby boy across the face. I screamed at Bryce, and then he pushed me away from my son and wouldn't allow me to comfort Nicholas. I knew then, resolutely, that I was leaving the bastard. I didn't know exactly when or how, but I was leaving with my children—and soon. He didn't deserve me, and he definitely didn't deserve our precious children.

After our team meeting the next day, my hands shaking like leaves, I called Jim aside and asked him if I could talk to him. He said, "Of course." We walked into his office and

BLACK EYE, BLUE SKY

sat down across from each other.

I scratched my head and crossed and uncrossed my feet. "Jim, I need to talk to you about something. I need to tell someone that I . . . um . . ." My chin trembled, and tears welled up in my eyes. I looked down at the carpeting, as if I had done something unforgivable and was in need of mercy.

The words were hesitant to come, but I knew I had to tell him. The time had come, so I pushed forward. "I've never told anyone this, but I have to tell someone." I met Jim's eyes, and his face was full of concern, anticipating, encouraging me to tell him. I averted my eyes and said, "Bryce is abusing me. He hits me, and I'm scared of him." My voice cracked, and I covered my mouth to hold back my cries.

Jim grabbed his tissue box that any good therapist has close by and handed me a tissue. I wiped my eyes and nose and continued on after I caught my breath. "The day after our honeymoon, he gave me a black-and-blue lip, and he almost broke my arm once." I covered my mouth again with a clean tissue. "He's spit in my face and calls me horrible names and tells me I'm stupid all the time."

At this point, I'm talking fast and crying, and Jim is trying to keep up and listen to every word. "But last night, he did something that was the worst thing to me: He slapped Nicholas across the face." I bent over and put my elbows on my knees, my forehead resting in my hands. It didn't even cross my mind to mention the violent sexual assault.

I was slumped over, and my body was shaking as I sobbed quietly. I wondered what Jim thought of me. *Does he think I'm a fraud?* Jim moved his chair closer to me, put his hand on my shoulder, and said, "Savannah, I'm so sorry that you've been living in this hell for all this time. Oh my God. Bryce is extremely violent. I've never really liked him, but I didn't know you were being abused like this." Through teary eyes, I looked at Jim and he leaned back. "It's shocking to hear these details. He sounds like a monster. You and the kids need to be safe."

He also said that in no way did God want me to stay in that cruel and dangerous marriage. At that, I started crying harder. Those words of love broke through to my heart, but I couldn't believe that God would allow me to leave this marriage.

Jim bit his lip and said, "I think we should go and talk with Mike. What do you think?" His eyes were staring directly into mine.

No! My heart leaped out of my chest. "Wait, no! I-I don't want to tell Mike. What will he think of me? What if he fires me? I need this job. I have two children to support, and I don't know where I'd go if I didn't have this job!"

"Hold on a minute." Jim had his hand up as if he were directing traffic. "I can assure you that Mike isn't going to fire you." Jim smiled softly. "Mike wants to help people in your situation, not make it worse. How would firing you help you? And it wouldn't line up with anything he's been teaching the last few weeks. Trust me on this, Mike's a good guy and he will be just as heartbroken and angry at Bryce as I am."

I thought about what Jim said and decided it was true. I took a deep breath and said, "Okay. You might be right. I think it'll be okay to tell Mike."

Together, we walked down the hall to Mike's office. On the way, an urge to run tempted my legs to flee and take me right out the door. I was afraid of this new path I was on. I was afraid and exhilarated at the same time. I was on the path of truth-telling. I was so used to hiding and covering things up. That's the way we did it in my family growing up, and I had lived up to that perfectly until this point. It was terrifying, yet I was ready to try this new way of living, because the old way wasn't working. Living this lie and hiding was a hard life, and I didn't want to live like that anymore.

Jim started out the conversation. "Mike, Savannah told me some things this morning that are very disturbing about her husband, Bryce. He's been beating her and now he's physically hurting the children. I think she's ready to leave him." He rested his eyes on me. "Is that right, Savannah?"

I was trying so hard to hold my emotion in, but my chin quivered and my voice was shaky and all I could get out was "Uh-huh." My shoulders shook, and tears streamed down my face, and Mike handed me his box of tissues. He said, "Oh, Savannah, I'm so sorry. I had no idea."

Jim told him that Bryce had slapped Nicholas across the face last night.

I could only whisper, "And that is the last straw for me." It took me a minute to get more of my voice back. I had to swallow and clear my throat. "For five years, he's been physically assaulting me, but seeing him slap my little boy's face was it for me." I wasn't thinking of the times he shook Nicholas as a tiny baby or let Sami fall off the porch in her walker or the time they witnessed him throwing a plate across the room.

Jim said, "Savannah was a little worried about what you might think, Mike. Like you might be disappointed and maybe she would lose her job if she divorced Bryce. I assured her that wouldn't be the case." Jim was hoping Mike would assure me as well.

Mike didn't hesitate. "There are no worries whatsoever about your job, Savannah. Divorce in your situation, first of all, is completely warranted. What Bryce has been doing to you is illegal and goes against everything we stand for. If you're not safe in your marriage, you must get out. There's no other choice. But doing it safely is of utmost importance. Do you have a plan?"

Jim said, "We'll work on one today, okay?" I wiped my nose and nodded.

Mike continued: "If you need anything, please let us know. HR is here for you, and we have a benevolent fund set up, so if you need help in any way, please don't hesitate to ask. We are here for you." He glanced out his window, thinking, then he said, "As a matter of fact, do you mind if I let Jean know what's going on? I will make sure she knows that if you need some financial assistance, your request is approved and will be processed immediately. I also want her to alert our security team. We don't want Bryce coming around here. We want our team to know he's not welcome here, and they're trained in how to handle these kinds of situations."

My mind was whirling. *Can this be real? Can freedom be this close for us? God isn't angry with me and going to punish me and make me stay in this second marriage? Oh, God, thank you!* I said with a wispy voice, "Thank you. I feel like the biggest weight has been lifted off my shoulders." My shoulders relaxed a little. " I don't know what I'd do without you guys."

When Jim and I left Mike's office, my eyes were red and puffy. People noticed, but all I could think about was that the fear I had had faded. I prayed, *Thank you, Jesus, for finding me and my children and for giving us a way out of the nightmare that we've been in.* I thought God was so disappointed in me that He had cast me aside. I thought I was a lost cause, trash to be thrown out. The kindness and respect I was given, as if I deserved to exist and take up breathing space, created a home where I finally belonged.

And there was something else: I realized there was no knight in shining armor, no savior coming for me. I was my own savior. It was *me* who was going to save *me*. I could save myself and my children, and I was beginning to feel a spark of love for myself.

That same day, I called Chelsea and told her everything. She and I cried together, and she called Bryce all sorts of names. She said she'd find an attorney who would be good for domestic violence, a smart and tough attorney who wouldn't be a pushover. I told her I was going to talk to Bryce that evening.

"What do you mean you're going to talk to Bryce tonight, Savannah?" Chelsea's voice was high and clipped. "You do realize, don't you, that this could set him off? With all he's done, I think you should move out first."

"Maybe you're right. I don't know, but maybe talking with him would help him see that I was serious about leaving him, and he would choose to get help because he wanted our family to stay together."

"Savannah, how can you say that after all he has done?" Her voice was raised, but she softened it when she pleaded, "Please take a few days to think about what you are saying before you go down that road."

"Okay, I'll think about it. I just want to do the right thing. Let's talk again in a couple of days."

27

A Nice Dinner Party

The next day, my phone rang in my office. It was our team boss, Kate. She asked if I would like to take a walk around the building with her. The sun was shining, and I was eager to feel the warmth on my skin, but not knowing what she wanted to talk to me about put my nerves on edge.

We met in the lobby, and she said, "I'm glad you wanted to walk with me. I do this most days of the week, and you're more than welcome to join me anytime. It helps me clear my brain when I'm overwhelmed or just gives me a peaceful feeling being in nature." Our office was surrounded by pine trees, maple trees, flowers, and a pond with ducks and geese.

I put my sunglasses on and said, "Thank you for asking me. I love being outside too." I took a deep cleansing breath in, and my body relaxed a little.

We rounded the corner of the building and were all alone when Kate said, "Mike told me about what you're going through, Savannah, and I'm so sorry. If there's anything

I can do, please let me know. I'm praying for you." Kate's eyes teared up, and she grabbed a tissue out of her pocket.

"Thank you. I appreciate all your prayers. I sure need them right now."

"I had no idea that you were suffering so much." Kate shook her head. "It's probably a good thing I didn't know; otherwise, I would have ended up in jail for what I'd like to do to Bryce." She laughed and touched my arm.

I laughed as well and said, "Yes, you and my sister too. She wants to do great bodily harm to him."

We walked a few steps in silence before she said, "I have a question for you, and if you can't, I completely understand given all you're going through. But would you be interested in attending the National Conference for Christian Counselors next week in Nashville? We hadn't budgeted for it this year, but an anonymous donor has donated money for your team to go. I've talked to your teammates, and they're all going. We'd love to have you there, and it might be a good distraction from everything."

I completely relaxed knowing this was her agenda. "Oh, wow, I've wanted to go to that conference for a long time. I was told last year was amazing." I smiled at Kate, but the smile faded. "I'd love to be able to go, but I'm just not sure that now is a good time. I'll have to ask my parents if they'd be able to watch my children for a few days."

"Just let me know—either way I understand." Kate smiled.

We finished up our walk, and I realized how different my workspace was than at home. At work, I heard words of support at every turn. I'd find notes on my desk telling me that "I'm praying for you and your children" or gift cards for the local grocery store. Often, I received hugs from people I didn't know that well. Love was in this place.

I wasn't about to leave the children with Bryce, so I immediately called my mother to ask her if she and my dad would be available and willing to watch the children while I was away. I knew I was asking a lot of them, and it would be three long days of missing my babies; I had never been away from them before. I already missed them, and the trip was a week away. Mother assured me that she and Dad could watch them; my parents' sour dislike for Bryce was obvious, and they seemed relieved that the children wouldn't be in his care.

When Bryce got home from football practice, I said, "I need to go to Nashville for work for a few days next week. I asked Mom and Dad to watch the kids so you can focus on work and the football league. I know next week starts a busy time of year for you." I was on high alert, staying positive and being unusually supportive of Bryce.

He looked at me with what I thought was skepticism, but that expression fluttered away and was replaced with compliance. "Yeah, that will work. I have some meetings so that will help a lot. When do you get back?"

"I come back on Saturday."

He gave the mail in his hand a slight slap on his thigh, winked at me, and walked into our bedroom. It seemed odd that he seemed happy about my trip—for now, anyway. I never knew when or if he would suddenly change his mind.

I started dinner with the kids at my feet, and Bryce came into the small kitchen too. He said, "I thought we could have Manuel over for dinner this week before you leave. And his mother."

My throat tightened. I didn't want to have a dinner party before a trip. I had so much to do to get myself ready, plus pack for the kids. And I wasn't feeling my emotional best.

"I'd really rather wait until I get back. I have so much to do before I leave."

Bryce picked up a soft toy Samantha was playing with and tickled her with it. "I'll help. You won't have to do everything and plus, they're casual people like we are. Valentina won't expect you to do anything special. She likes things low-key."

How does he know what she expects and that she likes things low-key? How does he know how casual she is? An odd feeling crept up my spine, but instead of firmly saying no, I said, "I guess it's okay, but I'll need your help, and please don't expect a grand meal." I cringed and turned away from him and rolled my shoulders as if my shirt was on wrong.

Two days later, I was rushing around the kitchen stirring the sauce and waiting for the water to boil for the pasta, breathlessly marking things off my list and making sure I didn't burn the garlic bread or step on one of the children who kept finding their way in. *Where is Bryce, and why isn't he helping me like he promised?* Just then, the doorbell rang. It was Manuel and Valentina coming for dinner.

"Thank you, Miss Savannah, for having us over. Me and my mom love spaghetti."

Manuel was standing in the doorway of the kitchen. He was taller since I'd last seen him, but he still had baby cheeks and full, round brown eyes. I smiled and put my arm around him while I held on to the sauce spoon, giving him a side hug. "You're welcome, honey. My mother taught me how to make spaghetti when I was around your age. Do you like to cook?" I walked back to the stove to stir.

"A little, I guess. I like to make *brigadeiros* with my grandmother. She's a great cook too. I love her *feijoada*!"

"What are *brigadeiros*? And fay-oh— what did you say? What's in that?"

"*Feijoada*!" Manuel laughed and got excited. "It's got pork and black beans in it and oh, man, it's so good! You say it like fay-jo-ah-da." He waited for me to repeat it, which I did. I was interested in his Brazilian heritage through his mother and grandmother. Then he added, "And the *brigadeiros* are so good too! It's chocolate, and you make it with condensed milk and cocoa powder, and then you roll it in sprinkles, man!"

"Manuel! Don't call Mrs. Savannah a man! Show some respect." His mother had walked up to us in the kitchen holding Samantha in her arms. Nicholas was by my side listening to our conversation, and as usual for him, he was taking in all the information. I wouldn't be surprised if later he asked me to teach him how to make some "bragadeers."

We sat down to eat and had an easy conversation, although I was busy with Samantha and Nicholas mostly and running into the kitchen to retrieve things. I didn't have the chance to join in the conversation as much as I would have liked.

After we finished eating, I got the kids cleaned up and the night was winding down. Valentina got up and said, "Manuel, it's getting late. We should probably go."

Bryce asked, "Would it be okay if Manuel stayed a little longer and I can bring him home?"

I wished Valentina had said no, but she agreed to it, and after saying our goodbyes, she went home.

About thirty minutes later, Bryce said, "Well, Manuel, I'd better get you home." I thought *Well, that wasn't very long. Why does he have to leave already?* Valentina could have taken him home. Something was strange about it, but I didn't say anything to Bryce because he was extremely defensive of "his kids."

I said, "Manuel, thanks for coming, buddy. It was great seeing you."

"Can I stay longer?" Manuel asked, with puppy dog eyes, disappointed that he was leaving.

Bryce quickly interjected, "No, sorry, I've gotta get you home. It's a school night."

I gave Manuel a hug and told him to come back soon.

After I put the children to bed, Kay and I talked on the phone for about an hour. Then I read a little and decided to go to bed. Bryce wasn't home yet, and it was 9:30 P.M. Where was he? Surely he dropped off Manuel by now. I didn't know exactly where he lived, but I knew it wasn't more than ten minutes away. *Gosh, why didn't I get his mother's phone number?* I could've called her and made sure Manuel was safely at home with her and found out exactly when Bryce dropped him off.

At 10:45, when he still wasn't home and he hadn't called, I dialed Bryce's cell phone several times. He didn't answer any of my calls, nor did he return them; I wondered if he'd gotten into an accident. I imagined him severely hurt and needing help. More calls at 11:20, 11:55, 12:30, 1:15, and, with my last call at 2:30 A.M., any fear I had changed to anger. I knew in my heart he hadn't been in a car crash or wasn't crumpled in a heap, dead on the side of the road, though a part of me wished he was.

Bryce had done this kind of thing before, being tremendously late, but never this audacious.

He did a masterful job of putting up walls around his life, compartmentalizing his home existence, work, coaching, church, and so on. I didn't know what was going on in any of these areas other than what he allowed me to know. My fear turned to anger as he sauntered in at 3:30 A.M.

I lay under a sheet pulled up tight to my chin, my head turned away from him toward the wall. *If he touches me, every fiber in my being will recoil,* I thought. Although he wasn't much of a drinker, I prayed, *Oh, God, don't let him be drunk or want anything from me. Should I pretend to be asleep, or should I get this conversation that will ultimately lead to an argument over with?* What I really wanted was to disappear. I wanted to be somewhere else. I wanted to miraculously rewind my life five years, never having met him.

The anger and sting of betrayal propelled me forward, and I looked over my shoulder and asked, "Where were you?"

"Out with friends," he replied. He stretched out his arms and yawned.

His nonchalance powered me further. "Out with friends?" I sat up to look at him. "I thought you were taking Manuel home. What friends?"

"John. And Matt." He enunciated each consonant. Suddenly the room lit up with tension as if we had a gas leak and one strike of a match would send us up in flames.

Should I keep going or keep quiet? That was my forever dilemma in this messed-up relationship. "Why didn't you answer my calls or call me? You said you'd be home at ten."

Bryce, who had been unbuttoning his shirt and putting his watch on the dresser, slowly turned toward me for the first time. "I never said I'd be home at ten." The space between his eyes wrinkled, and he shook his head.

"I've been wondering where you were for hours, and I can't believe you didn't call or let me know." Heat rose up to my neck and face.

Bryce's jaw tightened. He moved toward me, getting inches from my face, and put his hands around my throat. He pushed me down onto the bed, putting pressure on my windpipe, and, through clenched teeth, said, "Savannah, who the hell do you think you are to question me? I was out with friends." His eyes were dark and crazy, spittle flew out of his mouth, and his hands shook my neck. Then, as if fighting an internal demon, he released his grip, regained his composure, and wiped the side of his mouth with the back of his hand.

My heart pounded because I knew this altercation could have been much worse—a punch to the face, a slap, or twisting my arm, all things he'd done before. He walked around to his side of the bed, jerked the covers back, and covered himself up.

Almost five wedded years of this dark maze of power and control taught me not to push further.

The next day, I woke to an ominous sky and torrential rains. I dropped the kids off at daycare, and by the time I got back out to the car, my hair and coat were drenched. I drove downtown to find the high-rise building on the river where I was to meet the attorney Chelsea had found for me, Dave Smith. The rain wasn't letting up, so I was glad there was a parking garage in the building. Before I grabbed my parking ticket and got out of the car, I rubbed my neck and took a deep breath. My heart was racing a bit as I thought of all I needed to share with this lawyer.

When Dave Smith came out to introduce himself, I was confused because his booming, authoritative voice on the phone made him sound like a man of great stature, but out came a man five foot tall in a suit and bowtie. He swore like a sailor, which put me at ease, as I almost giggled every time he said the f-word. I had never been around someone so free to be themselves.

He made eye contact with me and nodded and said "Uh-huh," encouraging me to continue as he gathered the necessary information. I told him all about the physical, mental, and emotional abuse, the items I found in the backpack, and even the sexual assault when I was pregnant. When I finished, he put his elbows on his desk and said, "Ya know, I've never liked controlling, abusive bastards like your soon-to-be ex. Let's roast his ass." He abruptly leaned back in his chair and put his hands behind his head. "So when do you want to do this?"

I explained that I had a business trip the following week and that I didn't want my husband served divorce papers just yet. I still needed time to think through my plan of execution. I still had these lingering thoughts of guilt and shame that kept me tied to Bryce and our marriage. I'd hoped he'd change. I'd hoped my prayers would be answered and I wouldn't have to go through another divorce. I'd hoped that Bryce and I could be one of those success stories I read about and that our marriage, on the brink of disaster, would be saved from falling off the cliff.

The following week, I prepared to leave for Nashville with my coworkers and their wives for the therapist convention. Knowing that my children would be safe with my parents, I could relax a little and enjoy the reprieve.

Wednesday night, I said goodbye to Bryce. We hugged, and I quickly pulled away from him but kept the weak smile on my face. I took Sami and Nicholas to my mom and dad's, and we spent the night there so that the next morning, Mom could take me to the airport.

At the airport terminal, I asked Mom, "Did I give you their medicine, just in case they get a fever? And their snuggle blankets are in the guest bedroom—they'll need those especially while I'm gone. And Nicholas loves to be read to right before bed."

Mom smiled and squeezed my arm. "I've got this, Savannah. The kids are going to be just fine. You'll only be gone a few days." I continued to hug the kids until my plane was ready to board. I turned and waved and blew kisses. As I walked down the jetway, my nose tingled and I swallowed down a huge lump in my throat.

Once I settled in on the plane, I reassured myself that the children were fine and I focused on the week ahead. I stretched out, and the tightness in my back released. We were flying into Nashville that Wednesday afternoon just in time to register for the event and go out to dinner. Thursday and Friday would be all-day seminars, and then on Saturday, I'd fly home after the last speaker.

I tried to sleep for the short flight, but my mind wandered and kept getting stuck on when and how to tell Bryce about my wanting a divorce.

On Thursday after one of the seminars, Jim pulled me aside. "Savannah, how are you doing? You haven't really updated me on things between you and Bryce."

I didn't feel like getting into all the details with Jim. A heaviness settled down on me that I couldn't shake, so I picked the easiest thing to tell him. "I met with an attorney. I liked him, but I'm just not sure what to do right now."

Jim seemed like he was thinking. He sighed, changed his position, and said, "Savannah, I think you know what to do. You're just afraid. I understand—it's scary. But if you're thinking Bryce is going to change, I'm sorry to say, but the chances of that are slim to none." Jim stepped closer and said in a low, intense voice, "He's dangerous, and you need to get away from him."

My head started swimming as the bluntness of his words hit me in the gut. But I knew he was right. I got light-headed and rubbed my temples.

"You look sick, Savannah. Here, let's go over here and sit down. I'll get you some water." I sat down while my head swam with the fact that I was in Nashville, hundreds of miles away from my children. Things Bryce had done to me started caving in on me—*everything*—and my eyes misted over with tears. I was scared, and even though I had people declaring their support, I still felt alone. I wasn't sure I could do this, and yet I knew I didn't have much of a choice; staying with Bryce wasn't an option.

"I'm feeling sick, Jim. I think I need to lie down," I said when he came back with a cup of water.

Jim and his wife, Deb, helped me back to my room and made sure I had food and water. Deb stayed with me a little longer and even rubbed my back when I lay down. A migraine hovered over my head, threatening me with an all-out assault.

I knew Jim was right. I had to stop this fantasy of a happy marriage with Bryce. He was deeply troubled, and I needed to escape with my children soon. I shared my thoughts with Deb. "I should have left him years ago. I'm so afraid of what I have to do, but there's no way I can live like this anymore."

Deb put her hand on my shoulder and said, "I know this is scary, but we're here for you whenever you need us."

I rubbed my head as the intensity of the migraine started to swell. "I just feel so overwhelmed that I can't focus on the conference." A surge of nausea filled my throat, and I ran to the bathroom. I kneeled on the floor in front of the toilet, gagging and heaving.

Deb followed me into the bathroom and held my hair back. I finally sat back and leaned on the tub as she got a wet washcloth and drapped it on my forehead. She helped me back to bed and said, "Savannah, I'm calling Jim to tell him I think you should fly home early. You're in no condition to be here."

I could only groan and nod as she picked up the phone to call.

Jim agreed. "Of course she can go home. I'll arrange a flight for tomorrow morning."

Deb made sure I took my migraine medication, and then she stayed with me until my eyes got heavy. I smiled weakly and thanked her for helping me; her warm voice and soft touch made me melt into the covers.

I woke the next morning with only a vague headache, nothing like the earthquake I felt in my head last night, and my nausea was gone. I made it to my flight back home, and when I landed around noon, I took a cab directly to my parents' house; I wanted to see my children and talk with my parents. The cab pulled in front of their house, and I asked the driver to wait for me, as I wasn't sure if they'd be home. I knocked and rang the doorbell because I had forgotten the house key they gave me. Their car was gone, and no one answered the door.

I hopped back into the cab and gave the driver the address to my apartment. I thought that I could use this time to talk to Bryce. He'd be home from work by now. We pulled into the complex, but I didn't see Bryce's car. *Are you kidding me? Where is everyone?* I paid the cab driver, and the heat hit me as I jumped out of the car. I ran up the stairs to our place and unlocked the door.

Our air-conditioning was running, the cold air hitting my hot, damp skin. I tripped over a pair of shoes I didn't recognize and stumbled into the kitchen where everything looked like it had when I left just a couple of days ago. In fact, Bryce hadn't prepared a meal in there at all—not even my cast iron skillet had moved.

It occurred to me that my parents may have taken the kids to Chelsea's house, so I picked up the telephone and dialed her number. She picked up.

"Hey," I said. "Are Nicholas and Sami with you?"

"Yes, they're here with Mom and Dad. Why?" Chelsea asked.

"I went to Mom and Dad's to—"

Chelsea cut me off. "Where are you? I thought you were still at the conference."

"I got sick last night and decided to come home early to deal with Bryce. I couldn't get him out of my head. I'm going to tell him I want a divorce."

"Wait, Savannah, you know better than anyone how scary he is. He'll lose his mind, and there's no telling what he might do."

"I need to get this over with, Chelsea. It's affecting my health. I can't live like this any longer," I said with resolve.

Before I could say anything more, Chelsea had hung up the phone. I wondered if she was angry with me, but I couldn't focus on that right then.

The carpet muffled my steps as I headed toward our bedroom. I considered that Bryce may have parked his car where I couldn't see it and that he might still be in the apartment. I approached our bedroom, but the door was closed. A low moan came from the other side of the door, and I backed away with a sense of alarm traveling through my body. I leaned in to hear better, but I couldn't make out any of the sounds. Was someone other than Bryce in our bedroom? My heart pounded. I grabbed the doorknob and ever so slowly turned it. Locked! *Who could be in there?* My heart was just about to pound out of my chest.

I ran to my junk drawer in the kitchen and found a deck of cards and grabbed three or four. Quiet like a cat, I walked back to the bedroom door, still hearing moaning and other sounds I couldn't identify. Was it crying? I slipped the cards between the door and the doorjamb. Sliding down, I shimmied the cards between the door's lock and it clicked open. My heartbeat was so loud it was deafening. I pushed the door wider to see who was in the room.

Bryce. Bryce was in our bed on top of someone.

"Bryce! What are you doing?" My hand covered my mouth.

He turned around, red-faced, sweaty, oblivious that I'd

been breaking into our bedroom. He hopped out of bed naked and threw the covers on the person in the bed. He hastily put his sweatpants on and yelled, "What the hell are you doing here?"

"Bryce, who is in our bed? What are you doing?" I was screaming at him now.

"Get the fuck out of here!" Bryce came at me. He pushed me out of the bedroom, and I went flying backward, my head hitting the wall. He put his hands around my neck, as he had so many times before, and said, "God, I hate you. You fucking bitch! You aren't supposed to be here!"

He threw me to the floor and kicked me in the stomach, knocking the wind out of me. I doubled over in pain, trying to catch my breath, coughing and gasping. "I. Can't. Breathe."

I struggled to sit up, and when I finally could, Bryce grabbed the back of my head and pushed my head down toward my chest. The air forced out of my lungs, and the bones cracked in my neck. He crammed my head harder and further so that it seemed as if my lungs deflated like day-old balloons. I tried to get out of his stronghold, my arms and legs swimming, as you would if you were underwater and trying to reach the surface to breathe. I had no more air left; I was suffocating and I couldn't say anything.

My arms reached up to grab the wrist that was pushing my head down, but I couldn't push him away, his arm wet with sweat, a metal pole of muscles. I needed to let him know that I couldn't breathe, that my burning lungs felt like they would burst, but I couldn't talk. I believed in that moment that if I could explain to him that he was pushing too hard, he'd let me go, as if he wasn't capable of this level of savagery. I believed that he didn't realize he was going to kill me.

Spots blinked before my eyes, and I pushed up as hard as I could so I could get oxygen. I was able to inhale some air, but not enough to talk or scream, just enough to avoid unconsciousness. But he continued pushing, and soon, the room was spinning, then blackness. The last of the light fading away. I kicked and pushed with every ounce of my being I had left. I didn't want to die. My babies! I needed to live! *Oh, God, please help me. I want to live for my children,* I prayed. *They need me, and I don't want this to be the conclusion of my life.*

My world was drawing to a close. Lifelessness was closing in. The pain of my lungs searching for oxygen grew faint as I withdrew into the blackness.

I saw in my mind's eye my grandmother. She had on a housecoat with miniature periwinkle flowers all over it and pink slippers on her feet. She held Sami, and Nicholas stood next to her; they were smiling at me, and they were waving, standing on a grassy knoll next to a willow tree. I wanted to race to them, to throw my arms around them, but somewhere in my mind, I believed that I wasn't allowed, so I hesitated. Then a train whistle blew in the distance. I turned to see it, but there wasn't a train anywhere. When I turned back, my grandmother and children were gone.

But this wailing in the background—it was inconsolable. My eyes fluttered open, and I gasped for air. *Ah, oxy-*

gen! Oh, but it burned as it traveled down, and I coughed. My throat and lungs were on fire, but the sweet air came back to me. I woke up slowly, my chest and throat hot. I blinked my eyes open to see Bryce lying still, blood on his head. *Who is screaming?*

Someone standing over Bryce, but why is he in his under-wear? Skinny arms, holding my cast iron skillet, dipped in red. The pieces were coming together for me, and I felt sick. *He was in bed with Bryce.* Those weren't moans of pleasure. *Bryce. Molesting him. Oh my God, that son of a bitch.*

I struggled to stand up, almost falling. "Manuel. It's okay. Let me have the pan." He released it from his hand, and I held him as he sobbed in my arms.

Something moved near my feet. I tried to step toward the door, but Bryce's hand grabbed my ankle and pulled, all the while groaning and growling. I fell, one knee twisted, and I cried out in pain. Manuel stood motionless. "Manuel, run! Get out of here!" I screamed.

Blood dripped from Bryce's head wound, running into his eye. He snarled like a diseased animal, ready to attack. "You bitch!" He drew back and hit me full-on with his fist, slamming into my nose, causing me to fall backward. I screamed out as the blast of pain pulsated throughout my face and head, and I dropped the skillet near the couch. Blood filled my nose, making it impossible to breathe through it.

I lay on the floor crying and groaning, my head pounding as if I'd been hit by a sledgehammer. All of Bryce's cruel actions rushed at me. The lies, the verbal, mental, and physical abuse, the sexual assault, and now this: He's a child molester. I could not let him kill me. I couldn't leave my babies to be raised by a predator like him.

I stretched out my hand and touched the skillet. I wrapped my fingers around the cold handle as if my life depended upon it.

Bryce's eyes were blood red. He was coughing as he held his head and struggled to stand on his own. I was frozen in pain and fear watching him.

Bryce smirked, and then his expression turned murderous. He lunged toward me and grabbed me by the throat. His arms and hands shook as his fingers wrapped themselves around my neck.

This can't be the end of my life! Nicholas! Sami! With what little strength I had left, I lifted the heavy skillet and swung hard into Bryce's face. Blood splattered on me, and several drops landed on my lips. I heard bones crack as I felt the thud of the skillet hit his head. We both fell, and he ended up on top of me. I pushed him off like he was filthy and scurried up on my knees. Powering me, a conflagration of fear and hatred. I lifted the skillet high above my head and swung down hard on his skull again. As I lifted a third time, someone said, "Savannah!"

I stopped. I knew that voice. Chelsea came up next to me and wrapped her hand around the skillet as I held it. I released my death grip on the handle and surrendered it to my sister as Bryce lay motionless in a pool of his own blood.

28

Called to Be Free

Oh my God. Tears streamed down my bloodied face as the police handcuffed me. The officer's mouth was moving, but I had sunk to the bottom of a deep pool and I couldn't grasp what he was telling me. *I never meant to kill him. I just needed him to stop. What will happen to my children if I go to prison?* The officer put me in the back of his cruiser. Chelsea kept yelling, "He was going to kill her! She was defending herself!" but one of the officers explained that it's protocol to make an arrest in domestic violence cases even if it is self-defense.

Before the officer closed my door, I said in a raspy voice, "Chelsea, please take care Nicholas and Sami for me." I coughed, the pain searing my throat.

"Of course I will. They'll be fine. But we'll get you out, okay? I promise." The door slammed shut after Chelsea's last word. As we drove away, Valentina was getting Manuel into her car, and my chest tightened at the image of Bryce on top of him. My body shook as we drove the ten minutes to the station. They took photographs of my blood-stained face, my lips and nose were swollen, and I had a bruise growing on my left cheek and around my eyes. Then they took my handcuffs off and put me in a room by myself. I waited for half an hour in a foggy daze.

When the interviewing officer came into the room, he introduced himself as Officer Chandler. He sat down across the table from me and put his pad of paper on the table. Rubbing his chin, he asked, "Can you tell me what happened tonight?"

My head pounded, and I still could barely talk. I wrapped my hand around my throat and said just above a whisper, "My husband tried to kill me tonight." I swallowed, but that only made the burning worse. "Can I have a drink of water?"

Chandler nodded and left the room. He came back in with the water, and I said, "Thank you. I'd like my attorney with me in this interview." I had enough of a mind to ask for representation.

"As long as you insist on your attorney being present, you'll have to wait in jail until he comes," he said. Another officer, Ruiz, entered the room and escorted me to the jail.

"I'd like to call my sister," I said to Officer Ruiz.

"You're entitled to one phone call." She led me to a desk with a phone.

The phone rang only once when Chelsea answered. I got choked up and said, "How are Nicholas and Sami?"

"They're perfectly fine. I called your attorney, Dave, and he's arraigned for the bail hearing in the morning, but first he'll meet with you at the jail. I'm so sorry, Savannah.

Are you going to be okay there tonight?"

Adrenaline was still rushing through my body when I answered. "Yes, I'll be fine as long as I know the kids are safe. Thank you for everything."

I had to change into the jail's clothing as they took my bloodied shirt and pants. In spite of it being a jail-issued jumpsuit and two sizes too big, my body warmed and relaxed when getting out of my clothes that were covered in both my and Bryce's blood.

The cell door slammed shut behind me, and I jumped. I turned to watch Officer Ruiz walking away and I fought the urge to cry out, "Please don't leave me here!" I walked toward the bed and thought, *I can't believe this is happening.* I sat on the mattress, and the bed squeaked, then I noticed my hand on a dark stain. I stood up, and my lips curled in disgust when I saw a pile of folded sheets at the end of the bed. I hoped to high heaven they were clean so I could cover the scourge that was on the mattress. I leaned over to make the bed, but pain burst through my body, especially my head and neck. Even so, I couldn't get my children out of my mind, nor could I stop seeing Bryce lying on the floor with his head smashed in. I didn't intend to kill him. I didn't *want* to kill him. I lay back on the mattress and curled up in a fetal position with my eyes wide, staring at the wall.

The next morning, Dave Smith registered his name with the jail and waited for me in an interview room. I shuffled in, handcuffed, and he said to the officer, pointing to my wrists, "Hey, is this really necessary?" The officer mumbled something but unlocked the cuffs.

I absentmindedly rubbed my wrists and said, "Thank you."

Dave scowled at the officer.

When we were alone, Dave said, "What in God's name happened, Savannah?"

I softly touched my nose and winced. "I killed him, Dave. He tried to strangle me, but I fought back. Manuel was there, and—"

Dave interrupted me and said, "Wait, slow down. Who's Manuel, and why was he there? I thought you were on a business trip." He wrote down the name Manuel and circled it.

I told Dave everything, starting with coming home early from the conference. I told him about Bryce's relationship with Manuel and that he was molesting the little boy when I burst into the bedroom. I told him about the pure terror on Manuel's face after he'd slammed the skillet into his head.

Dave waved his hand and stopped me. "So, Manuel hit him first?"

"Yes. Manuel saved my life. I haven't shared with anyone but you that Manuel hit him, and I don't plan to."

"Okay, what happened after he hit Bryce? Was there anyone else in the apartment besides you three?"

I told him about how Bryce came to and attacked me and how I hit Bryce twice with the skillet. And then I told him that my sister was there near the end and that she could tell her side of things.

Dave sat back in his chair and put the end of the pen between his lips. He took a deep breath and sighed. "I'm not a criminal defense attorney, but I know enough to know that you have some things working for you. You have visible wounds, which, by the way, have you been examined by a doctor yet?"

I shook my head.

"I'll get that arranged for today. You also have witnesses, Manuel and your sister. The one thing that might work against you is that, if I remember correctly, you never called the police about domestic violence. Never in the five years of marriage, is that right?"

I bowed my head. "That's right." I watched Dave write notes on his pad of paper when it dawned on me. "I told my coworkers, though. Do you think that will help?"

He put down his pen. "Yes, that should help a great deal. What are their names?"

Later that day, a doctor examined me and reported that I had a broken nose, contusions on my face and arms, and damage to my spine and trachea. Dave received the report and came back to visit me in the jail.

"I've spoken with the prosecutor's office." He rubbed his forehead. "They're charging you with manslaughter." Dave shook his head. "It's a political game out there, and the prosecutor wants to make a name for herself. I'll call my colleague, Dan Fryer, to represent you. He's one of the best criminal attorneys in town."

My mouth fell open, but I was speechless. Tears trickled down my cheeks, and all I could think was, *What will happen to my children?* I put my hand on my chest and said, "What happens now? Do I have to stay in jail? Will there be a bail hearing?"

"You'll go before the judge today. There's a forty-eight-hour limit as to how long they can hold you here before your arraignment." He explained that since it was Friday already, waiting until Monday would have put them past the limit.

I walked into the courtroom in a daze. I almost missed seeing my sister and Dad; I tried to smile when I saw them. Dan Fryer, my new attorney, was there and put his arm around me and said, "I'm sure you'll be released on your own recognizance. And you need to plead 'not guilty.' Do you have any questions?"

I had a million, but I shook my head.

We both turned when the judge came out and the bailiff said, "All rise!"

I entered the not-guilty plea like Dan instructed, and the judge agreed to a personal recognizance bond until the trial, which would be set at another time. Dan said he'd call me on Monday to talk, I thanked him, and then I bolted through the swinging gate to hug my sister and Dad.

The next six months were a blur to me in some ways. I was ecstatic to be with my children, but my mind kept pulling me back to the fact that I was being charged for Bryce's death. *What will I do if I have to go to prison?* The thought tormented me. I couldn't imagine being separated from them.

Chelsea and her husband agreed to take Nicholas and

Samantha for me if the unthinkable happened, but they tried to reassure me that I'd be acquitted. I wanted to believe them.

The kids and I stayed with my parents, as I didn't want to go back to the apartment. It was the landlord's responsibility to have it cleaned, and I told him I didn't want anything in there. My dad reminded me that there may be important documents like tax returns and photos that I'd want, so he offered to go and check out everything. He came back with three boxes full of papers, special toys, artwork from the children, and jewelry and photo albums. I hugged him when I saw all the items he'd saved for me.

He pulled out an envelope and handed it to me. I opened it, and my fingers flipped through the stack of hundred-dollar bills. There must have been forty or fifty in there. My eyes widened, and I said, "Dad, where did this come from?"

"I found it in a secret drawer in Bryce's desk. He must have been stashing money away for quite some time."

I flipped through the cash again and shook my head. "Here, you take it, Dad. You're helping me pay for my attorney and allowing us to live here rent-free. Whatever's in there is yours."

"Savannah, you and the children need this money more than I do. You keep it, and we'll worry about the attorney's fees as they come."

As I awaited trial, Bryce's parents contacted me through my attorney. They wanted me to sign over his body so that they could have him cremated after the medical examiner was finished. I signed the papers in a conference room at Dan's law firm and slid them back across the table, avoiding eye contact with him. I wondered what the appropriate emotional response should be. I never wanted to kill anyone, but I also didn't shed one tear over Bryce.

I received phone calls from friends and cards in the mail, some with money in them. The notes read, "Praying for you. I hope this little bit helps in your defense"; "God is with you"; and "We love you, Savannah." I must have received two hundred cards and letters. The words of encouragement lifted my spirits during the darkest days of my life.

Days before my court date, I met with Dan to discuss my case. "I have two options for you," he said. "The prosecutor is offering you a plea deal. If you plead guilty to manslaughter, you may go to prison for up to five years."

"But I'm not guilty! Bryce was trying to kill me, and he was molesting a little boy, for God's sake! I can't be away from my children!" My blood pressure rose.

Dan lifted his hand off the table slightly and spoke softly. "There's another option for you. We go to trial, and you waive the right to a jury and let the judge decide the case. The judge who has been assigned to your case is knowledgeable and seems to care about domestic abuse victims. Last year, he ruled in favor of a woman defending herself against her husband who had beaten her to a pulp on several occasions and even held a gun against their two-year-old son's head. He raped her and beat her one night, and then she killed him with a kitchen knife."

I had so many questions and "what ifs." If I stayed with

my not-guilty plea and waived my right to a jury, what if the judge didn't agree that it was self-defense? What if the district attorney's office was able to convince him that it wasn't purely self-defense? And there wasn't an iron-clad guarantee that the judge wouldn't get sick or die, or the prosecutor wouldn't file a motion to have the judge reassigned. Could I risk that happening?

And yet, if I took the plea, I would be separated from my children for years—*in prison*! I pounded my thigh with my fist and said out loud, "No! I won't plead guilty to manslaughter." My only rational choice was to take my chances with this judge.

My day in court finally came, and both my parents and Chelsea attended. Jim and the other guys from my team were also there. As the prosecutor rose, so did my heart rate. She began by telling the judge I went to the apartment already angry and instigated a fight with my husband. She pointed out that I had never once called the police for domestic violence or filed a restraining order against Bryce. She also twisted the story that I had other options other than to kill Bryce. What those options were, she didn't say.

When the prosecution rested, Dan stood up slowly and asked to call two witnesses. Both Chelsea and Manuel testified that if I hadn't hit Bryce with the skillet, he would have killed me. Manuel's testimony had the judge, and me, mesmerized. I learned that he never left the apartment when I told him to get out; he was hiding behind one of the chairs in the living room and watched the entire assault. Dan questioned him about what happened in the bedroom of the apartment the day Bryce died; Manuel hung his head low and tears poured down his face. The judge's and the prosecutor's eyes were fixed on the young boy as he testified that Bryce had been molesting him for months.

Then my attorney read parts of the medical report. The judge wrinkled his eyebrows when Dan showed him pictures of my injuries.

In the end, the judge wasn't buying the district attorney's claims of my guilt. He said, "Mrs. Clark, it is clear to this court that on September 9, 1998, you didn't intentionally or recklessly kill your husband. Through testimony and medical reports, the evidence shows that you were attacked and suffered great bodily harm. It is hereby ruled that you acted in self-defense and all charges are immediately dismissed with prejudice." He hit the gavel, and I collapsed in my chair as the weight of the trial and impending prison sentence evaporated.

I said thank you to the judge and also whispered a thank-you to the Someone watching over me and my children.

I leaned over to Dan and hugged him. I asked, "What does with prejudice mean, though? Is that bad?"

Dan smiled and said, "It means that this case is over and done with. You can never be brought to trial again regarding Bryce's death. The judge believed you, Savannah, that you were in the fight for your life."

After my acquittal, my parents drove me to my small

townhouse where my children waited with their Uncle Spencer. I ran to my front door, leaving my parents and Chelsea as they were still getting out of the car, and when I swung open the door, the kids ran into my arms, laughing because we almost fell over. Spencer hugged me, and before I knew it, my best friend Kay grabbed me and screamed, "Savannah! I'm so happy you're home—for good!" Smiles, food, and long tear-filled hugs completed the evening.

I stayed in contact with Manuel and Valentina for a short while after everything that happened, but Valentina called me one day to tell me that Manuel wasn't doing well. We'd just had a visit and he was waking up with nightmares. After talking it through with his mother, we decided it would be best to end our visits. I also offered to pay for Manuel to go to a trauma therapist. I'd grown so fond of him, but I knew I needed to let him go, so we didn't see each other again. I also wanted to put the past behind me, so I chose a therapist for me and my children who had years of experience helping trauma victims heal.

At work one day, almost a year after Bryce's death, I was in my office writing letters, and a friend of mine, Katherine, walked in and said, "Hey, if you haven't found a church yet, I'd love it if you and the kids would come to my church on Sunday."

Her place of worship was near my townhouse, and I decided I needed to start attending again, not out of obligation, but from the little tugging at my heart. The story of King David from the Bible popped up in my memory, and I thought that if God could love him—the one who committed adultery with Bathsheba and then planned her husband Uriah's murder—maybe He still loved me too. I knew I had that one issue I still hadn't dealt with yet, and I wanted to know if I was too far gone for God's love and mercy to reach me.

Sunday came, and I don't know why, but as I listened to the pastor speak about God's love for me and His grace and mercy, it was like hearing it for the first time. Grace, getting something that I don't deserve, the love and forgiveness I hadn't earned. My heart expanded, and I opened my Bible.

I found myself leaning forward, wanting to hear every word the pastor said. I wanted more of God's love and grace. I *wanted* to enjoy a free and loving relationship with Jesus. As a tear made its slow decent, I wiped it away before anyone could see it. I knew He forgave me—I understood that in my head, but my heart didn't fully trust that.

The kids and I continued going to church. We enjoyed talking about what we learned at there. Sami and Nicholas enjoyed Sunday school and showed me their drawings and told me about the games they played in their classrooms.

One Sunday, I sat alone in the pew flipping through the bulletin and I read that there was a small group beginning for women who had had abortions. My heart stopped beating for a second.

Are they really talking about this? I mean, churches fly flags at half-mast for the millions of aborted babies, but I can't believe they're showing concern for the women who would do such a horrendous thing. I couldn't even think about what they'd talk about. But I knew I needed to talk to someone about this, as I had never told anyone about the abortion, not even my sister or best friend. There were times when I would rather have died than talk about what I did.

Several weeks later, a woman walked up on the stage. "Yeah, hi, my name is Karen. When I was nineteen, I got pregnant by my boyfriend, and we both decided we wanted an abortion." She had a New York accent, but a gentle tone of voice that made whatever she said easy to listen to, undemanding.

She continued: "For years, I denied that the abortion had any effect on my life. But when we married, I noticed I started feeling depressed, and when my third child was born, I had to go on antidepressants—that's how bad the depression got. I finally decided to go to a Christian therapist who helped me face the effects of the abortion and accept God's forgiveness so He could heal my heart. I wanted to enjoy my family and life, and I couldn't do it with that issue still lingering."

She ended her time by saying that she was leading a group to help women who've had abortions and invited women to call and join the group. She had her phone number listed in the bulletin. I liked this soft-spoken New Yorker right away and wanted to call her immediately.

Four weeks later, after hours of rallying my courage, I decided to call her. I knew if I didn't write down what I wanted to say, I'd fumble my words and she might wonder if it was a prank call. I wrote a script for myself and willed myself not to hang up and waited until I heard her familiar voice: "Hello?"

I swallowed and took hold of my paper and read, "Hi, my name is Savannah, and I'm calling about the small group you're leading." My voice was monotone, and I sounded like a recording. *I've got to stop reading.* I crumbled up the paper and continued on my own. "Um, I was wondering if it's too late to join the group, um, if you still have room? I . . . I know I'm calling late. I'm sorry about that—I was nervous—but I'd like to join if it's not too late and if you still have room." *Oh, I sound like an idiot! How many times did I say "late" and "room"?*

I waited, anticipating the words, "Oh, I'm sorry, we're full now, but we'll have another group some time in the future. You can join then." I was sure she was going to say that.

"Oh, yes! Yes, you can join. We'd love to have you! Actually, Savannah, is that what you said your name is? You're the only one who's called, so yes, yes, it's perfectly fine for you to join!"

We both laughed. My nervous-relief laughter balanced her "Oh, thank you, God, for sending someone!" laughter. God sure has a sense of humor.

I hung up the phone and lay down on my bed and started to bawl. The tears came down like a stream—tears of gratitude, relief, excitement, anticipation, remorse, a little bit of fear—watering the garden of my life. Sprouts of growth popping up here and there, as if winter were over and spring had pushed its way through, creating new life in my heart.

I had heard that there was a verse in the Bible that said

God collects our tears. He must have had to use a couple of vials that day. I was excited about what God was going to do, as He seemed to be doing some good things so far.

29

A New Beginning

One Sunday morning as I settled myself about five pews back from the front, I spotted a man sitting alone in church. He caught my eye because he was dressed nicely; he had a pressed white shirt and a tie, and he wore wire rimmed glasses. But best of all, he wore black wingtip shoes. I don't have a foot obsession, but he had me at the shoes. They brought me back to my dad wearing his wingtip shoes. *Who is this man? I must meet him! Wait, Savannah, no, focus on the sermon. Jesus wants all of your attention. Plus, you haven't had the best of luck with men. And he's probably married and waiting for his wife to show up. Now, settle down and pay attention to the pastor.*

So, I did. I opened my Bible and focused on the sermon. And I even prayed, "Lord, help me focus on you. I don't want to be distracted with another relationship, but if it's your will, let me meet this guy. And *soon*. Amen." No wife ever came to sit with him.

The next Sunday service, he was there again, sitting in the same row. Finally, our eyes met. I averted my gaze so as not to look sheepish. He approached me wearing his wing-tip shoes. A smile started to form on my lips as he stuck out his hand. "Hi, I'm Tyler."

I promptly shook his hand, and a sense of serenity washed over me. "It's nice to meet you. I'm Savannah."

The pit in my stomach that I'd had for years suddenly morphed into little butterflies.

Epilogue

"**G**randmama! Grandmama! Come here!"

"What? What is it?" I startled, as I had dozed off in a lounge chair on the deck. With an intensity on his round face, my young grandson, Graham, held out his hand for me to take.

I grabbed his tiny hand, and away he whisked me to where, I didn't know. But I trusted this little four-year-old and I knew there was a good reason. This time, as usual, he didn't disappoint. We ran down the sandy steps of the deck and ran toward my husband and my granddaughter, Maddie, where they were watching baby sea turtles hatch from their eggs.

A crowd had formed, including Nicholas and Samantha, now young adults, and their stepsister Amanda and her husband, Eric. We were all captivated by the tiny turtles breaking out of their shells and making their way to the ocean. Many struggled to find the water, and just as I wondered if I should help, a woman from the sea turtle protection committee, with a little creature in her hands, asked me if I'd like to take one to the water. I said, "Yes, of course!" and Graham and I cupped our hands around him. Carefully, we walked him as far as we could into the ocean, hoping with all our hearts this little turtle would be one of the few to make it.

In the chaos of people and baby sea turtles, we lost sight of everyone in our family, but then Graham waved down his grandpa and his sister, Maddie, who were approaching us. He said, "Grandpa, I helped a turtle out to sea!" He held out one of his hands and giggled. "And the little flappers tickled my hands."

My husband scooped him up, and Maddie said she got to take a turtle out to the water, too. She asked me if I thought the baby turtle would make it out in that big ocean. At almost nine years old, she was a very thoughtful and intelligent girl. She would know if I was telling her something that wasn't true.

I put my arm around her and said, "There are many predators out there, like birds and fish. But ya know what, we can pray for our little turtles if you want to. Because God cares for all of His creatures." So, we all prayed right then and there for Ava and Henry, the turtles we named from Fripp Island, South Carolina.

Graham wiggled out of Tyler's arms to see if he could get eyes on his turtle. My husband smiled at me and drew me in close, kissing the top of my head. He continued to hold me, not loosening his grip, as he said, "I'm the luckiest man in the world." He gathered his hands in my hair and softly pressed his lips against mine.

Samantha walked up and said, "Okay, okay, break it

up. Dad, did you get to carry a turtle? They're so cute."

"Yes, Maddie and I did," my husband responded.

Maddie slid her hand into her Aunt Samantha's hand and said, "It was so cool to carry a sea turtle! I can't wait to tell all my friends." She had a huge smile across her face.

"And I did it too!" little Graham said, jumping up and down, making sure we didn't forget his involvement.

My throat tightened, and I fought back tears thinking about how defenseless these baby turtles were to birds, fish, and humans. The odds weren't good—only one in one thousand usually survive.

Nick, Amanda, and Eric joined the rest of us at the water's edge. I took Graham's hand, and we stood under the big blue sky, watching the waves for a long time as his baby turtle, Henry, paddled out to sea. I think we were both wishing him well.

My little guy asked, "Grandmama, is he trying to find his mommy?"

"Yes, honey, I think he is looking for his mommy. And I bet she is looking for him too. And I think they'll find each other."

A Note to Readers

Family abuse and domestic violence damage us, but they don't have to be the end of anyone's story. Even with all that Savannah went through, she had the courage to face her fears and leave her abuser and create a life of joy for herself and her children.

I wanted to write a book that exposes the relationship between girls raised in abusive religious homes and then growing into women who marry violent men. There's not always a correlation; many women married to cruel husbands report that they grew up in loving homes. But I know far too many women whose parents told them that they loved them more than anyone ever would, immersed them in the teachings of the church, and then used their "biblical parental authority" to belittle, demean, abuse, and chip away at their self-esteem.

As young children, we believe our parents are always right. It was easy for Savannah to be fooled into thinking that abusive parenting was love, especially when her parent's violent behavior was justified by religious rhetoric. This helps explain how Savannah was trapped in the cycle of abuse in her marriage.

Using the Bible to justify, minimize, or overlook intimate partner abuse and to elevate men above women contributes to the staggering statistic of one in four women being abused by their partners, as does minimizing our daughters' (and sons') voices in the family. Children matter, and they're worthy of love and respect.

We can't be silent. We must keep telling these stories. If you're in an abusive relationship, you can call the National Domestic Violence hotline at 1-800-799-7233 to speak with someone who can help you.

I included the story of the abortion because there are countless women who have been demonized, marginalized, and silenced. Some of them carry a burden of shame and guilt from which they need freedom, but they continue to hide because they fear judgment. I want them to know that there is nothing that can separate them from God's love. They no longer need to hang their heads in shame, because no matter what, they are loved and accepted equally and unconditionally.

This journey was hard for Savannah, but all the pain, the hurt, and the brokenness were used to show the light that lived in her. And it lives in you too.

An African Proverb says, "When there is no enemy within, the enemies outside cannot hurt you." Savannah was her own worst enemy, beating herself up for the smallest of infractions. But once she became her own best friend, she experienced freedom and love. My hope is that you, too, will love yourself as the divine being you are and discover freedom from abuse and controlling relationships.

Acknowledgments

My gratitude to my amazing developmental editor, Alice Sullivan, who became a great cheerleader and support as I waded through the deep waters of writing for the first time. She understood my highs and lows and helped me through each wave. She pointed me to the equally amazing and wonderful Shayla Raquel, who has opened up my eyes to the world of self-publishing. She makes the impossible seem possible, and her copyedit was invaluable. Then, to the talented Melinda Martin for the perfect cover for this book. She captured exactly the tone and heart. I also want to thank my attorney and friend, Mark Haslem, for his guidance on writing about the bench trial, not to mention his expertise and professionalism over the years. Thank you to these four gifted and generous people for helping me forge through the unknown territory of writing and publishing. It's a miracle, and I couldn't have done it without you all.

I also want to thank all my friends along the way who encouraged me to keep going and to follow this crazy dream of mine. Jean Blauser, your support and humor kept me from jumping off the roof of my house—thank you. Judi Esposito, your love and friendship and cheerleading gave me the strength to keep writing when I surely thought, *What have I done?* Thank you for being there for me and reminding me why I started this in the first place. To Roz Clemens, your friendship and love for the past three decades have been a light in my life, and I've known you believed in me from the first. There's no way I could have started this book without you.

To my sister, we have a shared history that bonds us, and I definitely couldn't have finished this book without your sustaining support and love. Thank you for helping me keep my head above the water. I always called you when I needed to see the sunlight again. And thank you for the beautiful artwork for my JustOneYou logo. You are an amazing artist.

To my mother and father, thank you for teaching me so many things about life. Thank you for the laughter we shared and still do, Mom. I appreciate you and the way you show love to us, your family.

To my husband, the one who truly believed in me and supported me, literally, and never once complained about anything. You are God's gift to me. I love you so much!

Thank you to my children Andre and Aleigha and my stepdaughter Erica, husband Brad, and grandchildren Lilly and Paxton for being the sweet and bright stars in my life that you are. You bring me such joy.

I love you all so much. To the moon and back a million times.

About the Author

Allison Stevens is the author of *Black Eye, Blue Sky*. She holds a master's degree in counseling psychology and owns a private practice as a psychologist helping people with depression, anxiety, and relationship struggles. Her ultimate goal in this field is to help women find their power and courage. A fanatic dog lover, she provides dog-sitting for rescues and volunteers at her local humane society. Movies, music, and books trigger her imagination so she can tell beautiful and adventurous stories. Allison stays busy with her two grandchildren and husband in Grand Rapids, Michigan.

Connect with the Author

allisonleighstevens.com

Leave a Review

If you enjoyed this book, will you please consider writing a review on your platform of choice? Reviews help self-published authors make their books more visible to new readers.